Leah stared into the darkness of the cabin. The light was off. Funny. She didn't remember turning it off.

Lightning flashed soundlessly to outline the room and the man at the table, tipped back on two legs of his chair, stroking the cat on his lap with one hand, raising a dark stubby gun with the other.

"Turn on that light and you're dead," he warned her.

Fawcett Crest Books
by Marlys Millhiser:

MICHAEL'S WIFE

NELLA WAITS

WILLING HOSTAGE

WILLING HOSTAGE

Marlys Millhiser

A FAWCETT CREST BOOK

Fawcett Publications, Inc., Greenwich, Connecticut

WILLING HOSTAGE

THIS BOOK CONTAINS THE COMPLETE TEXT OF
THE ORIGINAL HARDCOVER EDITION.

A Fawcett Crest Book reprinted by arrangement with G.P.
Putnam's Sons

ISBN 0-449-23226-3

Printed in the United States of America

10 9 8 7 6 5 4 3 2 1

For my parents
Doris and Harold Enabnit

... virtue is an individual, not a group, attribute.
— ROBERT N. KHARASCH

The Institutional Imperative:
How to Understand the United States Government
and Other Bulky Objects

Chapter One

THE sign of the heron cast a distended shadow across double strips of pavement. The shadow, distorted and jetty, inked through sunlight to the ditch beyond, through barbed wire and a cow grazing alone.

Leah turned the yellow Volkswagen into the drive and stopped beside the gas pumps. The Volks was as dry as she was and Enveco was her only living credit card. The signs of the heron had been ominously few since she'd left Chicago.

She fell against the steering wheel and closed her eyes.

Fatigue exploded sunspots behind her eyelids, sent shudders through flattened muscles. Heat fingers searched along the dampness of her back where she'd pulled away from the seat.

. . . The whisper of leaves, the rubbery splat of tires on hot pavement as a car passed, the whining of dogs . . .

. . . A splatter of red across a soap bar . . . the smear of it across tile . . . the contrast against the white tub . . . the red stain oozing toward the drain. . . .

Relaxing muscles jerked. The acid of her stomach rose to her tongue. Leah pushed at the door as if the car were in flames and forced aching legs to stand on the concrete outside.

The whining turned to barking. Four medium-sized dogs with very large teeth fought the wire of their individual cages in the back of a pickup.

Leah glanced up at the familiar sign of the heron for reassurance. The neon bird stood on one leg, blue-gray, serene and supreme.

The dogs snarled as a door slapped its frame and they

7

turned stiffened tails toward Leah, then whimpered into silence as a man came around the pickup and growled at them. Tearing great hunks from a hamburger with his teeth, he climbed into the truck and drove off.

"Fill it?"

"What?" She swung around to find a cowboy leaning against the pumps.

"Your car. You want gas?" He didn't look like a friendly cowboy.

"Oh . . . yes. But don't fill it." She reached into the car for her shoulder bag. "How much would two dollars get me?"

"Not much."

"How about four?"

"Twice as much as not much."

"I'll take four dollars' worth." She had a credit card, but when and how would she pay Enveco? "Can you tell me how far it is to Ted's Place?"

"You're here."

"Here" was a building, gas pumps, and the cow still gazing across the double highway. The map had shown it as the first entrance to the mountains on the route she'd followed from Chicago. A place to stay overnight, rest, and gain courage before starting a new life.

"But on the map it showed a town."

"I don't make the maps."

The sun was too bright through her sunglasses. She felt like an alien on an enemy planet—a hungry alien.

The building didn't look like a gas station. It looked something like an Americanized version of a Swiss chalet. Interspersed with the dormer windows of the second story were the letters T . . . E . . . D . . . S.

"How far is the next town?"

The tree behind Ted's whispered its leaves in answer. It seemed to be the only tree for miles.

"Depends on which way you're going."

"That way." Leah pointed toward the dark shapes waiting on the skyline behind Ted's Place.

"The next town'd be Walden, over the pass. About ninety miles. Check the oil?"

8

"No." What were ninety more miles after today?

"Best thing this late in the day"—he smeared at the windshield with a rag—"go to Fort Collins. Spend the night. Start off in the morning."

Spend the night. Spend. "I just came through there." She found her Enveco card and handed it to him.

"Best thing," he repeated as she followed him toward the building. A dark-gold car parked beside it. Under the striped awnings the windows were full of signs—LUNCH; GROCERIES; SPORTING GOODS; COORS BEER; LIGHT OLYMPIA BEER; BUD; COLORADO HUNTING, FISHING LICENSES.

Three steps led down to the door where another sign declared NO PACKS, NO PETS!

But it was the smell that made her swallow and grab the doorframe. Hamburgers. Lovely, meaty, juicy, rich-smelling hamburgers.

Leah ignored the three men staring at her from a booth and the smiling dude behind the lunch counter under the Dr. Pepper clock. She walked around postcard racks and piled bundles of firewood to the sign at the back that read REST ROOMS.

Once in the ladies', she gulped water from the spigot, wetting her face and some of her hair. When it seemed that her stomach would accept the needed moisture, she brought the bottle of Maalox from her purse and drank from it.

A sign on the wall told her exactly how to dispose of soiled sanitary napkins. Another instructed her on how to release paper towels from the dispenser. She hated signs, but always read them.

The fire in her middle had subsided a little. Hadn't it?

The image of the three men in the booth slid before her own in the mirror above the sink. So there were three men in a booth.

But all of them had crowded into one side. And they were too large to sit comfortably that way. The one on the outside had grinned at her . . . expectantly? The dark one sitting so stiffly in the middle. . . .

Leah shrugged them off. She mustn't think of them. They'd been eating hamburgers.

The three were lined up at the cash register as she emerged from the hall. They didn't see her and she slid behind the grinner as the cowboy handed her the Enveco card, a ballpoint pen, and a clipboard with the gauzy layers of paper and carbons that would make her pay up. Environmental Energy Corporation was printed across the top.

"If you hadn't blown this," the grinner said to the dark man, still in the middle, "you could'a had a nice cushy job on the farm, showing off bag jobs or something."

She signed Leah Harper to the bill, but not before the dark man turned a look of murder on the jocular man so close behind him. It seemed to include Leah and she stepped away quickly.

If ever she came face to face with a murderer, she told herself, that's how he would look.

Hunger. It makes people fanciful. She selected a carton of milk from a glass-fronted cooler and a loaf of sliced cheese. On a rack not far away, she found bread. When she turned to the cash register, the three men were walking out the door.

As she left Ted's with her purchases, they were standing beside the dark-gold car. ". . . Illinois license plate?"

"Well what do you expect? It *is* a blonde in a yellow Volks."

Leah hurried to the Volks. This was one blonde who was interested only in food. But as the car and her stomach growled in unison, a face intruded through the open window.

"Are you Sheila?" His eyes seemed to be hidden because his grin pulled at their corners so hard that it pressed the upper eyelids down.

"No, I'm not Sheila." She stared into the eye slits that the grin left and experienced an odd sense of danger. No reason for that sudden feeling . . . but it was strong enough to add an unpleasant tingle to a queasy stomach.

"Charlie!" The cry came from behind them and she turned to see the two remaining men wrestle each other to the ground.

Charlie backed away and Leah jammed the Volkswagen into gear, roared out of Ted's drive, turned right and then right again where the side road heading west met the highway under the sign of the heron.

Charlie had joined the scuffle by the time she passed the side of Ted's Place.

A sign read WALDEN 92, CAMERON PASS—OPEN.

She should make Walden in under two hours. And she'd better. Two hours were about all she had left in her.

Leah steped hard on the gas pedal, anxious to put miles between herself and the strange trio back at Ted's. She didn't envy Sheila, whoever she was. What was a bag job done on a farm?

Fighting the bread wrapper with one hand until she'd extracted a slice of pasty tasteless bread, munching it as slowly as she could endure, Leah Harper faced the Rocky Mountains of Colorado.

Chapter Two

HER sisters' eyes had accused Leah over the lid of the coffin. Annette, her elegant clothes washing out her face. Suzie, adding the weight of another pregnancy. Two pairs of eyes, the same color blue. "This takes care of one of your problems," they seemed to say. "Where do you go from here, sister?"

That was the moment Leah had decided to go. Anywhere.

After the funeral, Ralph, Annette's doctor-husband, asked, "What will you do now that your mother is gone, Leah? Go back to New York?"

"No, I think I'll go west." She couldn't go *back* anywhere.

"West? What's west of Chicago?"

What *was* west of Chicago? She had been east and had seen oceans. . . . "I'm going to . . . to the mountains." The decision had been made that quickly.

Leah couldn't admit to her family that she was running *from* another failure and hadn't thought clearly about what she was running *to*. And so she'd said, "To the mountains."

And here they were. The mountains. Drawing closer. Hovering. Enormous, dark, ragged under a lowering sun.

Leah ate another piece of bread, poked her fingernails through the plastic cover of the Velveeta and peeled a slice off the loaf.

"But what will you do there, Leah? After the funeral expenses there won't be much left for travel."

"I'll have to get a job, won't I?" she'd answered flippantly and changed the subject.

The narrow asphalt led straight to the mountains, peaceful pastures on either side. A river flowed languidly to her left . . . a hint of pine soap in the air . . . the bell-like trill of a meadowlark.

Then the road rose, curved, twisted, and the river roared ahead of her. CACHE LA POUDRE, the sign next to the bridge told her. The river raced now, dangerously close to the road. Canyon walls swallowed up the Volkswagen. Leah wished she could get to the milk but needed both hands on the wheel.

A man stood on a rock in the river, a fishing pole in his hand, intent and as serene as the blue heron on its pole at Ted's Place.

There was no serenity for Leah. Monster mountains crushed in on either side of the cleft while the river roiled and crashed against rocks and rock-cliff banks. The sun would sink to the bottom of the canyon at one point and then she'd round a curve to gloomy shadow. She hoped it wasn't like this all the way to Walden.

The Volkswagen crawled as the grade steepened even though she pressed the accelerator to the floor. Danger signals from her mind kept shooting warnings at her senses. This canyon was so different from the canyons of the city.

At the outward edge of the next curve, the canyon widened to include a small treed area with picnic tables and trash cans and sunlight. She pulled over to eat and drink and calm tired nerves.

The sun felt cooler here than at Ted's Place. She sat at a picnic table and drank awkwardly from the tri-cornered fold-out of the milk carton . . . and pondered why it was that going back seemed such a sign of failure to her. Perhaps because she failed so often. Or because she'd had to return to her mother's house after her one real fling with freedom?

A car passed going downhill and soon another with a camping trailer going up. Leah felt less alone.

She'd even failed at being a daughter and fled guilt this time, guilt at not realizing how desperate her mother had become . . . guilt at her own relief at being free of the poor woman at last. How else would she have come to be in this deserted little park next to a roaring maniacal river?

Leah looked over her shoulder. There were probably few muggers in the mountains. But what about bears? She looked over her other shoulder.

A scrubby bush to the right of the picnic table moved, rustled.

The sun went down behind the mountain. It lit the tops of the cliff walls on either side of her, but Leah sat in shadow below.

The bush moved again.

Something fawn-colored uncoiled at its base. Leah stood and backed away as brakes screamed behind her. A car skidded around the curve, its rear tire biting gravel at the road's edge. And then it was gone.

A dark-gold car. Whoever sat at the wheel was alone. The sound of its engine had died suddenly. Had it stopped up ahead? Or was its sound drowned in the river's roar?

She turned again to the bush but the fawn-colored thing sat on the picnic table now, next to the food.

Leah shrugged. Just a cat. Wasn't it?

It had the color and markings of a Siamese but she'd never seen one that big. She'd never seen any cat that big.

"You aren't a cross between a house cat and a . . . a bobcat, are you?"

The cat answered her with a yowl instead of a meow.

"You sound like a Siamese." She reached for the food and the animal rubbed its neck against her arm, purring like a muffled machine gun.

"Hungry? Well, run on home and get your dinner. Be glad, you've got a home." Leah started for the car.

The cat gave a pleading and extended yowl. But the luminous blue eyes were cold, impersonal. There hadn't been a house for miles. "You do have a home? You weren't dumped?"

No answer. The cold eyes didn't waver. They reminded her of her sisters' eyes. Cats usually didn't look people eye to eye. Her mother's cats never had.

"I've got my own problems but"—Leah found a fairly clean plastic margarine bowl in the trash can—"you can have some milk."

The cat rubbed against her as she poured it. "I didn't like the looks of that last car, for one thing. Good heavens, you *are* hungry."

She broke up some bread and added it and more milk to the bowl. "Any cat who'll eat bread and milk is starving but you certainly don't look it." Her mother's cats ate nothing but liver or fish.

"You would have loved my mother, kitty. Too bad no one else did. Well, it's been nice," she said to the hypnotic eyes.

Leah put the food in the car and stood for a moment at the open door, looking up the lonely road and then down. Which way?

Was the gold car parked somewhere ahead? Waiting for Leah Harper? She was getting neurotic . . . the last few days had been too much . . . her mother, the funeral, the endless driving. . . .

Leah had been alone before and liked it. She was just tired. And the sun wasn't getting any higher. Walden lay ahead and she refused to go back . . . anywhere.

She slid behind the wheel and the Volks worked hard just to get her up the incline to the road. Her stomach felt

14

better and she was *not* going to worry about that gold car. It, like the giant Siamese, was not her problem. It had nothing to do with her.

But her conscience pricked her enough to look as she passed. The picnic table was empty except for the little margarine bowl. The cat's home probably lay somewhere ahead. Cats wander.

Leah set a course for Walden, hoping the anemic Volkswagen could make it. She forgot the hungry cat . . . but not the dark-gold car with one passenger.

Chapter Three

"BUT you'll be gone for your birthday, Leah," Suzie said with a knowing glance at Annette. "After all this sadness, we'll need something to celebrate. Won't we Ed?" She leaned against her husband in that proprietary way.

"Yeah. Remember last year, Leah?" Ed's leer indicated that even a death in the family hadn't stopped the open season on spinster sisters-in-law.

Their mother had been alive then and had brought her liquor and her cats.

The air moving through the car window was cold now. And strangely fresh.

But her mother never got drunk, just sadder, emptier.

Leah had romped with Suzie's little boys and sidled away from their father's hands. Ralph and Annette had quarreled in their married way.

Suzie whispered to Leah, "It's just that they don't have any children. That's what makes Annette so pinched and old. Children keep you young."

And later Leah had overheard Suzie tell Annette, "Leah's twenty-nine and no husband in sight. I'm worried for her. That's what makes her so nervous, the ulcer and everything." At one time Leah had wanted a husband, a home. Now she wanted freedom. From what she wasn't sure.

The canyon opened into a wide valley. Twilight illumined the side of jagged trees, rumpled mountains, of water spilling over rocks.

Well, she wasn't twenty-nine anymore. This very day she'd turned thirty!

Tents, trailers, and campfires along the river, children chasing each other, mothers pulling things from boxes on picnic tables, fathers carrying firewood. That would have been a cheap way to travel, but Leah, the city girl, wouldn't have known how to handle it . . . alone.

"You've been independent long enough, Leah," Ralph, the doctor, had said one year ago today. "The time will come when you'll wish you had a man to take care of you." Old Ralph didn't grab for her like Ed. "You've still got your looks and figure, the grace you had as a model. It's your damned independence that turns men off."

Ralph wasn't the first man to mistake Leah's flippancy for independence. If only she were as independent as people thought her. Now that Iris Harper was dead, Leah had a real chance to prove that she could be. Not like the last time she'd fled the family and gone to New York, only to be called back two years later to help care for her mother. But the New York experience hadn't been a success either. All she had to show for that was a scrapbook.

No dark-gold car. But it was harder to distinguish the colors of cars that came up behind the Volks and invariably passed it.

A ranch and two brown horses with white flashes stood at the fence with their ears back, glaring at her, reminding Leah that she was an alien.

And finally a lake, long and narrow, with more campers around more fires. Leah felt alone in the little car surrounded by darkness. The road rose away from the lake in curves that twisted back on themselves.

"Well, I want to be alone. To start fresh, new. . . ."

A yowl came from the back seat. Leah's start forced

the car off the road and up the side of an embankment. Headlights stared into space. The engine died.

"Damn you!" she yelled at the luminescent eyes suspended above a suitcase. "I thought I left you back at . . . are you trying to kill us both?" The Volks slid down off the embankment and stuck. She revved the engine but couldn't back up. The motor stalled again.

The Siamese purred behind her.

Leah set the emergency brake and stepped out to peer over the embankment. She thought she saw the tops of trees far below. Her stomach lifted breathlessly at the thought of the Volks flying out and over the bank, falling down as if from the sky in a sickening free flight.

"Sorry, kitty, but you're going to have to go." She reached into the glove compartment for the flashlight. "No hitchhikers allowed." She swiped the flashlight at the glowing eyes.

The cat swiped back, its claws making a scratching sound on metal. The eyes disappeared and the narrow beam of light could find nothing in the jumble of luggage that had upset when they'd climbed the embankment.

"Look, kitty, I'm so tired. I'm a stray, too. I can't help you. You're too big to lose yourself in this tiny car." But it had. It either moved every time she moved a suitcase or a dress bag or had crawled under the front seat.

She gave up and flashed the light on the back tires. They sat in a small indentation with water running down it. A car came up and passed without slowing. "Nobody helps strays," she muttered.

Strange rustling sounds in the darkness. . . .

Leah jumped back into the car, put it in reverse, and tried rocking her body and the Volks. She put the gear in first and the front end lowered as part of the embankment gave way.

Into reverse again . . . the door ajar . . . one hand on the handle in case she had to jump. Tires whined, then buzzed . . . then caught. They all backed onto the road.

"I don't know what I'm going to do with you, cat, but if I don't get to Walden soon I'm liable to twist your neck. You picked the wrong stray."

An answering rustle behind her.

The Volkswagen groaned up and around curves. Shadow pines tried to block the stars, crowded in on the road.

No houses, no campfires. Just the headlights that seemed to be keeping a constant distance behind her. Why didn't that car pass her like all the others? Was it dark-gold?

Slow, grinding mile after mile. Her bottom ached with the flatness of the seat, her back with fatigue. Her vigilant stomach began its sour burning.

Sleep and nausea waved through her alternately.

A sign loomed in the dark, CAMERON PASS. Surely Walden was near.

Stars winked on one side of the sky and lightning on the other before trees closed in on the road once more. The lightning revealed a strange nature world with which Leah could not identify.

The cat crawled to the back of the seat next to her and purred in her ear.

"I wish you'd go away. You remind me of Mother." *Her mother with the long tapered fingers hanging over the side of the tub, blood oozing off the nails to drip to the floor. . . .*

The pavement ended and Leah fought gravel. Enormous road machines slept in a hollowed-out space in a mountain. Over two hours since Ted's Place and still no Walden.

The gravel ended finally, and the bump as she hit the pavement knocked the big cat onto the seat beside her.

Still the headlights showed only trees and road. Still the headlights behind her kept watch.

She was half asleep by the time they passed a lighted sign that she thought said Pair-O-Vancy. A motel?

"Kitty, let's see if that car is following us." Leah pulled over and turned off the lights. "Or maybe I'm as neurotic as I think I am."

Lights appeared behind her, moving slowly. The car passed in the dark.

Leah waited.

"It doesn't look like it's coming back. Should we go see what a pair-o-vancy is? What do I mean, we? You're get-

18

ting dumped again the minute I get a chance."

The sign, at closer, slower inspection, read PAIR-O-, with a picture of two dice burned in the wood followed by the word CABINS.

Leah turned into the drive. "Paradise. That I can use right now."

A gas pump directly in front of her . . . STANDARD. OIL. GAS. SORRY, NO GAS.

Shadow cars and unlit cabins and in the center a log house with a light over the door. . . .

The rustling of a mountain night settled over her as she walked to the house. A heavy chill wrapped Leah and the smell of pine and dirt in a dark bundle. She knocked.

No sound from within. She knocked again.

Leah decided to sleep in the car, here in this oasis of civilization. But as she turned away, the door opened and a man stood on the step tying a rope around his bathrobe.

"I'm sorry to get you up, but the sign said there was a vacancy."

"Don't matter." He had a beautiful warm smile that was missing two teeth. "Thought we were done for the night so I turned in. But there's a cabin left." He looked toward the Volks, sitting dimly beyond the porch light. "You alone?"

"Yes. I've been traveling all day. I was trying to get to Walden."

"I know." His chuckle was sleepy, soothing. "You're a flatlander. Long way to Walden still. Good thing you stopped. Flatlanders always think they're going to make good time. Not used to mountain roads." He yawned and stretched his arms above his head.

"I don't have much money. . . ."

"All I have left is a double." He stepped off the porch into shadow. "They go for ten a night. But I'll let you have it for the price of a single since it's late. That'd be seven."

"Seven dollars?"

"These are only fishing cabins. Not the Holiday Inn. But you'll sleep better without all that machinery controlling your air. Real mountain fresh air. Good for you, believe me."

A few minutes later Leah believed him. She stood under a hanging sixty-watt bulb with a chain and felt the real mountain fresh air coming in through cracks in the roof, the walls, the floor. Leah was cold to her teeth.

Two iron bedsteads covered with worn white chenille, more chenille hanging on wires at the windows, a refrigerator, a round table with oilcloth and four wooden chairs, a stove with a sign that warned: DANGER—OVEN DOES NOT WORK. DO NOT HEAT WATER IN WATER BUCKETS. THERE ARE TEAKETTLES FOR THIS. THERE IS HOT WATER IN LAUNDRY ROOM IN HOSE BEHIND WASHING MACHINE. THANKS, THE MANAGER.

The manager walked in with a pail of water and set it on a stand beside a metal pan. He hung what looked to be a huge gravy ladle with a curved end over the edge of the pail. On the wall behind the metal pan another sign: IF YOU LEAVE DIRTY DISHES, LEAVE THREE DOLLARS.

Shaken by more than just the cold, Leah walked out to the car and drove it up to the door, carried her coat, purse, food and a suitcase into the cabin.

The manager was now stuffing raw boards into one side of the stove.

"I thought the oven didn't work."

He stuffed some newspapers on top of the wood and lit it. "This part of the stove is for heating. It'll take the chill off quick."

She handed him seven dollars.

"I see you're not quite alone." He looked to the floor. The Siamese sat proprietarily next to her left shoe.

He bent to pet the cat. "He's a beaut. Looks well cared for. You'd be amazed how many people dump their animals around here. Makes me boil." He stood and looked into Leah's eyes. "I can see you're not that kind of person. If I thought you was, I wouldn't even rent my last cabin to you. The bathroom's lit all night and it's behind my house. Hot water in the shower. Have a good sleep."

And Leah was left staring at the Siamese, who jumped onto the round table and settled next to the groceries.

She looked under the chenille on one of the double beds. There were four heavy wool blankets. The cabin was

20

scrupulously clean and the snapping fire in the oven began to warm it.

She pulled the chenille curtains across the windows and tried to feel cozy.

Odds and ends of dime-store dishes sat on a shelf. Leah poured milk into a thick white mug and met the chilly blue eyes on the table.

"You're going to eat me out of pocket and you're not even mine." But she poured milk into a bowl for her companion. "You know, I used to have dishes like this in my apartment in New York?"

The animal hunched over the milk, studiously ignoring her.

Leah sat on a straight chair and lowered her face to his whiskers. "I used to try to paint little flowers on them to class them up, but the paint came off in the dishwasher."

The big cat raised his head to sniff the tip of her nose and returned to the milk.

"I had the paints left over from a sorry attempt at oil painting. But I couldn't afford the lessons." She whispered it into his ear and the ear twitched in irritation. "That was after needlepoint and before ceramics or was it macramé? I know it was before short-story writing and poetry."

The cat licked the last drop from the bowl, then yawned in her face.

"I dabbled. Leah, the dabbler, that's me. I worked so hard to pay the rent on that apartment I was too tired for hobbies and too broke. I don't like roommates," she said pointedly and remembered the tiny bedroom she'd shared with two sisters in the redevelopment house in Chicago. "An apartment is very expensive for one person, even a tiny. . . . Kitty, are you listening to me?"

The kitty was washing behind his ears.

"And I class you with roommates. Oh, I've had plenty of offers, but nobody moves in with me. Get that?" Leah sat back and watched the cat ignore her.

Dabbling had led her nowhere. She'd scrapped each project after a few weary weeks. Scrap. . . . Leah turned to the suitcase on the bed behind her. "This time, kitty, I'm really not going back!" She stood so suddenly that the cat arched and spit, elongated eyes widening to a circle.

Leah opened the suitcase and reached beneath her clothes for the scrapbook. "My only claim to fame. But not something I could display on a coffee table." She tore out the first page and looked at Leah Harper smiling comfortably in a girdle she didn't need. Lifting the metal circle above the fire by its handle as she'd seen the manager do, she consigned page one to the flames.

"Look at this." She displayed page two to her feline companion. "Would you believe that is Leah Lorraine Harper? How could I ever show this to my grandchildren?" The bottom half of Leah, in panty hose, went into the fire. And the next page, and the next . . . Leah in bras with invisible stuffing in the cups. And one of her hands with a diamond ring . . . long tapering fingers like her mother's. . . .

"Of Iris' three girls," she had heard someone say, "Leah is the spitting image of her mother in looks and temperament."

"I will not be another Iris, kitty. I will never fail that completely."

But the cat slept, curled blissfully between the Velveeta and milk.

Leah burned the scrapbook and threw the plastic cover into the wastebasket. "Here I go, burning my bridges again."

The moon lit the encampment when she stepped out of the cabin to look for the bathroom, but there were clouds around it and thunder rolled through the pines.

The ladies', and men's, and the laundry room shared a building. She showered behind a folding screen feeling sleepy again as she groped her way back to the cabin, wearing her coat over pajamas.

Warm air greeted her as she opened the door. The loud purring of the Siamese seemed homey and welcoming.

She could barely see the light chain in front of a lighter patch of covered window, had actually started to reach for it before she remembered that she hadn't turned it off before she left.

Lightning flashed soundlessly to outline the room and the man at the table, tipped back on two legs of his chair, stroking the cat on his lap with one hand, raising a dark stubby gun with the other.

"Turn on that light and you're dead," he warned her.

Chapter Four

LEAH HARPER had never had much sympathy for namby-pamby women who allowed themselves to be victimized by men.

But this was the first time she had faced one holding a gun.

During the second that thunder detonated over the cabin's roof, Leah thought of a surprising number of things she could do. She could run for the door, scream, kick the gun out of his hand, overturn the table, pretend to faint. . . . Could he see her better than she could see him? Was the weapon real?

Her mother's often-repeated advice to her daughters had been, "If a man gets funny with you, knock him in the nuts with your knee."

But these nuts were well protected by a fat cat and a hard-looking gun. Leah began to sweat. Each tiny pore seemed to react with a sticky, sickly ache.

"Sit." His voice was low and flat. Lightning had revealed the face of the man with the murderous look at Ted's Place. He had a voice to match.

Leah's hands found a chair. She sat.

Even when she heard the cat hit the floor, even when the man came to feel in her coat pockets, run his fingers over her pajamas, Leah sat meekly, hating herself for her fear and the sickly sweating.

23

She didn't fear rape. The man's hands, his breath were as cold and impersonal as the big cat's eyes. He was searching her.

Leah feared death.

The air still hung with the chill of the passionless tone of the few words he'd spoken. She knew the weapon was real. And that it was loaded. She knew the man was dangerous.

Cracks on top of the stove blinked red. He moved behind her and her suitcase clicked when he opened it. How could he see?

But she was beginning to see. Not just the red glow from the stove or the yellow-blue flash of cat eyes on the table, but other shapes. Her purse between the cat and the dark milk carton. The Maalox bottle—he had already rifled her purse. The shadow of the chair he had vacated, even, dimly, the door. . . .

A mosquito buzzed her ear, landed on her neck. Leah found herself rising from the chair, taking a quick step toward the door.

"Don't." It came with swift, sharp finality from behind her. The image of his gun, the estimate of his size, the tone of that one clipped order stopped her.

And then, in astonishment, she heard her own voice saying, "If I'm going to die, it won't be sitting down." She felt her foot rise for another step.

The brutality of the arm that encircled her from behind and the force of the hard metal in the small of her spine left her breathless.

"No tricks, Sheila."

"I'm not Sheila," she gasped through the crushing of the arm across her chest.

"You'd better be. Or we're both dead."

Headlights turned off the road and brightened chenille curtains. Leah relaxed against her captor, hoping for more room to breathe.

He had stiffened, alert to what was happening outside.

A car door slammed. A repeated knocking sound and then the manager's voice telling someone that there were no cabins left.

The arm loosened and Leah took a deep breath. One more and she could scream. His hand moved up to cover her mouth, leaving her free for a fraction of a second. She swiveled to face him . . . brought her knee up hard . . . fingernails finding his face. The gun clunked as it hit the floor.

God, he was big. Her knee struck too low.

She managed only the beginning of a scream before his fist in her stomach took care of any air she might have used for voice.

Leah doubled over with her face almost against her knees. Something hit the back of her neck. Lights sparked behind her eyeballs and then darkness.

Her first awareness, even before she opened her eyes, was the instant recollection of all that had happened. Her second was that she was all in one piece. And every piece hurt.

She heard the asthmatic rattling of the cat and felt a measured poking, prickling on her chest.

Leah opened her eyes to discover her hands were tied together above her head to the metal bedstead, and her ankles to its foot, her body stretched savagely taut between, a gag rapidly drying out her tongue.

The Siamese stood with its front paws rhythmically kneading her sternum where the coat had pulled away, its claws pricking her skin through pajamas. He purred exuberantly, his eyes half closed. It was the dance cats do when they're full, safe, contended. Those cold-blooded eyes, closed to slits now, pretended that they loved Leah, were thankful for her protection and care.

Leah raised her head and saw the outline of the man at the window. His gun held aside a corner of the curtain. Agony moved from the back of her neck to her head. There was an answering fury from her ulcer. What was he watching for?

The Siamese stepped off her chest, turned around three times, and curled up, using her armpit for a pillow.

Damned useless animal. Why couldn't he have been a Doberman pinscher?

Raindrops plopped on the roof. Lightning snapped. Thunder rolled in close behind. The man added wood to the fire in the stove.

Leah's hands and feet were without feeling, the muscles in her back, legs, and arms stretched to the limit.

The man left the window to rustle around on the shelf. And then he stood over her, lighting a candle stub in a saucer.

Holding the saucer, he sat on the bed, his thigh against her thigh, and put the gun to her head.

Chapter Five

LEAH closed her eyes and waited. She thought of the violent way her mother had died a week ago.

Tears pushed beneath her eyelids. This couldn't be happening. No!

Burning juices surged up her throat and lay rancid on the back of her tongue. She choked against the gag in her mouth . . .

. . . and felt it being loosened . . . and then removed.

"No screaming." The gun proded emphasis at her forehead. "When your friends come, Sheila, you're my hostage. When were they supposed to get here? I saw you talking to Charlie."

The candle reminded her that it was her birthday, probably her last. Her tears cleared and the flame narrowed, undulated. Leah opened her eyes and saw two flames.

"Sheila?" His voice sent both flames into a frenzy.

"Maalox. The bottle on the table that was . . . in my purse. Please!"

Her stomach gurgled dangerously in the silence. The cat lifted its head and looked at Leah's middle.

The candle moved closer until she could feel the heat of the flame. "Are you on something?" he asked.

"No. I'm sick. Oh, please."

The flame and the cold metal moved away. Now was the instant to scream . . . and to be shot while helplessly tied to a bed. At least her mother had made a play for dignity by doing it herself.

The man and his candle returned with the Maalox. He tasted it and spit, cleared his throat, put the bottle to her lips. The candle and the gun were in the same hand.

Leah drank the last of the thick chalky fluid. The cat lay warm across her stomach.

The man sat against her again. "Now—"

"I'm not Sheila. I don't have any friends coming. My name is Leah Harper."

"I know. And a damned poor cover. What's happened to old Welker? He could have done better."

"I don't know any Welker. I'm—"

"An innocent bystander, I know. We don't have time for this, Sheila. When's Charlie due? He couldn't have been far behind me."

A car on the road behind the cabin, its headlights brightening chenille. He lowered the candle and she could see the scratches her nails had left above the stubby beard line.

His head turned with the sound of the car's passing, his eyes in shadow because of the slight overhang of his forehead, the thickness of his eyebrows. Something desperate in the tense way he sat listening to the car. It made him seem all the more dangerous.

"We'll just wait then. I've got you, at least."

"You won't have me much longer if you keep me tied so tightly."

He bound the wet gag across her mouth, felt her hands and feet, and loosened the bonds. He'd used her clothes for ropes. Her feet were tied with a blouse and a button clanged against the metal bedstead as he worked.

Leah moved her hands and feet up and down and around to warm them. She lay in that degrading position and watched him blow out the candle and sit on the other bed to wait for "her friends." The cat left her stomach and crawled up beside him. He stroked it automatically.

Rain pelted the roof, dripped somewhere on the floor. The cat purred.

Leah drowsed because she didn't dare to, fought it off, drowsed again, slept, dreamed of her mother in her bloody bath. . . .

She awoke to dim light. The rain had stopped. The man and the cat and the gun slept together on the other bed, the man's feet still on the floor. He'd fallen over where he sat, a mass of black ruffled hair curling around his face, a long black sideburn blending with the stubble on his jaw.

The fire had gone out and it was cold.

Birds sang in the trees around the cabin and the Siamese raised his head to listen, stood to stretch and yawn.

Still the man didn't awaken. Wouldn't it be wonderful if he'd died in the night? But the steep slope to the massive shoulders rose and fell peacefully.

Even asleep he exuded an aura of strength. Leah was surprised by a sudden memory of another tousled head she'd seen asleep in the dimness of dawn. But sleep had robbed Jason of his strength. It was with Jason that Leah first realized her attraction to strong men and the dangers inherent in that attraction.

But the danger presented by the man on the other bed was obviously more serious. The danger here was death.

Leah lay staring at a sign on the wall beside the bed. NOT RESPONSIBLE FOR FIRE, THEFT, ACCIDENT OR PERSONAL INJURY.

The cat padded to the door, yowled, and turned to look at Leah.

As if she could get up and let it out.

Her companion must be very tired if he couldn't hear the commotion at the door.

She wiggled her wrists in their bonds. Her opponent was good at knots. She slid her hands up the metal, bent her head back till she could see them. They'd been tied with two of her belts.

28

The man spoke clearly in a foreign language. He hadn't moved.

Leah and the cat stared at him. There hadn't been a trace of an accent in his English.

He muttered a phrase that sounded like Spanish and rolled over to face the ceiling, the hand of his gun arm slapping the wall on the other side of the bed, leaving the gun where it lay beside him.

He grunted and opened his eyes.

The Siamese called a request again and the man sat up and shook his head, stared at the cat as if he'd never seen it before, gazed around the cabin with a bewildered look, and gave a start when his eyes fell on Leah.

Wouldn't it be wonderful if he'd had temporary insanity last night? . . . If he suddenly regained his senses and released her, apologized for his behavior?

But he blinked, then seemed to get it all together. He picked up the gun, moved to the door, opened it slightly and looked, then widened it to let the cat out.

He didn't appear Spanish. His size, his manner, everything about him seemed American. He checked the view from both windows, gobbled a slice of her Velveeta, used the giant gravy ladle to dip water from the pail into the metal pan and washed his face in cold water.

There was no towel and he still dripped as he reloaded her purse, put the groceries back into the paper sack.

Lifting her suitcase onto the bed, he pulled out a pair of blue jeans and a yellow jersey top.

Working quickly, roughly, but expertly, he untied her feet, pulled off her pajama bottoms, slipped on her jeans, untied her hands, ripped off her coat and pajama shirt, slammed the jersey over her head, and slid on her coat and shoes. Leah had never been dressed so fast in her life.

"Pick up your purse and the food," he ordered and threw everything that wasn't on her into the suitcase, removed the gag and stuffed it into his pocket.

Leah tried to stand. She fell but he jerked her upright. It hurt to walk and she staggered to the table. "I'm not Sheila, you know." Her mouth was so dry from the gag that it was painful to speak.

"If you're not, I don't need you alive, do I?" Again he peered through a crack in the door. Then he pulled the covers on the bed aside to make it look as if she'd left them that way as she crawled out.

Leah shivered in the dawn's cold. Those four wool blankets would have been heaven.

"Now, walk out to your car and get in on the driver's side, start the engine." He handed her the keys. "I'll be right behind you. Just open your mouth once." He waved the gun in her face.

He'd thought of everything. The cabin would look normal. Nothing left behind to warn anyone of the danger she was in. If she could just leave one little thing as a clue. But what?

There was no time. The gun prodded her out to the car. With muscles aching from the rack he'd made of the bed and the chop he'd given her neck, Leah slid into the driver's seat and put the key in the ignition.

No one stirred in the other cabins.

When her captor placed her suitcase in the backseat, the Siamese jumped in to join it.

The three of them pulled out of Pair-O-Dice in the yellow bug.

"Left," he said.

Leah turned left and no one saw them leave. At least she was headed toward Walden.

Would she get there?

Chapter Six

"WHAT are you going to do with me?"

"I don't know."

"May I have some food?" She hated the meekness of

her tone. He'd stripped her dignity as easily and as surely as he'd stripped off her pajamas.

"Ulcer?" He handed her a slice of Velveeta and one back to the cat. Surprisingly, the animal seemed to be eating it.

"What do you care?"

"I don't. Just asking." He sounded defensive.

Had she found a soft spot in this hard man? She dared a glance in his direction and decided she hadn't. He looked tired, sagging, somehow hopeless. But the gun did not.

His legs and shoulders filled the Volkswagen to suffocation.

A high plain stretched ahead to distant mountains. Vast herds of cows and their calves grazed behind fences. An occasional ranch building brightened in the rising sun. The sky was cloudless now, but puddles glistened beside the road as scavenger magpies cleaned up the grisly remains of small animals, the night's work of automobiles.

"If you're not Sheila, you've got yourself involved in a real mess." Was that doubt in his voice? But the gun still aimed its barrel at her head.

Leah allowed herself a twinge of hope.

Chartreuse-yellow weeds, bushy and lacy, misty with raindrops, filled the ditches. A tiny brown animal stood on its hind legs at the road's edge.

"Welker would have used a professional." A heavy sigh, and he slapped his knee. "You could have had me twice." There was a cleft in the middle of his chin where the whiskers didn't grow.

"What do you mean? I was tied to the bed." Leah could have bitten her tongue. Why couldn't she keep her mouth shut? His thinking was going in the right direction.

"Before and after that." This time his fist hit the dashboard, his growl like that of an animal. He reminded Leah of an animal, hunted, cornered. What did she know of animals? He was just a dangerous man, with a gun. She was the one who was cornered.

If she pretended to be Sheila, he would keep her alive as a hostage, but he would keep her. As Leah Harper she

31

wouldn't be needed as a hostage or alive either. Was she dangerous to him alive? Wouldn't it be easier, less messy, to just let her go?

A rumbling noise behind them. Leah checked the rearview mirror, but the road was empty.

"And then again, you could be a clever trap . . . but. . . ." He talked more to himself than to her.

The rumbling grew louder. He swiveled to look through the rear window, then to the sides.

But the sound came from above. A shadow darkened the Volks and spread to each side, as if a giant scavenger bird was about to pick them off the highway. The shadow of a small airplane gradually moved onto the road ahead.

Her companion swore. Leah slowed the car. The plane appeared behind its shadow, rose, banked, and turned to buzz them, flying dangerously low.

"Keep going slower," he ordered. "But don't stop." He hid the gun. "I've decided to buy your story. I'm dead anyway."

The sound of the plane was distant behind them.

"See that culvert ahead? Slower. . . ." He opened the door. "You've got a great cat and a great body. So long." He jumped from the car.

Leah slowed more now in reaction to her surprise than because she wanted to. She looked back but couldn't see him in the ditch. Reaching across to slam his door, she stepped hard on the accelerator.

He'd gone from her life as quickly as he'd come. But the small plane had not. It came behind to buzz her again, so low that she automatically hit the brakes. She'd had no time to let down after her encounter with the stranger and the fear of death that had gripped her for hours. She accelerated in panic just as the car had almost come to a standstill.

She turned to look at the one remaining occupant of the car. "Kitty, what do we do?"

The stupid cat was asleep!

Leah looked back to find the plane coming toward them, head on, swooping at the last minute. Its sound on top of the noisy Volks was deafening and more than her beleaguered nervous system could stand. Leah watched as the poor bug shot ahead when she'd meant to stop it. The plane was trying to stop her, her disrupted judgment was trying to kill her, and the end result was a phenomenal burst of speed from the old secondhand Volkswagen.

Eventually she regained enough control to take her foot off the gas pedal and steer to the right-hand lane. Leah was suddenly alone on the endless road.

She pulled over and stopped, stepped out to look at the sky, her heart jumping, her ulcer demanding that she vomit, her knees so shaky that she clung to the door to keep upright.

The little plane was flying away into the sun. And there was a lonely car coming up behind her. Why had the plane flown off when she'd finally stopped?

And then she saw the answer in the approaching car. Its top bore twin gum-ball machines.

Leah let go of the Volkswagen to wave it down, almost fell into the road in front of it. She saw the insignia and COLORADO STATE PATROL lettered on the door as it stopped in front of her. Leah ran toward it, and fell into the arms of the uniformed man who stepped out.

"I've been attacked, Officer! Please, help me."

"Take it easy." He seated her gently in the patrol car, then sat beside her. "Now tell me everything."

He was so young-looking. Leah could have used a daddylike figure. That dark stranger wasn't so professional either. "He really should have killed me," she thought with a jolt, "because I'm about to rat on him." Professional what? Gangster? Murderer? Bank robber? Indian chief?

Leah shrugged off the dark memory of the man who'd said hopelessly, "I'm dead anyway." She told her story to the patrolman, who looked stern and military in his uniform, but whose questioning was gentle.

And she did fine, had him with her all the way, until she described the attack by plane. That was the point where he smiled and blinked at the same time and had to work his tender young face back into an official mold.

"Have you left out anything?" he asked when she'd finished and he pulled the speaker from the radio set in the dashboard. "I mean, were you molested?"

"I was punched in the stomach, chopped in the neck, and tied to a bed all night . . . if that's not molested—"

"But were you sexually assaulted?"

"No. But—"

"Are you sure?" His eyes followed her from shoes to hair, softened with understanding. "Do you want a doctor?"

Leah groaned inwardly. This kid'd had the new training women's lib forced on the law. "I'm thirty years old. Old enough to know if I'd been raped. I have been attacked, but not sexually. No permanent damage. I do not need a doctor. But I could use some breakfast."

He replaced the speaker and smiled soothingly. "So could I. I was headed for the best breakfast in Walden when I met you. But first, let's check out that culvert." The patrol car made a U-turn.

Leah sat inert, while he checked the culvert . . . and found no trace of her attacker.

"Let's get that breakfast," he said when he returned. He drew up beside the Volks. "Can you follow me in? It isn't far."

Minutes later they'd both parked in front of a clapboard building in a tiny treeless town. The patrolman reached in the window to pet the Siamese, asleep on top of her suitcase. His hand came out crossed with bloodied scatches.

"He prefers murderers," Leah said dumbly.

The patrolman laughed and guided her into a building pulsating with wonderful morning odors. "Order me a number one with ham and have them hold it for ten minutes. Order for yourself. I'll be back."

"Where are you going?"

He wrinkled his nose and grinned. "I'm going to look up the local fuzz. Couldn't get him on the radio."

Leah felt human for the first time in a week. Even law and order had a sense of humor in the West. She picked up the menu stuck between the napkin and the salt and pepper holders. The café was worn and dingy, but obviously patronized by the locals.

Knowing her ulcer would have ordered a poached-egg-on-milk-toast, Leah ordered the number one with bacon and hot chocolate. She deserved a binge. The gregarious waitress didn't seem to mind the hold on the patrolman's order and brought Leah's hot chocolate right away.

Tempted to human kindness by the comfort of her hot drink, Leah stopped the waitress as she came by with a tray of dirty dishes. "Do you have doggy bags?"

"No. Do you have a doggy?"

"There's a stray cat in my car and he—"

"Oh, poor starving thing." She set the tray on the table.

Leah blinked. "If you can imagine a blimp starving, you've a better imagination than I have." She felt foolish to have brought up the subject.

"Fur," the waitress said and sat down across from Leah.

"What?"

"Well, some cats look fat because of their fur. Had a good feel on this cat? Probably all ribs under that fur. What does it like to eat?"

"Anything."

"Honey, no cat eats anything, even if it's starving. I know. I've got three. Hubby hates them but. . . ." She rose and lifted the tray. "All kinds of scraps around here."

"I don't have much money."

"Forget it. They'd be thrown out anyway. Any cat lover is a friend of mine, honey."

Leah finished her chocolate and pondered the cat. Having one opened strange doors.

She remembered having an insane desire for a dog when she'd had to leave New York and return home. She'd met a dog once who would have been perfect. He was a large bony red, with a tail in constant happy motion and soft amber eyes.

Leah read his tags, took him home, and called the owner. That was how she met big, strong Jason, who always asked after scraps for his "Mutt" when he visited a restaurant and who invariably left with a doggy bag.

The relationship was Jason lasted about three months. Leah discovered that he wanted her on a leash as tight as

Mutt's. When it was over, Leah missed Mutt more than she did Jason.

She'd finally begun to tremble with delayed reaction and letdown when the number one with bacon arrived. Two beautiful fried eggs, hash-brown potatoes, three strips of bacon, two pieces of buttered toast, and a huge mug of coffee. Leah hadn't tasted a fried egg or coffee for two years. She stopped only once, to reflect on whether or not her dark attacker would have any breakfast. A body the size of his would demand a lot of it.

She didn't pause even when the patrolman and his companion slid in across from her. The patrolman's breakfast arrived with a brown bag for Leah and a wink from the waitress. "For Goodyear, your blimp."

"Goodyear?" The law looked up from his number one with ham.

"The cat . . . in the car. He's kind of big and fat like a . . . Didn't you ever see the Goodyear blimp over cities or football games?"

His look was blank but he said, "Oh, the cat." He made Leah feel old.

When she'd finished her breakfast she retold her story to the "local fuzz." She assured them both that she had left marks on the man's face, that she had not been raped, that she did not need a doctor, that even if it sounded crazy it was all true.

The sheriff's deputy had her repeat her description of the attacker, told her of a cheap motel, and left.

Leah was stunned when the patrolman insisted on paying for her breakfast and escorting her to the Shangri-La. "Not every day I run into a beautiful blonde in distress." He blushed.

She felt like giving him a motherly pat on the head and hoped that Shangri-La would prove less exciting than paradise.

Shangri-La stood at the very edge of the treeless town. On a treeless hill. Across from a treeless cemetery.

"You stay right here now, so we can contact you when we hear something. Okay?" He'd carried in her luggage, even emptied the trunk.

"Okay." Leah felt a long way from Shangri-La as she looked around her room. She was getting the shakes again.

"Should we feed your blimp?" He looked at the greasy bag in her hand and the Siamese next to her left foot. God, did the creature heel, too?

"Okay." She was so tired and at last so sated with food, she couldn't think. She'd forgotten the cat.

The patrolman spread out a feast of bits of sausage, bacon, and ham. There were five little cartons of half and half and he poured the cream into an ashtray. "You need sleep. I'll keep in touch. Good-bye, Miss Harper. You too, Goodyear."

Goodyear was too engrossed in the feast to look up. Leah managed a wave and a "Thanks."

After the cat had gobbled all but the bag and the ashtray, he yowled at the door.

Leah opened it. "Good-bye, Goodyear, go find yourself a good home. I can't afford a pet and I don't really like cats. My mother had five and. . . ."

But Goodyear was gone. He hadn't even looked back.

Chapter Seven

LEAH reached for the hot and cold handles of the bathtub . . . and saw the tub in the house in Chicago . . . and her mother's body . . . the bloody razor . . . heard her own uncontrolled screaming. . . .

Would she ever be able to look at an ordinary bathtub again and see just an ordinary bathtub?

A shudder joined the shakes she already experienced. She lay back in the hot water and stared at the steam slowly clouding the tile. She must relax, soak away the soreness of her wild night, think of something other than her mother's suicide . . . what?

The cat. He'd entered her world and left it as quickly as the big man with the shadowy eyes . . . no, she wouldn't think of the man either. But he'd said she had a great body. That was nice to hear at thirty, even from a murderer. There were ugly swollen places on her wrists and ankles.

She'd think of the good days before her father died, when they lived in the comfortable house in the suburbs. Or she could think of later, her college days before the lawyer informed them that the money was running out, that they'd have to find a less expensive life style, that Leah would have to leave the university and find a job if her younger sisters could hope for even a junior college.

Leah's mother had never used her college degree. Unable to face the working world after her husband's death, she couldn't even manage the family finances. Widowhood had been a hard blow to Iris Harper, but the sale of her home and loss of her cleaning lady, bridge club, car, charitable committees, affiliation with the suburban church and its women's functions, membership in the country club, its golf course, and all the things that had summed up her identity to herself—all these losses had wiped out an entire personality.

She closed herself away from her unfamiliar neighbors into the little house in a redevelopment section. Leah and Annette took over the younger Suzie and everything else, and worried every minute they were away from their mother. But Iris just watched TV, talked to her cats, drank, vegetated, grayed. . . . Until a week ago. . . .

Leah washed quickly and stepped out of the tub. Perhaps in sleep she could find forgetfulness.

When her father died, Leah discovered that the mother she'd considered a pillar of strength was not. Leah had been surprised at how unsettling this discovery had been. When Iris took her own life, her daughter strengthened her resolve never to depend on anyone but herself.

There was a scratching at the door as she left the bathroom. "Oh, no, you don't. I said good-bye, remember?"

She ignored the plaintive yowl and slipped into a nightgown. Checking the watch in her purse, she found it was only nine thirty in the morning.

The Siamese had moved to the windowsill, staring in at her with evil slanted eyes framed by the metal rims of the picture window; the barren cemetery with old-fashioned gray headstones provided a haunting background for the "evil eye."

How had he come to adopt Leah? Had he been dumped from a yellow Volkswagen? Had he hopped into the next one that came along? Or did Leah resemble a former owner? Maybe the food hadn't suited at home. Food was obviously at the top of his priority list.

Leah closed the drapes and crawled into bed, lay listening to the noise and prowlings at the window and at the door.

Goodyear did not have the fine aristocratic bone structure of a true Siamese. Although she thought of him as Siamese because of his coloring and markings, his bones were built more along the lines of alley-massive. He was probably the result of a chance encounter between a treasured purebred and a big back-street tom.

A dog—it sounded large and very near—growled low in its throat. Goodyear hissed. Leah leapt from the bed.

The cat collided with her ankles the minute she opened the door. She stood looking at a German shepherd with a surprised expression on his face and blood dripping from his nose. The dog turned and ran.

Goodyear calmly washed himself on her bed.

"Looks like I've been taken in again," Leah muttered and locked the door. "You were in about as much danger as a. . . . Oh, just turn off your motor so I can get some sleep." She lay down again and tried to feel some ribs through lush fur. The ribs were well padded with fat.

But the fur was soft, squishy, warm. It felt soothing under her hand, accompanied by the loud purring, the scratchiness of the animal's tongue as it extended its washing to her wrist.

"You can take on a German shepherd but just get chummy with a murderer. Someday when I can afford a pet, it's going to be a dog." But she continued to stroke the luxurious coat. It had the tactile allure of rich velvet or worry beads.

Leah went to sleep, still seeing the haphazard dark knots on the pine walls surrounding her and thinking of the tall, cruel man who had tied her to a bed. He'd automatically stroked the cat, too.

She awoke to a persistent sound she could not at first identify. Goodyear lay curled in the hollow of her arm.

Someone was knocking at the door. She pulled her coat over her nightgown and slid the safety chain into place. A man stood outside the slit the chain allowed, but he was not dark and threatening.

"Leah Harper?" A stiff, mechanical smile.

He hadn't called her Sheila. She relaxed. "Yes."

He slid an open wallet through the crack and she read the intimidating words "Federal Bureau of Investigation." She'd slipped the chain from its lock before she remembered where she'd heard the name on the card below the badge—Welker. Joseph Welker.

He was in the room, closing the door behind him before she could protest.

Leah pulled the coat around her tightly and backed away. "Welker."

"Yes, Miss Harper. You don't know me, but"—he slid sideways along the wall and peered through an opening he'd made in the drapes as the dark man had done the night before; what was supposed to be out there this time? —"the local authorities have informed me of your problem, the man who held you captive last night?" He sat in the room's one chair and his smile warmed a little before it vanished. "His mistaking you for someone named Sheila?"

Leah backed as far as the bed and sat. Tendrils of anxiety chased away the grogginess of having slept all day. Anyone could have a badge made. She'd never seen a real one and wouldn't know the difference. "But the FBI. He didn't take me across any state lines or—"

"I know. And I realize this must seem strange." His neck wrinkled over his collar and his eyes continually

40

scanned her face as if he were trying to read her thoughts . . . or her character.

"He mentioned a Welker. He said you goofed because you didn't send a professional." The Siamese crawled onto her lap and hung over on both ends. He too watched Joseph Welker with suspicion.

"That's because he thought you were Sheila. She *is* a professional. But you somehow got in the way." Resting his elbows on the chair arms, he put the tips of his fingers together and continued to study her over them. Behind his brown hornrims, Welker looked like a lawyer or a doctor. In fact, he resembled her brother-in-law—the calculated ease, the controlled posture, the slightly receding hair clipped short and combed back away from his face, the air of authority. . . .

"Miss Harper, I'm afraid we have a problem." He crossed his legs and ran a finger down the crease in the pants of his brown suit.

"We?" Leah sensed her most recent set of troubles were not over, after all. She buried a hand in the comfort of cat fur.

"I have just arrived from Washington to find a certain situation in a very nasty mess."

"Why is that *my* problem?"

"Because, quite innocently, you've become involved. You have twice been mistaken for a woman named Sheila, you've also been in contact with Glade who—"

"Glade?" It sounded like an air freshener.

"The man you met last night. He's in a great deal of danger and—"

"*He's* in danger! He's the most dangerous man I've ever met."

"Well, there are even more dangerous men after him, Miss Harper. And if they even suspect that you might be able to tell them where he is or give them a clue, their questioning might not be pleasant. The word is probably out that he was seen with a blonde in a yellow Volkswagen and . . . I understand that there was an aircraft involved this morning before he jumped from your car?"

"Yes. It tried to run us off the road."

He stood to survey the jumble of luggage on each side of the bed. "I don't suppose you have a wig with you? That isn't blond?"

"I don't own one."

"Well, then I suggest you wear a scarf over your hair for the next few days and that Volkswagen will have to go. They couldn't have seen you too clearly from a plane."

"But the Volks has been sitting out there all day."

"Yes . . . well, we mustn't tempt fate any longer. Every minute that car sits there puts you in jeopardy." He picked up the phone on the bedside table and dialed. "Brian? Is the Vega ready? . . . Well, hurry it up! . . . No, she's all right, no thanks to you and Sheila. . . . I haven't asked her yet. Just keep your eye on this place and hurry that Vega. Better send Sheila for the Volks." He hung up and picked her keys off the dresser. "Do you have all your belongings out of the car?"

"Yes, but . . . now wait just a minute! How do I know you are who you say you are or that any of this is true? How do I know you're not just stealing my car?"

"Miss Harper, no matter who I was, do you think that if I were going to steal a car it would be that little yellow mess outside your door?"

She had to admit he had a point. "But this is all going too fast, I don't understand—"

"I realize this seems heavy-handed at the moment and I will explain everything shortly, but too much time has been lost already. It's partly our fault that you've become involved in this and it's the least we can do to replace your car with a safer one. There's a blue Vega on the way. It's newer than your Volkswagen and just the thing for you." He leaned toward her and Goodyear gave a warning moan with his mouth closed. Maybe this man was with the FBI. The cat was not fond of the good guys.

Sheila couldn't have been far away because a knock sounded at the door just then and Joseph Welker handed the car keys out with a "You know where to hide it. Now step on it!"

Leah reached for the phone and caught a glimpse of troubled blue eyes in a pale face and a wisp of flaxen hair peeking under a stylish presewn bandanna.

Welker closed the door and turned as Leah dialed the operator. She asked for the police and expected him to try to stop her, but he merely brushed cat hairs from his suit and waited patiently as she announced, "This is Leah Harper, Room Ten at the Shangri-La Motel. There's a man in my room who claims to be—"

"The FBI," the languid voice of the deputy Leah had met at breakfast interrupted. "It's okay, Miss Harper. He's legit. Just be a good girl and do what Mr. Welker wants."

"But—"

"You're outa my league now, lady." And he hung up.

Leah stared dumbly at the silent receiver until Welker replaced it for her. "Now that the Volkswagen and my identity are taken care of, perhaps we can talk."

Leah swallowed. "About what?"

He took her back over every detail of her adventure from the time she'd met Glade and his companions at Ted's Place to the moment she'd fallen into the arms of the state patrolman.

"And you haven't been disturbed or seen or heard anything suspicious since this morning?"

"Not until you came."

"Yes. Well, you've been lucky." He pried more cat hair from his pant leg, studied the varnished knots on the pine paneling. "Miss Harper, I understand you are presently unemployed and"—he gestured to the tiny crowded room —"and low on funds." He stood and walked around the bed and back as if he would have liked to pace but there was no room. "I have a job for you. If you weren't already involved I wouldn't suggest this but . . . I have to get a message to Glade. It's urgent."

"But I don't know where he is."

"I don't either. But I do have a list of probabilities and not enough people to cover them all. I'd like to send you to one of the places where he could show up." Joseph Welker pulled his wallet from an inside breast pocket and Leah glimpsed the strap of a shoulder holster.

"Mr. Welker, I do need a job, but not a dangerous one.

43

I've been through a lot in the last week and last night was—"

"If I thought you'd be in any danger, I wouldn't propose this, believe me. But with a different car and your hair covered there's no reason why you should be." He removed some bills from the wallet and laid them on the dresser. "All I want you to do is to take the Vega and go to Oak Creek, a small town not far from here. Stay here tonight—I'll have a watch kept on this place—leave in the morning. That'll give him time to get there if that's where he's headed. I'll have people watching other areas. Hang around Oak Creek tomorrow. If you see him give him this message. One, Welker is willing to meet any reasonable terms for the property, and two, the company has hired goons and they don't want him alive."

"What property?"

"The less you know about that, the better. Then take the money and the Vega and leave this part of Colorado. Just stay six, eight hours in Oak Creek, walk around so that he can spot you. If you don't make contact, leave before dark and go on your way, a richer woman driving a better car."

"Why me?" Just the thought of seeing the dark man with the gun again made her shudder.

"Because he knows you, should know that you're no danger to him. He's desperate and running and he's not likely to show himself to me or my people. It's a long shot, I know, but you just might bring him out of the woodwork. The chances are good that even if he sees you in Oak Creek, he won't let you see him, but all I ask is that you try." He added another bill to those on the dresser.

Leah licked dry lips. "Is that real money?"

"Yes, Miss Harper. And all you have to do to earn it is to go to Oak Creek. Probably the easiest money you'll ever earn. But most important, you might save a man's life and your government a good deal of trouble."

"Were Charlie and his friend at Ted's Place goons?"

"No, they're . . . with another organization."

44

"How do you know I won't just take the money and not go to Oak Creek?"

"I admit I haven't had time to check you out. About all I know for sure is that you don't have a police record in this country and that you haven't traveled abroad. But I've learned to be a fairly good judge of people. You seem levelheaded enough and frankly I'm pulling out all the stops, doing everything I can to reach this man before he's murdered. You are only one of a number of plans being set in motion."

Leah looked at the pile of bills. It was a lot of money. "If I did make contact with this Glade, how do I know he wouldn't murder *me?* I find him a lot more frightening than any goons."

He appeared startled for the first time since she'd met him. "I'll admit he's capable of it. But he can be a reasonable man and he has no reason to harm you. He knows you're not Sheila. You don't pose any threat now that he knows who you really are. He's also known to have a special weakness for blondes. That's why I sent Sheila to—"

"He doesn't have any weaknesses and—"

She was interrupted by the sound of a car in front of her unit. Welker stepped outside and she could hear him talking with another man. At one point he exploded with "Holy Jesus!"

She pushed Goodyear off her lap. "You know, kitty, it would be heaven to not have to worry about finances for a while but—" She opened the door almost to collide with Welker.

"Listen, something's come up. I have to run." He handed her a set of car keys. "Think it over tonight and I'll talk to you first thing in the morning. You can go out to eat. I've put a tail on you. But don't wander all over town."

"Hey, wait! I've decided not to take the job. Hey. . . ."

But Joseph Welker was gone and Leah was left staring at a blue Vega.

Chapter Eight

"GIVE me one good reason, kitty, why I should want to save that big brute's life." Leah slid into a dress and zipped it up the back. "No way am I going to Oak Creek. Not for all the money. . . ." The bills still lay on the dresser. She looked away and yanked a comb through her hair.

"I'm going out to dinner. Why don't you just go? I keep telling you I can't afford a pet."

Goodyear jumped to the dresser and sat sniffing the strange pile of money.

"Oh, no, that's not mine. I'm not taking the job. I'm going to find something more relaxing."

The cat moaned a warning and struck at the money.

"What's the matter? Is it counterfeit? Or does it just smell like the law to you?" Leah went into the bathroom to wash her hands and returned to find the money on the floor, Goodyear still crouching smugly on the dresser.

Next to her shoe lay a twenty-dollar bill. "Cat, you were right. This has got to be counterfeit." She picked up more twenties, some with wet, frayed corners. "Of, for . . . Government jobs must be cushy in a depression. No, this has got to be fake."

Leah counted. "Goodyear, if he'd pay me this much to make an uncertain contact with Glade what's-his-face, what must he be willing to offer Glade for the property, whatever it is?"

Goodyear answered in Siamese fashion, the irises of his eyes vertical slits in the devil's fashion.

"Well, I'm not going to do it, you devil. He's probably with the Mafia. They've always got lots of money. He probably conned the local sheriff's office with phony papers or something." But she tied a scarf over honey-blond hair. Too much of it showed underneath, so she wound the long strands into a knot and pinned it tight to the back of her head.

"I can't just leave all this money lying here, though." She stuffed the bills into her purse. "I am going to get dinner and you are going."

Leah grabbed the cat and carried him to the door, where he squirmed out of her hands and disappeared into the room. She searched under the bed and the chair, in the bathroom. No Goodyear. Her ulcer rumbled. "When I get back, I just may make kitty stew out of you," she yelled at the infuriating critter she couldn't see and locked the door behind her. She turned to face the Vega.

It was hate at first sight.

She walked around it, kicked a tire, looked in the windows. The car smelled new, strange.

Leah walked to the drugstore to replenish her supply of Maalox, glancing over her shoulder often to see if she could spot the "tail" Welker referred to. She saw no one. She paid for the Maalox with a twenty from the FBI-Mafia-whatever and watched closely as the clerk examined it. But the woman just put it in the till, returning the change to Leah. "Thank you and have a nice evening."

Leah stood outside, listened to the click as the clerk locked up behind her, watched an enormous round weed tumble by, saw a man with a cigarette hanging out of his mouth, lounging in a doorway across the street. The tail? A goon? Other than Welker's this was the only business suit she'd seen in Walden.

She hurried toward the café, peering down side streets for the yellow Volkswagen, feeling lonely without it. All the shops were closing now, only a few people ambling on the sidewalks. Rush hour in Walden was a slow affair. The little town seemed harsh, dusty, almost as alien as the mountains. If the man in the suit was following her, she didn't see him when she entered the café.

For dinner, she dared her ulcer with a steak and sat by the window to watch for the Volkswagen, or Welker, or

47

Sheila, or the tail or even a sign from heaven to give her direction.

"Are you the gal with the stray cat?" A strange waitress stopped at her table.

"How did you know?"

"Well, Betty described you from this morning and you're kind of hard to miss. She told me to send some scraps home with you if you came back. Just a minute, I'll get them."

When she returned with the brown bag, she said, "Funny, her thinking of your stray after getting the boot this morning. But she's crazy about 'em."

"Boot?"

"'Yeah, she got let go today. Not many tourists going through this summer and lots of local people are leaving to see if they can get work in the shale towns. Not enough business. Feel sorry for Betty, though. Her husband's out of work, too."

Later, Leah found herself standing on the sidewalk, wondering what an ex-model, ex-secretary, ex-clerk, occupational failure, guilt-ridden ex-daughter with three years of college and an ulcer could do in an area where even the waitresses were being laid off.

The sun was setting in eerie pink and lavender cloud drifts behind the cemetery when she reached Shangri-La. Goodyear appeared for scraps of steak, liver, chicken, and hamburger. When she let him out, his stomach barely cleared the floor. But this time she didn't say good-bye.

Leah felt very full herself and a trifle nauseated. Feast and famine and worry were no way to live with an ulcer. She brought out her array of creams, astringents, and hair rollers for something to do and because it was a comfortable routine, and worried about her problems anyway.

She searched for wrinkles, crow's feet, gray hairs, and found none. She didn't look any different at thirty. But she felt different. That birthday was just one more step in a downhill decline. Finally she turned on the black and white television and stared at it, but her thoughts kept getting in the way.

Leah did her fingernails, did her exercises, put on her

nightgown . . . found herself listening for a cat at the door. Perhaps she would keep Goodyear for company. But she couldn't afford his appetite. Of course, there was a great deal of money in her purse. But it wasn't hers. She opened the door to semi-dark. "Kitty, kitty, kitty?" No Goodyear. Just the strange Vega.

The evening stretched on interminably. After sleeping all day, she resigned herself to a long, slow night.

Leah missed her scrapbook and for the very reason she had burned it. Going back didn't look quite so bad after the last twenty-four hours.

"Economy worsens, congressional committee probes tax write-offs of major oil companies," said the flickering black and white face. "Chicago woman kidnapped near Cameron Pass"—Leah jerked alert from her TV trance —"and more rain for the high country. These and other items in the news, but first this word from Enveco."

Chicago woman kidnapped? No, it couldn't be. . . . She watched impatiently as a well-dressed middle-aged man dug a hole in a sandy beach with a shovel. He dumped money into the hole and explained that oil companies poured millions of such dollars down dry holes to find a few producing oil wells to provide America with the power to run its cars, industry, and homes.

They weren't talking about her, surely. But how many Chicago women could have been kidnapped near Cameron Pass recently? She sat through a depressing report of Dow-Jones, the Detroit auto industry, unemployment, and an ad for denture wearers who ate blueberry pie.

Then a host of congressmen expressed shock in bureaucrateese over the "laundry list" of major oil companies. They all strangely resembled the man dumping money down a hole in the beach.

Words and phrases flew about the room from the flickering tube. "Special favors . . . loopholes . . . tax breaks . . . privileges . . . percentage depletion . . . dry holes . . . foreign royalties . . . intangible drilling and development costs . . ." But over it all Leah continued to hear "Chicago woman kidnapped."

If Welker was with the FBI and had worried enough

about her safety to exchange cars, surely he wouldn't have allowed her story to reach the news wires.

Two clear plastic stomachs digested aspirin at uneven rates and then: "A Chicago woman, thirty-year-old Leah Harper. . . ."

Good God! Her name and everything.

". . . was held captive at gunpoint last night at Pair-O-Dice Cabins, a fishing resort fifteen miles west of Cameron Pass. According to Miss Harper, her alleged assailant. . . ."

Alleged! Leah threw a plastic hair roller at the screen.

". . . beat her and tied her to a bed, but didn't rape her, the woman said."

Although there was no emotion in his voice, he made it sound as if there was something wrong with the "Chicago woman" because she wasn't raped.

"Jackson County authorities are searching for a black-haired, muscular man. . . ."

Leah began pacing the room.

". . . probably in his mid-thirties and on foot, wearing dark blue shirt and trousers. The man forced Miss Harper to drive him to a spot a few miles east of Walden, Colorado, on State Highway Fourteen where he released her unharmed. A look at weather and sports after this message."

"Welker, you bumbling idiot!" Leah hissed at the elderly lady in a porch swing who tried to discuss laxatives. "Now everybody will know my name, where I am. . . ."

Leah unlocked the door to peer cautiously out into the dark. "Kitty, kitty?" she called softly. She needed somebody to talk to. The shadow-Vega hunched between her and the road. She was suddenly relieved that it wasn't a yellow Volkswagen.

"The Denver area will be warm and dry again tomorrow," said a voice behind her. "But there is more rain in the two-week forecast for the high country, where rivers and streams are dangerously swollen already, officials say. . . ."

"Kitty?" But the world was dark and empty. Leah spent her night in Shangri-La alone with her fear.

Chapter Nine

LEAH looked suspiciously at everyone who entered the little café the next morning. Her hair was again knotted up under a scarf and her head ached from worry and lack of sleep. She finished her poached-egg-on-milk-toast quickly and hurried back to the Shangri-La, hoping she'd find Goodyear waiting to get in the door, hoping she would not find some menacing type waiting in the room.

But the front step and the room were empty. Welker had said first thing in the morning. Where was he?

Finally, Leah packed her bags and loaded them in the Vega.

She called softly for the cat, and when there was no answer, she locked herself in the room. Were there goons out there looking for Leah Harper? How much of all this could she believe? How much did she dare not believe?

The minute Welker came she'd hand him the money and leave Walden in the dust. She'd keep the Vega because she had no choice. Where could she go with so little money? With jobs so scarce?

Leah would find something. She had to. Something far away from a place called Oak Creek.

She placed the wad of bills on the dresser and took the car keys out of her purse, fiddled with them nervously.

A faint rustle at the door. . . .

"Goodyear, thank God!" But she opened the door to a man with his knuckles poised to knock. "Oh—"

"Brian Kruger." He flipped open a wallet with the now-familiar badge and stepped inside. "Joe Welker sent me." He checked the street and closed the door. "Listen, don't waste time. You have to get out of here."

"You're telling me! I saw the news on TV last night. What—"

"We're really sorry about that." He had soft brown eyes that reminded her of Jason's Mutt and hair so thin that his scalp showed between every third strand. But he couldn't have been over twenty-five. "Joe and I worked all evening to get that story off the wires but we were too late. Now, Joe wants you to—"

"You can tell Joe to take a flying. . . . Here." She pushed the money at him and opened the door. "I'm taking the Vega because you took my car, but I'm not taking the job. I'm not going to Oak Creek. You can tell that to your Joe."

"But. . . ." He followed her out to the Vega.

Leah slid in, threw her purse on the seat beside her, and put the key in the ignition.

But Brian Kruger held the car door open. "Wait, listen, you mustn't come back to Walden. We're leaving right away and we don't have enough people to keep a watch on you here."

"Don't worry. If I never see Walden again, it'll be—" A dark tail, unmistakably feline moved rhythmically along the motel wall above a line of low shrubs.

"Goodyear!" Leah struggled out of the low car and pushed Brian aside. "Kitty, kitty." The tail turned the corner by the office and Leah followed. "I'll even go to the café and beg you some breakfast if—"

A large black tom with yellow eyes emerged from the shrubbery and sauntered off toward the filling station next door.

Leah turned back to the Vega. How could she miss a cat she didn't want? When she didn't even like cats?

Brian still stood by the car. "Listen, I wish you'd change your mind about—"

"Good-bye, Mr. Kruger." Leah got in, slammed the door in his face, and backed out into the street.

A sign at the edge of the desolate cemetery read STEAMBOAT SPRINGS 62, and a lonely road stretched west. Why not?

Brian Kruger watched her from the parking lot of the

Shangri-La Motel. Leah headed the Vega across the valley for Steamboat Springs. It had the same four-on-the-floor shift as the Volks and even a working radio. But she heard a repeat of the newscast she'd watched on television the night before, complete with more rain for the high country and a Chicago woman kidnapped near Cameron Pass. She turned it off.

She missed the cat. Had the big Siamese found a new home already? Cats were independent. Leah was independent. Her mother had depended on cats when she was in trouble. Leah might well be in trouble now. But Leah would depend on Leah. She checked the scarf over her hair. If a blonde in a yellow Volkswagen was in danger, who would notice a girl in a scarf and a blue Vega?

She would look for a job in Steamboat Springs. Maybe it was bigger than Walden. Anything was bigger than Walden.

Leah'd had a vague impression, perhaps from school maps, of the Rocky Mountains as one jagged barrier running north and south along the western end of the United States, the impression that one drove through them as she had in getting to Walden and then came soon to California and the sea. But more mountains rose across the treeless rolling plain ahead of her, and from what she could remember of the map, still in the Volkswagen, there was a lot more Colorado after Walden.

The expanse of sagebrush and fence posts, the infinite view of distances, the empty road added to her loneliness. She could be attacked by an airplane here and no one would ever know.

Why hadn't the newscast mentioned the plane? It had given away everything else.

As she left the valley floor and rose again onto a tortuous mountain road, Leah finally admitted to herself that she'd made a mistake. She was running from guilt and failure and she had run to the wrong place. Just as her sisters and brothers-in-law had warned her.

The harsh and stunning beauty all around her was the kind that should be viewed on television from the safety of an easy chair—like the surface of the moon. This was no place for Leah Harper, born and bred to the city.

Even if she hadn't met an attacker on her first night in the Rocky Mountains, the strangeness of this country would have added one more element to her burden—fear.

And the more time she put between herself and Walden, the more she thought of the silly cat. How was he faring? She missed having him to talk to.

Keeping her eyes on the devil road, Leah reached into the purse beside her for a Kleenex. Her hand met a pile of jumbled paper. She knew what it was even before she dared to glance away from the road. Brian Kruger had stuffed the money into her purse, probably when she went off chasing the wrong cat. But why? She told him she wasn't taking the job. She couldn't go back to Walden. Welker and Kruger would have left by now, anyway. What was she to do? If she kept the money it would be like stealing because she wasn't going to Oak Creek.

"Politicians and corporations steal from the government all the time."

RABBIT EARS PASS, ELEVATION 9,880, and soon Leah started down again.

Of course, they had practically forced the money on her. She had refused it and returned it. What more could she do now? And she certainly could use that money.

She rounded a curve and found herself facing another valley, the jagged peaks that loomed on the other side of it. The valley itself was far below, jade green and lush, with a river snaking through it. The road catapulted down a ledge on the mountainside.

She'd heard of breathtaking views. This one left her limp. So did the appalling grade of the road. As she started down, she noticed a settlement on the valley floor and hoped it was Steamboat Springs.

Had Brian Kruger stuffed the money back into her purse so that when she found it she'd feel she had to carry out Welker's orders, after all? Were they playing on her honesty, vulnerability?

STEAMBOAT SPRINGS 4, the sign read at the bottom of the grade, with an arrow pointing ahead. But the words below almost sent her off the road, OAK CREEK 16, with an arrow pointing to a side road.

Thinking she'd been running from it, she'd actually been heading for Oak Creek all morning.

Leah stopped at a drive-in for lunch. While she ate, she could see the side road that led to Oak Creek. Her layer of guilt had doubled once she passed it. She wasn't a politician or a corporation. She had no right to take the Vega and the money and not go to Oak Creek. She didn't want a job in Steamboat Springs.

Leah wanted to admit defeat and get the hell back east. Not to Chicago and the family, but to New York where she knew she could get a job, lose herself comfortably in the canyons of the city.

When she drove out of the drive-in she headed back the way she'd come. She couldn't help being dumb and honest—the blue Vega pulled onto the road to Oak Creek —even though she knew that people like Welker and the man pouring money down a hole in the beach used and abused the honesty of people like her. She couldn't use that money unless she did as Welker asked.

She'd stay around Oak Creek for four hours instead of eight because she was only half as dumb as Welker thought her. She'd make no attempt to look for the brutal Glade, who had miles of other places to hide anyway. After four hours she'd have earned the money and the car and use them to head for healthier climes.

Feeling better for having made a decision, Leah traveled the green valley, wondering about the man's odd name. Glade evoked either a spray can or a peaceful clearing in a forest. But there was no peace in the misnamed man with shadows for eyes and a gun in his hand.

Leah was not eager to carry out her instructions. The Vega made no attempt to reach the speed limit and two vehicles came up behind her and passed. The first was an empty dump truck with coal dust flying from its bed. The second was a yellow Volkswagen with a blonde at the wheel and a giant Siamese cat blinking back at Leah from the rear window.

Chapter Ten

LEAH chased the yellow Volks all the way to Oak Creek but lost it after it passed the dump truck.

She drove around the town, which was even smaller than Walden and placed half in a narrow valley and half up the side of a mountain. She didn't see her car. But she did see a small airplane fly up the valley along the road and circle Oak Creek.

Not knowing if it was the same aircraft she'd met the day before or not, she felt sickly in the midst of things again. She parked the Vega on a side street and left it.

Tightening the scarf around her head, she headed for main street to mingle with other unknowns. Like Walden and unlike New York or Chicago, there was no one to mingle with. She felt exposed to all eyes in the sky.

Leah spent the afternoon entering, leaving, and reentering the few shops—her plans in disorder. The plane left, and just as she was calming down, it returned.

Oak Creek contained curious inhabitants. She couldn't have met more than thirty in three hours, but half wore cowboy boots and Stetsons, and the other half, sandals and long hair. They seemed to blend amicably. The straights and the long hairs divided the businesses—one shop offering hardware and the one next to it crafts in wood and pottery. Both shops sported identical signs in their windows offering a fifteen-hundred-dollar reward from the Cattlemen's Association for information leading to the arrest and conviction of cattle rustlers.

In another, she met a Siamese cat presiding over a display counter of Indian jewelry and obviously the prized possession of the girl in the granny dress who ran the place. But this cat was a true Siamese with the slender head and sleek body. Goodyear would make two of him; still there was the same rich cocoa-brown face, paws, and tail, the same fawn-colored body between.

Leah left the shop with tears in her eyes and wondered what this strange country was doing to her. "This is just not the United States of America, that's all."

Finally, Leah realized she hadn't heard or seen the plane for some while and literally fell into a restaurant she had passed six times. The smell of sauerkraut hit her in the face like a fist. She would have reeled out into the street again, but a spurt of customers propelled her inside.

Leah found herself in a minute cafeteria. The room was large enough but the short counter offered a selection of exactly two dinners, sauerkraut and Polish sausage or barbecued ribs—the vegetables and other side dishes didn't care which. She grabbed a tray and a hot plate, filled it with ribs and extras, and staggered to a table.

"Coffee, milk, or Dr. Pepper?" asked a boy in a dress next to her elbow.

"Milk."

The milk and the bill arrived immediately with a flounce and gorgeous smile. Was it a boy? Leah concentrated on her dinner and decided she was too spaced out to know the difference. It was probably a girl, but if it was, she needed a shave.

Leah was halfway through the ribs when she felt eyes staring at her.

At the next table four men in leather shorts with embroidered suspenders and knee socks stole glances at her, but they were not exactly staring. Bright-colored backpacks leaned against the table legs. The men looked like young replicas of the little old Swiss Colony Winemaker.

Beyond them two cowboy types with shaggy crew cuts were looking, too. Why should everyone notice her? She had to be the only normal person in the room.

Her search stopped at the next table. It had a lone occupant whose eyes were shadowed. But she knew they stared at her over grim lips and cleft chin. Leah looked away, signaled the boy in the dress for another glass of milk, and kept her eyes on her plate.

When she gathered enough nerve to look up, his table was empty.

Leah found the rest room. There was only one. It sat next to the pinball machine and was labeled "Their's." She threw up the ribs and extras.

When she sat again at her table she ordered ice cream and it melted to pudding. She drank a slow cup of tea. Then a glass of milk. She didn't want to go back onto the street. She drawdled over a piece of pie. Eventually the place closed up around her.

Leah was on the street. It was dark and cold. Not daring to peek into any of the recessed doorways, she raced for the Vega, fumbling at the door handle in panic. When it opened, the light in the roof came on and she made a quick check of the floor in the back. He was too big to hide there anyway.

It seemed to take forever to find the keys in her purse, put the key in the ignition with a hand that shook. The sound of her rapid breathing filled the car before the engine drowned it out. Just as Leah leaned across to lock the door on the other side, it opened. . . .

Chapter Eleven

HE crawled in beside her, closed the door so that the light went out, grabbed her wrist as she moved to press the horn, turned off the engine, and took hold of her other wrist. It all happened too fast for Leah to think.

They sat in the dark, in silence. She couldn't even see him.

"I'm supposed to give you a message," Leah managed

finally. She pressed her knees together to stop their shaking. But it made the shaking worse.

He tightened his grip until she cried out.

"Welker . . . I'm not Sheila, honest . . . but he took my car and my cat and gave me money."

"Who?"

"Welker. He said he was from the FBI and wanted me to come here to give you a message."

"Looked like you were trying to run away."

"I panicked. I didn't expect to see you in a restaurant . . . in the open like that."

"I was hungry. What's the message?"

"You're hurting me. I can't remember."

The hold on her wrists didn't loosen. "The message."

"There's someone after you."

He laughed. The laugh held no mirth.

"Company people . . . goons? And he will meet your terms for the property."

"I don't know what you're talking about."

"Neither do I. That's all he told me."

"How did you know to come here?"

"He said you might come to Oak Creek. He didn't say why. He said I was to give you the message, that you would know what it meant, and then I could leave."

Glade took both her wrists in one hand and passed cold metal across her fingers, then let go. "Drive." The cold metal poked at her neck.

"You can have all the money. You can have the car. Take them and let me go. I'm not in this. I'm being used—"

"Drive to the corner and turn left. Now."

No denying the steel at her throat or the steel in his voice. Leah started the engine, turned on the headlights, released the emergency brake in an automatic dream—and wondered at the incredible stupidity of honest people.

The Vega left Oak Creek on the road by which she had come and he soon ordered her off onto a path by the river. A pile of wooden debris showed white in the headlights and he made her drive through a hole. She found herself in a tumble-down building with a dirt floor.

Leah shivered as they left the car. The river roared back from its bed through the slits in the building. Every other board in the walls and ceiling was missing.

"Are you going to kill me?"

"I'm considering it." He smelled unwashed. He threw her coat around her shoulders and forced her to sit on the cold dirt. "You're not Sheila?"

"No."

"How am I supposed to contact Welker?" He stood behind her.

"He didn't say. I supposed you'd know."

"Then there must be somebody else coming. You were the bait."

She remembered seeing the blonde in her yellow Volks on the way to Oak Creek. "Maybe—" Leah closed her mouth.

"Maybe what?"

"Nothing." Helping him would not be helping herself.

He yanked off the scarf and grabbed the bun on the back of her head. Bobby pins flew, one of them slid down the skin under her dress. The cracking sound in her neck mingled with the sound of hair pulling out at the roots.

Leah told him about the blonde in her Volkswagen.

When he let go, she almost fell over backward. She huddled into her coat, her hair falling about her face and shoulders, and hated him.

"Probably the real Sheila, if you're not."

"I'm not."

"Where are your jeans?" He was at the car, pulling the keys from the ignition, opening the trunk, dragging out her suitcases.

Leah stared at the stars through the open slats in the roof. The brute had a penchant for blue jeans.

Glade rummaged through a bundle of something in the corner and came back with a flashlight to attack her luggage again. Muttering low, he dumped her hair dryer and rollers from the duffel bag and replaced them with clothing.

Bars of light and dark crossed his face and body as night light filtered through slats.

"Get into these." He dumped a pile of clothes in her lap.

Ice in the air fingered her body as she slipped out of her dress and into jeans, blouse, wool sweater, and an oversized sweat shirt.

He'd lost all interest in her "great" body and was pawing through her purse. "You're a hell of a lot richer than the last time we met." He held up the wad of bills, then slid them into her wallet. Adding her wallet and the Maalox to the contents of the duffel, he threw her luggage, coat, and purse into the trunk with the clothes she'd removed and locked it.

When she'd tied her tennis shoes, he pushed the duffel at her and gathered his bundle from the corner. They left the shedlike building to hurry between shadows to the river.

"I can't swim," she lied. Maybe he intended to drown her. Maybe she could swim away if he thought she was helpless in water. Maybe. . . .

He grunted in answer and pushed her along the bank until they came to a log over splashing water. His grip kept her balanced as she crossed it. They stood on a tiny island, the river—really just a stream that sounded like a river as it crashed over rocks—surrounded them with sound and a moonlight shimmer of spray. There was a smell of coal dust in the air.

Glade looked up and down the bank, as if trying to find a crossing. The frogs resumed their debate in baritone burps. Her alleged assailant turned, stooped, and put his shoulder in the pit of her stomach. "Hold onto your bag," he said and stood to wade across the stream with Leah flopping breathlessly across his shoulder. He put her down on the other side and they headed toward a dark mountain. Glade started straight up the side of it.

Leah was already winded by the pace he set. "I can't—"

"You will."

And on they climbed until her legs screamed with aching. It seemed forever before he stopped to let her rest.

"Why . . . why don't you just . . . kill me down here? I can't—"

"I haven't decided what to do with you." Again the viselike grip on her sore arm as he dragged her to her feet. "But don't tempt me." And they set off.

Leah's heart was pounding and her throat stung from gasping when he stopped on top of the ridge. He surveyed the countryside while she sprawled at his feet.

Crickets sang. Wind whirred in the trees below, moved closer until it ruffled their hair and whirred past. Leah shivered and sat up, holding her head in her hands.

Glade offered her a drink from a cloth-covered canteen. "It's just water," he said when she hesitated.

The water tasted of metal.

He stood towering over her, big and hostile like the country around them. "Let's go."

They started downhill, Leah stumbling and slipping each time the grade steepened, her duffel bag dragging on the ground behind her, but always the cruel hand to steady her and force her onward. The night was bright with moon and stars and he didn't use the flashlight.

Finally, he stopped and drew her back against him. A darkened building loomed ahead in a small clearing, its roof sloped steeply on both sides like a capital A. His bundle hit the ground with a soft thump and his other hand covered her mouth. They stood in this fashion, listening to each other breathe and to little rustlings in the trees.

He picked up the bundle and they moved slowly toward the clearing, stopping again at its edge. Glade pulled her toward the building, unlocked the door with a key from his pocket, and ordered her inside.

Leah faced a wall of window in the same A-shape as the roof. The moon flooded a room that was a combination bedroom, living room, kitchenette, and bar. Her tired tennis shoes sank into thick-piled carpeting.

He turned on a dim light in a cubbyhole bathroom, told her he'd give her three minutes, pushed her in, and closed the door.

When she opened it, he was mixing himself a drink using only the moon for light. She went to her duffel for a gulp of Maalox.

Glade ordered her to take off her sweater, sweat shirt,

and shoes and to lie on the bed. Pulling a rope from his bundle, he tied her wrists and ankles leaving a foot-long connection of rope between. He pulled the covers to her chin.

She watched, hating him, as he stood at the window and finished his drink, took something white from his bundle, and disappeared into the bathroom. She heard the shower running, the thumping of his elbows against the shower stall. Leah worked frantically at her bonds.

But she was still tied when he stepped out of the bathroom, looking darker in white T-shirt and jockey shorts, rubbing his hair down with a white towel.

Glade pulled back the covers and crawled into bed beside her.

Chapter Twelve

LEAH felt along the rope that bound her ankles. Where was the knot?

The man had sprawled on his stomach and fallen asleep the minute he'd hit the pillow. He'd turned the back of his damp head to her and now he smelled like a wet dog. Leah was still trying to locate the knot and making grandiose plans for escape when she too fell asleep.

She awoke to daylight, sounds of small animals skittering on the roof, and to find herself snuggled up to Glade's warmth.

Easing away to the cold part of the bed, she hoped the hungry rumble in her middle wouldn't awaken him. The knot must be around her wrists somewhere . . . and then in disbelief, Leah realized that during her quiet struggle one ankle had come free. The rope was under her heel.

This careful man had slipped up and that renewed her confidence.

She slid the foot out and then the other ankle from the loosened loop. Elated, she crept from beneath the covers and edged over the bottom of the bed to the floor, her wrists still tied.

It was a small but elegant bachelor's pad, complete with stereo and moss-rock fireplace and even. . . .

Leah stood shivering and incredulous . . . a telephone sat atop one of the boxed stereo speakers.

Glade still had not moved. For someone on the run, he slept like the dead. Leah stepped carefully toward the telephone, the rope dangling from her wrists. She picked up the receiver . . . and heard a dial tone. Her luck was finally changing.

She glanced over her shoulder and froze with her finger in the O on the dial.

Leah hadn't been able to describe the color of Glade's eyes to the young patrolman or the sheriff's deputy at Walden. But she could have now. Because they were open. And directed at her.

They were as dark and deadly as the rest of him.

He sat up, blinking away sleep. "Do you know?" he said with a yawn. "You are a real honest-to-God, first-class pain in the ass." It was the longest sentence she'd ever heard him speak.

For his size, he moved with incredible speed to cross the room and cradle the telephone receiver.

They studied each other silently, Leah forcing her eyes to meet his. There was passion there, after all, but now it was busy with other things behind the dark stare. She had the feeling that her fate was being decided at that precise moment.

The phone rang.

Leah jumped and dropped her eyes, losing the staring contest. Glade seized the rope between her wrists and twisted it. Leah slammed to her knees in front of him.

"Make one sound and I'll twist both arms off. Understand?"

She nodded, staring now at the black hair on his legs,

and heard the ringing stop as he picked up the phone.

"Yes?"

The voice on the other end of the line came through like static but she couldn't make out the words.

"He didn't show. But someone else did. . . . No. . . . I'll need another pack, bag, kit, and parka—medium and dark green. Can you do it? . . . And rations. . . . I don't know but I'm taking her with me. . . . Yes, her. . . . Thanks for everything. . . . No. Just stay out of this, it's getting deadly. . . . Say you don't know me and stick to it . . . I'll try to make another contact. . . . Right. I'll leave the key. Good-bye and thanks." He hung up and then said to the phone, "I probably won't live to repay you."

Glade pulled her to her feet and untied her. "Your toothbrush and comb are in here." He shoved the duffel at her. "And wash out that cut on your wrist."

By the time Leah left the bathroom he had dressed in clean clothes, made the bed, set coffee to perk, had crisp bacon draining, and was cracking eggs into hot grease.

"If you'll just let me go, I won't—"

"Make some toast."

They consumed an enormous breakfast, wordlessly, sitting side by side on stools at the kitchen bar. He set her to washing dishes while he shaved with the bathroom door open. A sweet domestic scene—except for the gun resting on the edge of the sink in front of him.

He found thick socks in a drawer, brought a pair of ugly boots from a closet, and made her try them on. "They'll do if you wear two pairs of socks." He put additional socks and her tennis shoes in the duffel bag.

Everything was tidy when they left, Leah in the ugly boots, the key on the bar. They crossed the road in front of the cabin and walked downhill, stopping to bury his dirty clothes under a rock.

"Glade, please—"

He caught her up short, swinging her around. "Welker even told you my name?"

The thunder on his face, the suspicion in his voice told Leah she'd made a mistake. "Just Glade, not the rest. If you're running away from someone, I'll just slow you down. I won't tell anyone I saw you if you let me go."

"I either take you with me or shoot you here. You have a choice."

They started down again.

"Tell me everything he said." The hand on her arm squeezed mercilessly but they didn't slow. "Everything."

She would have a bruise on her arm to match those on her wrists. She told him all she could remember because she sensed that he'd begun again to believe she wasn't Sheila . . . until she'd used his name. It wasn't healthy to be Sheila.

They had walked miles in what Leah thought to be the direction of Oak Creek, and she was dragging, when a woman's scream brought them up short.

"Quietly," Glade warned and they climbed through trees to the top of a ridge. He pushed her down behind a boulder and lifted himself to peer over it.

A car started somewhere and drove away. The hand on her back lifted. "Stay here." Leah was alone. His bundle lay beside her.

She couldn't believe she was free. She raised herself over the boulder to see him slither down a weedy slope. Beyond the slope was a meadow of wild flowers and at the far side of it a narrow dirt road . . . and a yellow Volkswagen. Someone slumped over the wheel.

Leah turned to run in the other direction but a muffled explosion stopped her. The front of the Volks burst into flame. The hood flew back over the bug's body just before Glade reached it.

A dark smoke ball enveloped the scene and she stood undecided. Something round, with feet, burst from the smoke and raced across the meadow toward her. Glade followed with a woman draped across his arms. They reached the bottom of the slope as another explosion disintegrated the Volkswagen. Burning pieces flew across the meadow and a smoking ball of fur cleared the ridge, raced past Leah, and bounced off a tree trunk.

Leah drew off her sweat shirt and wrapped the stunned animal in it. The end of his tail was singed and smoking, the back of his hind legs blackened. "Poor Goodyear, poor thing." She cradled him, crooning. He lay trembling in her arms, his eyes dilated with shock.

There were dark smudges on Glade's face when he stumbled over the ridge. Long flaxen hair rippled over his arm as he laid his burden on the ground. Sheila was naked below the waist, her legs blackened from the knee down. Angry red patches mottled her face.

"Sheila?" he bent over her. "Sheila?" Had he saved her because there was a humane instinct in him, or just to get information?

The poor creature moved her lips and answered him in a whisper. Tears crept from sightless, staring eyes. He studied her a long moment, rubbed his forehead, then stood.

Smoke billowed from the meadow.

"We'd better get out of here." He reached for his bundle.

"You can't leave her. . . ."

"She's dead."

"Are you sure?" Leah found a tree to lean against. She'd seen too much death lately.

"Yes." His shoulders drooped as he stared at the woman at his feet and then at Leah. "That could just as well have been you, Leah Harper. Your friend Joseph Welker sent you straight back into this mess. The damn fool."

"Was it . . . goons?"

He touched the woman's bare thigh with his toe. "Looks like it."

Sheila's empty eyes still stared at Leah. Leah moved away.

"She's been tortured. They probably thought she knew where I was." He picked up her duffel. "I'm getting out of here. Coming?"

"Why should I? You've put your gun away."

He sighed and ran his hand over dark curls. "Listen, damn it! She was in your car, had your cat . . . she's blond . . . They probably thought they had you—not Sheila." Glade walked off.

Leah looked again at the disfigured body and shuddered. Had Sheila taken Leah's place? Cradling the singed cat in her arms, she ran after him. "Wait."

He stopped but didn't turn.

"What did she say to you? I saw her speak."

"She said she didn't want to die." He started off at an angle to the meadow, almost at a run, as if to escape the woman on the hill.

Chapter Thirteen

"NOW let me get this straight." Leah drank from the canteen and passed it to Glade. "If I go with you I'm in danger because you are in danger. If I don't, I am in danger because I'm alone." She rubbed her arms, sore from carrying Goodyear. "I know I'm tired but it still doesn't make a lot of sense . . . somewhere."

Glade poured water into his cupped hand for the cat. Except for a singed tail and hind legs, the Siamese seemed in good shape. He'd condescended to let Leah carry him uphill and down for two hours like a litter bearer.

"Your cat's got a lump on his head."

"He ran into a tree and you're changing the subject."

He looked at her directly for the first time since they'd left Sheila's body. "It's your decision."

"I can't make a decision without any information and why should I trust you?"

"You trusted Welker."

"And look where it got me. When I saw you at Ted's Place with those two men . . . were they goons?"

"No." A deep tan fitted his face like a hood, but stopped where he had shaved that morning. Had he been bearded until recently?

"But you said before you jumped out of my car that

you were dead, anyway. If you didn't know about the goons till I told you in Oak Creek . . . were Charlie and friend going to kill you, too?"

"I think after they got what they wanted I would have had an accident—fatal." Shadowed eyes didn't blink.

"What will the goons do if they catch you?"

"Kill me."

"This is getting pretty hard to believe . . . what you've told me. And what you haven't makes it hard to understand."

"I don't really know you are who you say you are, do I?" Hard suspicion in his voice. He fingered a small rock, turning it over in his hand. He seemed to be turning something over in his mind as well. "I can't tell you any more," he said finally.

"Then I can't go with you willingly."

"Suit yourself. I guess it's your neck." Glade started up the treeless slope. When he reached the top he looked back.

Leah cringed. Would he shoot her as he'd threatened to that morning? But he just threw the rock to the ground, shrugged, and disappeared down the other side.

Leah stared at the cat lounging gracefully on her sweat shirt and saw instead Sheila's body. She'd tried not to think about it when following Glade but now the savage horror of what had happened to Sheila was beginning to sink through the protective numbness that followed shock. Tortured, he'd said. Had she been raped, too? Leah wanted to forget Sheila but she felt so alone and exposed on the rocky hillside. . . .

The sun was high and hot. She shed the wool sweater and tried to feel relieved that he had left her.

Surely her decision had been the right one. There couldn't be any safety with the dangerous Glade.

The goons had been after Sheila, not Leah. How could they have known about Leah anyway? From Welker? Or the newscast . . . they couldn't have missed that.

Strange scenery loomed around her and it all looked the same. Bees hovered over tiny flowers almost lost in the grass. A clear, sun-drenched world. No roads, no signs, no people to give direction. How long might she and Goodyear wander to find a way out, with no food or water? Even carrying a gun, Glade had been company.

Had the goons flown the plane that had tried to force her off the road? But that had been before the newscast.

Leah drew up her knees, wrapped her arms around her legs, rested her chin, and tried to ignore her surroundings . . . just as she used to do when she was small and her younger sisters seemed to be getting all the attention. She would love to have had a phone handy at that moment, to call Annette, to reassure herself that the real world still existed.

To go back to the Vega, providing she could find it, might be dangerous if "they" really connected her with Glade and Sheila. If she were one of the hunted now, where could she go and to whom? She didn't know who the hunters were.

Leah hadn't wanted to believe she was numbered among the hunted when she'd talked to Glade. Now that he was gone, she perversely feared she was. She decided to cut her losses, leave the Vega and belongings, and catch the first flight east. Checking her wallet in the duffel bag, she found the FBI money still there. She'd certainly earned it.

"The first order of business, cat, is to get us to civilization and hope we don't meet up with any bad guys along the way." She picked up the duffel and pulled her sweat shirt from under the cat. "You can walk this time."

Goodyear turned his back, then humped with racking spasms that rippled under his fur along his sides to his throat. He vomited, coughed, vomited again, and gave her a nasty look over his shoulder that said, "Now see what you've done?"

Leah scooped him up and started downhill. "The trouble with you is you're male. Males are behind all the problems I've ever had. Because of men I haven't been able to get anywhere and because of you I might not even get out of—"

The sound that interrupted Leah turned her insides to water. She ran down the hill with the twisting cat trying to claw her and the duffel flopping under the other arm. The enormous boots tried to trip her.

The sound of a small plane drew closer. And while she chided herself for fearing every motorized vehicle aloft—they couldn't all be looking for her—she felt truly among the hunted now. The hill was too open, but a thicket of scrubby bushes ran along the gully at the bottom. Before she reached them, there were other feet pounding behind her. But she ran faster toward the thicket without turning, almost losing the struggling animal in her haste.

Goodyear would be a dead giveaway.

An arm and heavy breathing loomed behind her, the arm propelling her even faster until her feet seemed to paw the air. "Don't let go of the cat," Glade warned and pushed them all under the prickly bushes.

They lay on their stomachs, watching through brambles as the plane cleared the crest of the hill. Glade gagged for breath, his face dripping. He'd run a long way to get back to her.

"Cover your hair." He pulled Goodyear under his chest. Leah reached for her sweat shirt and couldn't find it. She pulled the green wool sweater from the duffel to cover her head and slid the white duffel under her.

"Lie still," he ordered, but his own body shuddered as he struggled to breathe. She was afraid he was moving the bushes.

"Is it the same plane?"

"I don't know."

It flew in very tight circles around the hill. Leah could see two men in the cockpit. One of them had binoculars. The circle began to widen. It was the same plane.

"Put your head down so they can't see your face."

Her eyes snapped an automatic picture of the hill as she lowered her face to the damp smell of earth. But the picture of the hill remained. Because there was something there that shouldn't have been. And it lay like a dark calling card not twenty yards from their hiding place.

"My sweat shirt," Leah whispered under the sweater. "It's out there. It's navy blue but very obvious."

"Oh, Jesus," he said in the same flat, hopeless way he'd

71

said, "I'm dead anyway."

Goodyear complained with a warning and she could feel Glade struggling to keep the cat beneath him.

The sound of the widening circles roared closer until it was directly over them.

"Will you tell me now what all this is for?" she said without moving her head. "What if I get killed for something I know nothing about? It's not fair." There had been a not too subtle change in their relationship. She was now on the same side of the hunt as he. The wrong side. The next time the plane made a pass over her sweat shirt she knew she'd be sick.

At first she thought he hadn't heard her but finally he answered in a strangely muffled voice, "It's all about oil shale."

"Is the property Welker offered you money for some land with oil shale?"

"No. It's . . . information. Get ready to move." The muscles of his leg tensed next to her.

She raised her head. The circle was taking the plane over the crest of the hill.

"Now." He lifted her by the arm.

"My sweat shirt."

"Leave it. They've seen it. Don't drop anything else."

They ran along the gully full of bushes until the sound of the plane indicated it was turning. He pushed her down again. One of her legs lay in water as they hid under bushes. Goodyear laid his ears back, slanted his eyes, and moaned murder as he was tucked under Glade.

"Why should the FBI be interested in oil?"

"Everybody's interested in oil. Come on."

They moved every time the plane turned its tail. Leah, expecting a bullet in the back at any moment, had a light, floating feeling until she slammed safely to earth again. They gradually left the plane's circle behind. Maybe it was staying with her sweat shirt.

"What if we run out of bushes?"

"We're dead."

By the time they emerged the plane was only a sound behind them. "Can't we hide here till they run out of gas?"

"They've radioed for men and dogs by now. Let's hope we don't meet them on our way out." They ran upright through trees. Leah could still hear the plane.

Keeping to any cover available, they came finally to a surfaced road. He checked the sun and headed them to the right along the road, but back in the trees.

"We're going in the direction of the plane, aren't we?"

"Yes, and in the direction of the truck, I hope."

"What truck?"

"My . . . our ticket out of here." His beard was growing out already. Goodyear had added scratches to those she'd left on his face.

One of her ugly boots squeaked as she ran, soaking from her periodic sojourns near water. He kept her moving at a killing pace.

"How many people . . . or groups of them are after you?"

"Your goons make three."

"I reported you to the local police in Walden."

His look made her shudder. "That makes four. Can't you run faster?"

"No." She'd seen that look before . . . at Ted's Place.

A gray pickup was parked at the edge of the road ahead. "Stay here." He thrust the cat at her and moved cautiously toward the truck.

Leah glanced back down the road. He was neither a "nice" nor a safe ally. If she wasn't so tired she could escape him now. Was she safer with or without him? Goodyear ran a set of claws down her neck. She slapped him and glanced toward the truck.

Glade peeked under a tarpaulin that covered the truck bed and gestured.

She hesitated, looking back down the road. At least he wasn't pointing a gun at her.

She could hear the sound of the plane again. It came from ahead.

Sheila's tortured body shimmered behind her eyes.

Leah pushed the struggling cat's paws from her face and ran toward the sound of the enemy plane and the dark man crawling into the cab of the pickup.

Chapter Fourteen

"SEE what's in the box." Glade drove sedately. The plane appeared to their right, still making its circles.

"Cold chicken."

Another pickup approached, a car behind it.

"Get down," he ordered.

Leah folded herself over the chicken. She heard dogs barking as the vehicles passed. So did Goodyear. He climbed the back of the seat.

"Were those the dogs I saw at Ted's Place?"

"Probably." He took a chicken breast. "See if that thermos on the floor has coffee in it."

It did. Goodyear slithered down between them. With the smell of chicken he'd forgiven all.

"Give him the wing if there is one."

"Why are you so nice to cats and so mean to people?" Leah handed Goodyear a wing.

Glade's teeth showed white between dark stubble in the first smile she'd seen. "That's a good question, Leah Harper." The truck no longer moved sedately. "Is it just chicken?"

"There're rolls and packets of honey." She took a closer look at the side of the box. A helpless, disbelieving mood made her laugh until she feared she'd choke on the chicken in her mouth. "It's Colonel Sanders!" A gift from the normal world. It must still be out there.

"Civilization is a creeping disease." He laughed with her, but his laugh was hollow, like his voice. "Spread me some honey and have some coffee. Good old Ben is a civilized beast."

"Who's Ben?"

"A friend who . . . provided all this." But again suspicion tinged his voice.

The chicken vanished between the three of them. Goodyear ate bread and honey but showed no interest in coffee.

Leah dozed and slept. She remembered passing through a small town but aching muscles and a satisfied stomach succumbed even as she fought sleep. The next she knew, they were on a narrow dirt road sweeping endlessly through more scenery.

"Good morning." Glade shifted his weight around Goodyear, who lay peacefully curled between his legs. "No one's following . . . yet. Any coffee left?"

"Where are we going?" She handed him the thermos cup and felt a twinge of panic when their fingers touched. What *was* she doing here?

"We're going to get lost."

She swigged Maalox to fight the chicken. If they weren't lost already she didn't know the meaning of the word.

"Go easy on that stuff. You'll have to ration it. No drugstores where we're going."

A winding lane led away to a desolate ranch house far below and the tiny prosaic figure of a woman gathering wash off the line.

"Why am I going there with you?" She looked back longingly at the woman.

"Look"—his sigh was impatient—"you are not a much-desired gift from heaven. Like you said, you'll only slow me down." And then, almost under his breath, he added, "But I can't very well let them do to you what they did to Sheila, can I?"

"Why can't you?"

"If I had to, I'd kill you myself first."

"What's the difference?"

"I'd be kinder and quicker. Let's just hope it doesn't come to that." He reached across her to open the glove compartment and she shifted her legs to avoid his touch.

"You've killed before." She couldn't look at him.

"Yes." The glove compartment held a bottle of whiskey, an envelope, and an assortment of tools. He removed the bottle and envelope.

The fences stopped. The truck rose from a treeless grassy valley to pass through groves of aspen with tall white stalks and shaking lime-green leaves.

"I knew you were a murderer the first time I met you." And here she was riding off to nowhere with him and all because some unknown criminals tortured and killed a woman who he said had been mistaken for her and because an airplane had chased her under some bushes. Things had happened too fast and Leah had made another of her famous mistakes by coming with him. She was sure of it.

"It's men," she said miserably.

"What?" He took a drink and handed her the bottle.

"Men have constantly ruined my life. You are merely one in a long string." She dared a drink and choked, wondering again what people saw in the stuff.

"Don't spill it." He grabbed the bottle and capped it. "We'll have to ration this, too." His sudden flow of conversation dried up and his look was black as the pickup flew over ruts and rocks and bumps till Leah thought every organ in her body would mash itself to jelly. He was either angry because of her comment on men, or disgusted because she choked on raw whiskey, or he was just planning on how he would kill her quickly if he had to. Had he come to her rescue at the sound of the airplane for her sake or because her presence would give away his own?

They swooped down on a guest ranch on a river bottom and left it just as fast. Leah looked back wistfully. Surely that ranch would be lost enough.

"Why didn't the men with the dogs recognize you when we passed them on the road?"

He swiped dark curls from his forehead. "They make mistakes, too, I guess. I had my head turned away."

A sign read ROUTT NATIONAL FOREST. At least there were signs. How much more lost could they get? But the incredible jolting journey continued.

"The FBI and the police are after you. That's two of the four groups. And the goons make three. Welker said he was trying to save your life. If you gave or sold the property to the FBI, would the rest leave you alone?"

"No. And they're after *us*."

"Why me? I don't know anything."

"I doubt if Sheila did, either."

"She was with the FBI, too."

"So I hear. They didn't used to use women but I've been out of the country. . . . She was supposed to intercept Charlie and talk him into turning me over to Welker." His smile was bitter. "Charlie was looking forward to the meeting but had no intention of——"

"Could Charlie have done that to Sheila?" She remembered the grinning man who stood beside her car at Ted's Place and her own uneasy sensation.

"No. She was an FBI operative. That would have been too far out of line even for Charlie. He specializes in accidents anyway . . . and games." The truck slowed and turned onto a side road at a sign that read TRAPPERS LAKE, 10 MILES.

"So Charlie's not with the bad guys. Welker said a company hired them. What kind of——"

"An oil company."

"And everyone is after the property and——"

"But if they get us they won't get the property. Because I won't tell where it is and you won't know." His tone was icy.

"Oil goons, FBI, and the police. That leaves a fourth group."

"That's . . . another organization," he said in that muffled way. Those were the words Joseph Welker had used when she'd asked about Charlie. Both Glade and Welker had grown uncomfortable.

Another sign. WHITE RIVER NATIONAL FOREST. Surely they were lost by now. But did Leah really want to be? Need to be? Her glance slid to the powerful man beside her. In a way he reminded her of Jason . . . and there had been other Jasons in her life. But no one remotely like this man.

"This other organization must be even more secret than the FBI the way you and Welker look when it's mentioned. What is it? The Mafia? Or the CIA?"

The truck braked. Leah was flattened against the windshield. "The Mafia? The—"

"Woman, if I answer that one question, will you get off my back? I need to think, damn you!"

"The CIA? In Colorado?"

His hands on her shoulders lifted her from the seat. "I can't think when. . . ." He shook her once and let go. "I don't need you. Remember that." It was almost a whisper. Blood vessels bulged on his forehead.

She had driven him to the point he had driven her. Leah could feel it. "The FBI, the CIA . . . is this property-information stolen?"

"Yes."

"You're a thief as well as a murderer. And you ask me to trust you, go with you for something I know nothing about. Why should I? Sheila is dead and you say she didn't know. If you hadn't mistaken me for her, I wouldn't even be involved at all."

"That, Leah Harper, is the only reason you are sitting next to me now. It's my fault you're in this. I'll try to get you out." He started the engine and the pickup moved down the road. "But I can't promise anything. For either of us."

Men. Always men. Her father hadn't wanted her mother to be any more than a dependent keeper of his house and family. When he died, Iris Harper had no training to head the family, no economic sense. His oversight ruined them all and eventually led to his wife's suicide.

Leah had enrolled in journalism her freshman year in college. There had been eight girls and two hundred and eighty men in the class. The male faculty had cut it down to one girl and two hundred and eighty men in two weeks. The one plucky upstart had stuck it out to graduate with honors. But Leah had moved out of journalism into liberal arts, the catchall for the undecided, unwanted, or undeveloped. And the dabblers.

"And then there was Clifford," she said aloud, not meaning to.

"Clifford." Glade glanced at her and then past her through the window. The truck slowed to a crawl.

"At the travel agency," she explained.

An entire field of yellow daisylike flowers with brown centers appeared on their left, too large for daisies, too small for sunflowers, alight with sinking sunlight—too vast and bright for any postcard to capture.

They had stopped. Her companion stared at the field of flowers. Leah wouldn't have expected a murderer-thief to appreciate the golden glory on the other side of the window.

They eased forward, Glade scanning the roadsides. The flowers ended at a line of pine forest and then another clearing. At the back of the clearing sat a white wooden wagon that looked like an old gypsy home on wheels. The truck stopped again.

"Shepherd's wagon," he said and watched it.

It looked deserted. There was a long handle meant to be hitched to a horse; its end lay on the ground. The wagon seemed to be shut up.

Glade checked the rear-view mirror and the sky, then turned the truck off the road into the clearing, driving in behind the shepherd's wagon where they couldn't be seen from the road.

"Are we lost now?"

"No. But we'll wait until dark before we go on. You can get out and stretch your legs, find yourself a tree."

"A tree?" They were nearly surrounded by trees.

"All that coffee has to go somewhere. Just stay out of sight of the road."

"You mean—But I can't—"

"Suit yourself. You're a long way from a flush toilet." He left the truck and disappeared into the trees. Goodyear crawled out after him.

Leah sat deserted, staring at her ugly boots, wishing she could get back to the United States of America. He'd taken the keys with him. Finally, she shrugged, opened her door, and crept off into the trees.

When she returned, Glade was bent over a green backpack on a metal frame. It was like those she'd seen in the restaurant in Oak Creek and before that on hitch-hikers along the highways.

He looked over his shoulder with a smile of insolence and a raised eyebrow. "Manage?"

Leah considered answering with a well-placed kick but decided against it. She still wore bruises from her last tangle with this beast.

"At least you didn't need a dime." He drew another pack from under the tarpaulin that covered the back of the pickup.

Above her the aspen rattled its leaves and Goodyear appeared like an overweight eagle's nest clinging to a slender silver branch. He returned her stare with cold-blue malevolence.

Glade scratched his head over a foil packet. "I've been gone a long time. I don't suppose you can cook." It wasn't even a question. An assortment of strange packages and metal containers lay at his feet.

Leah studied him. He wore cowboy boots, but he didn't look or act or talk like a cowboy. The CIA, FBI, information. . . . "Are you an enemy agent?" she asked suddenly, embarrassed by the melodramatic question.

Bewilderment was replaced by amusement on his face and then his smile opened to laughter. "Lady, at this point I don't know what I am." He stuffed the varied paraphernalia into the packs. "But I think I'm still an American citizen."

His answers always confused her more than they helped.

He lifted the smaller of the two packs. "Let's see if this fits." He put it on her back and adjusted straps around her shoulders and waist. It felt as if it weighed as much as a used car.

"Are we hitchhiking?"

"Hardly. These are survival packs." He put both packs in the pickup and took the envelope that had been in the glove compartment from the dashboard, sat on a rock and examined the papers he drew from it.

"Nineteen twenty-seven," he muttered and threw down the first paper. It was mostly green with swirls of brown and white and tiny lines of black. "Department of the Interior, Geological Survey" was printed in one corner.

He threw the next paper down with a shake of his head and Leah picked it up. It was a letter.

Glade,
Sorry about the age of the survey map. The Forest Service is getting jumpy about telling people the whole truth about the last of the wilderness. I don't blame them. As far as I know this is the last survey map of the area. I've included the latest tourist brochure—not too complete or accurate but maybe you can figure things out between the two.

I did the best I could with the second pack on short notice. She? I see you haven't changed, after all. You both should be outfitted for as long as I thought you could carry. Don't forget to leave the note with the truck. Sure wish I knew what the hell you're up to now. But good luck, whatever it is.

Ben

Glade sat staring at the yellow blaze of daisies through the trees. Leah read the letter he held in his hand, over his shoulder.

Dear Crocker,
Thanks for the loan of the truck. It sure made the move into my new pad easier. Sorry I couldn't stay for a beer but this nice lady who followed me out in my car was eager to get back. (Heh, heh.) Next time I'll stay awhile and we'll catch us some fish.

Ben

Ben's "pad" must be the cabin where Leah had spent the night before.

In his other hand Glade held a folded map with ROUTT AND WHITE RIVER NATIONAL FORESTS printed across the top and a picture beneath of a fisherman standing up to his crotch in a lake ringed by snow-capped mountains. It made Leah shiver just to look at it. Surely he didn't expect her to go fishing.

Finally, he stirred and spread both maps side by side on

the ground. He must have studied them for a half-hour while Leah's teeth chattered as the last of the sun faded.

He rubbed the stubble on his chin thoughtfully. The brute grew beard like he grew muscle. "We've got ourselves a challenge, Leah Harper." He put the maps in his jacket pocket and stood to stretch.

"Why do you always call me Leah Harper instead of just Leah?" She was pacing near him and he clamped his hand on her wrist and swung her around so hard she collided with his chest.

"I'm convincing myself that was Sheila back in the burning car." His other hand grabbed her hair and snapped her head back so that she was looking up into his face. "And that you are indeed Leah Harper."

She saw nothing but cruelty in his eyes.

"You'd better pray that I become good and convinced," he said in a tight whisper.

Chapter Fifteen

"YOWL. . ." Cat eyes glinted back silver moonlight.

"Be still, you good-for-nothing creep." Leah nuzzled her cold face against the warmth of lush fur. "You're a bad kitty." She scratched him under the chin until he purred. "And we are involved with a bad and unpredictable man."

She stood beside the backpacks and watched through the trees as Glade drove over a small bridge in front of a lodge made of logs. The lodge was lit and so were several cabins to the side of it. People moved behind windows.

A stream chattered under the bridge. Trees moaned low in the wind. Frogs croaked and crickets answered. A horse whinnied. Wood smoke wafted by, occasional voices.

She wasn't alone with him now. She didn't know for sure that she faced the same danger as Sheila. Might she be in as much danger from Glade?

Leah could run, elude him and find people here and tell her story, ask for the police and protection. That had to be the wisest course.

But still she hesitated, even as the truck disappeared into a shadow next to the lodge and car lights moved up the road. Glade would be captured if she publicized his whereabouts by turning herself in. Who of all the people after him would be the first to find him?

Would the goons torture Glade as they had Sheila to get the information-property? Why should she care if they did?

The car turned to cross the little bridge; its headlights pierced the shadow that held the pickup, but she couldn't see Glade.

Leah moved from one foot to the other, clutching the cat, trying to decide what to do. She didn't want Glade captured. She didn't know why. But she did sense that her habit of hesitation was the very fault that had let Welker push her into this position to begin with. Glade had told her just enough to make her unsure but not enough to let her make an informed decision.

A shadowy figure moved across the bridge and she damned herself and gullible people like her who let people like him and Welker and governments and giant corporations use them and then Glade was across the road, through the trees and beside her and the moment was lost.

Brushing the cat from her arms, he slung a backpack over her shoulders, and cinched the waistband. He crawled into the other pack and stared at the shadow of Goodyear at his feet. "We can't leave him here," he whispered. "He's so weird, he's recognizable."

"You aren't going to kill him," she said through her teeth.

"I should. And bury him deep. He'll only get in the way. Cats are unpredictable."

"I won't let you. I'll scream."

"I can't anyway. If you think you're an innocent by-stander, that poor cat. . . ." He scooped the Siamese up in his arms. "I guess once you've broken training you might as well go completely berserk. We're going to regret this, though."

They walked in the trees beside the road until they came to a pickup-camper and a roaring fire. A man, woman, and three teenagers sat in folding patio chairs around the campfire and rock music blared from a transistor radio. The couple argued in harsh voices, the teenagers—all boys—looked stony with boredom. A dog barked. Other campfires and vehicles loomed beyond.

Leah could smell charred steak and so could her ulcer. Goodyear moaned.

They moved onto the road and walked between campgrounds with the homey sounds of crying babies, music, crackling fires, and human voices.

Again Leah considered breaking away and causing a commotion. Again she saw the disfigured Sheila and hurried to catch up with the man ahead of her.

"The trail head is supposed to be straight on to the end of this road. There'll be a sign of some sort," Glade whispered.

"Trail to what?"

"Escape."

"I've been escaping for a week and all I've done is get in more trouble."

"It's been ten months for me. Faster!"

"What are you escaping from?" she asked.

"I've told you."

"No. You haven't told me anything that makes sense."

They left the campfires behind and walked through dazzling moonlight and oblique shadows. The road curved.

"Thanks for not bolting back there, if you are Leah Harper," he said in a shadow.

"I'm not Sheila," she said in a patch of moonlight and wondered why she hadn't bolted.

"It's this goddamn cat," he said in the next shadow. "I've heard of fog tactics, but a giant Siamese. I can't figure an operative with a cat. You even seem to like him, aren't just using him as a—"

"I hate him. He adopted me. I hate you. You got me into this. And where for God's sake are you going? And why am I going with you? I can't carry this load on my back much longer."

He gurgled a low laugh. "We've just begun, Leah Harper."

They climbed an earth embankment to find moonlight glimmering on a board sign, making the print, merely etched into the wood, stand out dimly white.

"Flat Tops Primitive Area. No motorized vehicles," Leah read aloud.

"Warning," she continued. The sign was worn. "Something about trails and in the open . . . and beetles. Beetles?"

A dog growled not far away and a voice snapped, "Sasha!"

Goodyear climbed Glade's face.

"Sorry," said the voice. "Come along, Sasha." The dog followed the figure into a streak of moonlight on the road below. It was indiscriminate in shape, but big. Thank God, it was leashed.

"Come on," Glade whispered and she followed him into the trees.

"I'm so stiff after today I hurt everywhere. It's the middle of the night."

"You'll loosen up." He moved ahead of her briskly. "And it's only nine o'clock."

The trail was a narrow path between trees. In the shadows Leah stumbled over rocks and tree roots she couldn't see.

"Pick up your feet," he ordered.

"I can't walk this fast. Slow down."

Glade stopped ahead to wait for her. Wind moaned down the trail and they were surrounded by cracking, creaking groans. Leah grabbed his arm. "What's that?"

"Dead trees rubbing against live ones. They fall over against their neighbors sometimes when they die. Wind makes them rub." His entire face was in shadow as he turned his head from side to side. "Seems to be an awful lot of deadfalls in among the trees. Some kind of pine beetle's been through here, killing trees. That's what the sign was about."

His long legs carried him so fast that several times he was out of sight ahead of her and she had to run to catch up, panicked at the thought of being left alone. Although she didn't feel that comfortable with him either.

They crossed streams, fallen trees, and open meadows where bogs sucked at their boots. The weight on Leah's back dragged on her shoulders, her head felt as if it would tear itself open. Dead trees creaked eerily with the slightest breeze. And then one splintered, cracked, and thundered to the ground somewhere. Leah could feel the earth under her feet vibrate with the impact.

"What if one of those trees fell on us?"

"It wouldn't hurt for long." He started off with Goodyear blinking back at her over his shoulder.

What kind of a man was he? A man who could slug a woman in the stomach and who had admitted he'd killed, but who carried a twenty-ton Siamese up a mountain because he couldn't bear to do away with it.

"And what kind of woman am I?" she thought. "Even to be up here with this man?" But she hooked her thumbs under the padded straps of her pack to take some of the pressure off her shoulders and plodded on behind him like a squaw. Leah found the wilderness around her more frightening than anything human, including the man ahead of her.

The distinct odor of skunk . . . Leah's eyes moved to either side of the trail. Dead trees stood naked and ghost-white next to their shadowed pine-covered neighbors. When they had passed the skunk smell, other odors took over—sharp pine and the softer scents of earth, leaves, and mold. The sour smell of horse droppings on the trail and a faint fragrance of flowers.

After an hour Leah's lungs burned. She fought for air but it seemed thin and unsatisfying. Her feet ached, her knees felt rubbery. Her heart pounded at her ears until she couldn't hear her boots hitting the ground. The pack seemed to tear her shoulders away from her neck.

And still he moved ahead of her. She could see her breath on the crisp air but felt the dampness of perspiration on her face and under her arms.

Finally, Leah sat down in the middle of the path and burst into tears.

Glade lifted the pack from her shoulders, offered her water. "Not much farther now."

Goodyear crawled up her legs and stuck a cold inquiring nose in her hot face.

"I'm going to die," she blubbered. "My heart can't beat right."

"How long have you been in Colorado?"

"Four days." It seemed like four years. She hadn't thought of her mother for hours.

"You're not acclimated yet. Here, eat this."

It was a bar of chocolate that tasted like mousse. "If you think I'm sleeping in some moldy unheated barn or something tonight, you're crazy."

"It won't be a barn," he said soothingly, rubbing her legs.

"I'm dizzy."

"Just rest awhile. It'll be all right." The man who had chopped her in the neck and tied her to a bed positioned her between his legs so that her back rested against his chest. "Isn't it beautiful?" His breath tickled the top of her hair.

Leah made an attempt to focus. Giant boulders lay jumbled and moon-white, like the dead trees, in a field that stretched to the face of a cliff.

Goodyear crawled out onto a boulder and hunched. Moonlight glistened on the tips of white twitching whiskers.

"I can't get enough air."

"It's thinner here than in Chicago, but cleaner. You're not athletic, Leah Harper. But you're plucky. You'll make it." He leaned against the tree behind him and she moved with him. "Try to relax."

The rigidity of the gun in his pant's pocket made that hard to do. She'd wondered where he kept it.

A long cliff with a flat top rose straight and rugged to

the skyline across the boulder field like an immense uncut gemstone. Moonlit facets reflected dull chalky light.

Why couldn't she stop thinking of Sheila? That sight had been even grislier than the one of her mother in the bloody tub. Two such experiences in a little over a week must have unhinged Leah's mind. Why else was she escaping with a murderer to avoid being murdered? She even believed his fantastic story, what she could understand of it. The tension he carried with him like his gun convinced her that people were out to kill him as Welker had said. His was a life-and-death kind of tension.

Leah, who had been sweating a moment before, now shivered with cold and he pushed her away so that he could stand. "Let's get going. You'll freeze if you don't move."

At the crushing weight of the pack, her body screamed in protest. She hadn't been this miserable, physically, in her life. Unless it was the night he'd stretched her to the bed. "You enjoy torturing people, don't you? You steal, murder, torture. I'll bet you run over little old ladies at crosswalks just for fun."

He walked across boulders to retrieve the cat and they were off. Goodyear crawled onto Glade's shoulder but found he was too big to balance even on that Mr. America expanse, so he maneuvered to the top of the pack behind his bearer's head and gazed with slit-eyed contempt upon Leah struggling behind. The desire to croak the haughty creature grew stronger each time Leah looked up.

But she soon hadn't the strength to strangle an ant. Her heart was back to its palpitation tricks. She gulped for air that wasn't there and walked into Glade's pack before she realized he'd stopped.

He drew her around to stand beside him. "Tell me what you feel, looking at that."

She dragged bulging eyes from her ugly boots and saw more trail. "Agony," she answered.

The trees had stopped. The trail snaked back on itself across the open mountainside as did some of the roads in this forsaken country and, like them, it went nowhere but onward . . . and up.

"Look again." His voice came as close to dreamy as so hard and passionless a voice could. There was almost a hint of love in it.

Leah sagged against him and had the vague notion that he hugged her. Dutifully she looked again. Moonlight on a mountainside, an ever-steepening trail, a waterfall splashing below, no human habitation in sight, nothing.

"Paralysis?" she tried again.

"You are a cold and heartless woman."

Leah stopped to cry and catch her breath at every switchback and there must have been fifty of them.

"Think about all those men who've ruined your life and pretend you're stomping on them," he suggested. The freak wasn't even puffing and he had the strength to laugh at her. "But keep stomping."

She pretended she was stomping on Glade and Goodyear.

The muscles in the front of her legs, between knee and hip joints pulled in growing, numbing pain and she worried that they'd lock forever with the next step.

Leah was dreaming, futilely she knew, of the Holiday Inn, a hot shower, and poached-egg-on-milk-toast when they finally reached the top. The top of nothing but core scenery with a cold, coarse wind sweeping across it.

Not even a moldy unheated barn.

Chapter Sixteen

"THIS isn't what I expected." Glade slumped to the ground beside her, his eyes sweeping the landscape. "That's what I get for using a 1927 map."

"Not what *you* expected? Where are we going to sleep?" Fatigue and misery curled like weights around her head.

"No cover, damn it!" The icy wind buffeted his words away from them.

If the beetle had been merely busy down below, he'd been deadly here . . . rolling grassy terrain . . . a few clumps of trees scattered widely apart and all of them dead.

"We'll camp here and walk farther in tomorrow . . . hope to God it gets better."

"Camp? In what? We don't have a trailer. I don't see a cabin, even a tent. There're no people—"

"That's why we came here. We'll camp over there in that patch of trees for tonight."

"But they're dead. They might fall on us." Even she could hear the note of hysteria in her voice.

"Leah, those trees have been dead for fifty years by the looks of them," he said with a grudging patience. "They'll be some protection from the wind. We'll take the chance that they won't fall tonight."

"You called me Leah. Just Leah."

"Even female operatives don't go down with a whimper," he said rudely and stalked off into the wind.

She left the cat attacking tufts of grass and forced hardening muscles to move after him.

Glade found her a puffy parka stuffed into a nylon bag in her backpack. But the inside of her bones were cold and nothing short of a scalding two-hour bath could warm her now. She sat on an uncomfortable log, hugging her knees, as he fought the arctic wind to build a fire from the deadwood littering the area.

"I'm hungry," she said miserably.

"You're a pain in—"

"I don't know enough nasty words to describe you, Glade-whoever-you-are," she snapped back and moved closer to the fire.

He tried to read the mysterious instructions on foil packages by wind-flickered firelight. Leah was merely waiting for death by the time he'd boiled water on a tiny one-burner stove that resembled a holder for a carafe candle.

They ate silently—hot chocolate, cheese, sausage, and

thin pieces of rye bread. Goodyear wandered in for cheese and sausage.

"Where do we sleep?" Leah asked resignedly, almost falling into the tiny fire that couldn't have warmed a thimble against the ice on the wind.

"Sleeping bags." He pulled some material from another nylon sack. It puffed and ballooned when he pulled it out as a magician would draw endless scarves tied together from an impossibly tiny container, and blossomed into a sleeping bag.

"But where do we put the sleeping bags? On the ground?"

"Yes, city girl, on the ground." He placed his bag across the fire from hers, stripped down to his shorts and T-shirt and crawled in.

"But what if it rains?" She was still standing.

"Won't tonight. There's a tent in my pack but I'm too tired to put it up."

Leah unlaced her boots. When the wind moved instantly through two pairs of socks, she decided to sleep in her clothes for the first time in her life. She rolled up her parka for a pillow and pulled the bag's zipper to her chin.

One hummock of grass hit her between the shoulders; another pushed up the left side of her rump so that the right side pressed down on a sharp rock. The other hummocks lumped themselves in between.

"Glade, what if the kitty wanders off?"

"With our luck, he'll come back."

She'd never dreamed that there could be so many stars or that they could seem so close.

Her nose felt as if it was catching frostbite. What would her poor complexion do without the creams and proper cleansing?

The scope of the sky and the land around her was terrifying now that the hike had stopped and she could no longer ignore it. She felt diminished, unimportant, frightened.

And she was alone in this vast wild place with an unexpected man. No one would know she was here. He was good at covering his tracks. That note left with the pickup would hide all trace of the fact they'd even started up the trail. There'd be no vehicle below that anyone could ascribe to them.

"You really are trying to save my life, aren't you?" she asked, trying to reassure herself. "Why else would you work so hard to get me up here? Why else would you go to all this trouble . . . but if you're a murderer, why—"

"Have you ever met one before?"

"No."

"Then possibly you've misjudged us. Go to sleep."

Leah tried to forget the two solid blocks of ice that had once been feet. She rolled over on her side to get off the rock and the sleeping bag rolled with her. "Do you think there might be bears up here? Or wolves?"

"No. You make enough noise to scare off an army."

Silence. The wind moaned, the grass rustled, the dead trees creaked, but to Leah it was still a silent alien world. Her body, excluding her feet, began to warm itself in the sleeping bag, but chilling tendrils slithered in through the opening at the top to her shoulders and crept down her spine, giving her shuddery spasms. "Glade, I'm cold. . . ."

"Jesus Christ, woman!" His roar evaporated the silence and suddenly he stood above her in his underwear, blocking out the stars. He knelt with his hands outstretched as if to strangle her.

Leah screamed.

"Shut up. I'm just pulling up your drawstrings."

The neck of the bag pulled around her face like the casing for a mummy. She was totally trapped now. "What if a wild animal—"

"Listen to me"—the deadly voice was anything but reassuring as his knee in her stomach pinned her and the bag to the lumpy earth—"I'm running for my life, and now I'm running for yours, too. Help me, Leah, please? Go to sleep, please?"

"Okay." What else could she say? She was immobile, lost and miserable in this weird place meant only for wildlife specials on television. "Just get off me."

He was back in his bag and, by the sound of his breathing, asleep in seconds. How could anyone human sleep in such discomfort? Maybe murderers weren't human. But how many said please?

The fire died to red coals that glowed brighter in each gust of wind. Trees creaked like spooky doors on unoiled hinges. Dead-white branches curled over her like gnarled fingers. Danger rustled behind every tuft of grass.

A studied, stealthy sound drew gradually nearer the campfire. Leah and her sleeping bag sat up.

Goodyear slithered toward her with round flashing eyes. He sniffed her bag and wandered off, whiskers twitching, tail alert, throwing a departing yowl over his shoulder.

Leah slept that endless night in half hour intervals. During waking intervals she heard unexplainable noises and felt the strain of cramped muscles that had drawn her into as tight a fetal position as the bag would allow. She awakened once to see an owl with iridescent eyes glide above her, around and through dead-tree fingers, wings spread and nasty-looking talons curled. And again later to find dawn graying a night sky and Goodyear wrapped around her head.

Leah awoke finally to the smell of coffee and to a dead mouse deposited on the foot of her sleeping bag.

"A secret admirer brought you a gift in the night." Glade laughed over the steam of his coffee. Even he wore a parka this morning.

The reason was obvious once she'd disentangled herself from the warm down bed. He'd built no fire. She worked at the interminable boot laces with cramped fingers and then started off to find a tree. "Don't turn around," she said. Dead trees provided no privacy.

There wasn't an inch on her body that didn't ache. The pain caused by the mere act of walking and squatting took her breath away.

When she limped back, he handed her a cup of coffee and dished something steamy from a frying pan on the little stove to a cold metal plate that chilled her hands and the food in seconds.

"What is it? It tastes like Styrofoam."

He picked up a clear plastic bag of pale yellow powder.

"It says here it's scrambled eggs. Cat wouldn't eat it, though."

That indeed was indictment of any food. Goodyear sprawled motionless on Glade's sleeping bag after his big night.

If Leah thought this world out of proportion to herself and to reason by moonlight, by day it was twice as much so. The vista was unending. It was like finding herself suddenly set down in the Stone Age. She felt grubby and a little Neanderthal.

They sat on the rim of the steep sloping valley they had climbed the day before. Parts of the snaking trail appeared below and in the distance tiny lakes reflected an orange glow back at the fireball sun sitting on the ridge to their right.

The valley was surrounded by mountains with their tops sliced off and, like the one on which she sat, they were mostly treeless. Grass covered them like soft green fur. Patches of white dotted the green.

"What do you do when you're not murdering people or stealing things, or is that your profession?" She helped herself to more coffee.

"I'm a mining engineer."

"That sounds a little prosaic for—"

"TV tends to glamorize us. We murderers are mostly just plain folk." He grinned and began to do up their dishes, which consisted of dribbling a few drops of water on a plate and scraping it across the grass.

Leah was in no mood to help him. She took a perverse pleasure in watching a man do the domestic chores. The cups, plates, and pots all nested neatly into each other, ending in one compact bundle.

"But last night you said something about breaking training. What kind of training would an engineer—"

"That was my other job." He rolled Goodyear off his sleeping bag and stuffed the bag into its sack. "You might say I moonlighted."

Leah began to do the same with her own bag. The sleeping bags, their stuff sacks, even the parkas were all the same grass-green color as the backpacks. She was beginning to loathe that color.

"What was your moonlighting job?"

He knelt to help her and his dark face was very near when it closed, hardened, and he became the old dangerous Glade. "I worked for the government."

"You mean like in the army or what?"

He watched her in a still, curious way that made Leah hold her breath. This went on for so long she thought he might not answer. A muscle twitched in his cheek and another at one temple. "No. I worked . . . for the Central Intelligence Agency."

That gave Leah enough to chew on for the rest of the morning.

This was fortunate because she hadn't the breath to talk under the heavy pack. Even here a trail, almost too narrow to walk in, cut deeply into the turf so that when her boots hit the sides she tripped. But when she tried to walk outside it, the clumpy grass turned her ankles.

She plodded on behind him, afraid to lose him, afraid to go back alone even if he'd let her, but alarmed that she might not be up to what lay ahead.

Goodyear, forced to walk this trip, complained loudly behind her, lagged, but kept them in sight. She would have expected him to wander off and get lost, being a cat, but he too seemed to sense that this man was their only safety in the wilderness. This, she was fast deciding, was no ordinary cat.

The terrain was hilly, but not steep. Yet any rise, no matter how gentle, exhausted her.

Silent agony. Growing shame at a body she had always been proud of, a body she had kept fit and slim even on an ulcer diet, a body that had been photographed and praised. But a body that seemed to fail her now. Was thirty *that* old?

Eventually, shame gave way to anger. Consuming anger at the stalwart figure ahead who didn't tire, get thirsty, fear this vast empty world, or have to talk to someone of his own species for reassurance. Finally she was spitting mad and she stopped.

"Wait!" Leah tried to put her hands on her hips to pose

a defiant stance. But she was so tired her knuckles slid off her jeans and her arms hung drunkenly at her sides.

He turned, eyebrows raised in question marks over shadowed sockets, his own body straight and nonchalant under a pack that must have weighed twice her own.

"Glade *what?*" she croaked, trying to sound aggressive with a dry, airless throat, demanding some small payment for this pointless, endless journey.

Glade walked back to her, uncinched her waistband, and slid the pack off her shoulders. They had stuffed the down parkas into sacks as they had the sleeping bags, and he'd insisted they wear only wind-shirts over their clothes, thin pullover jackets with hoods. Now he drew off her shirt, tied it by its arms around her waist as he had his own, and replaced her pack. The sun was higher and she'd been hotter than she'd realized. The slight chill was invigorating. But when he started off, she didn't.

"Glade what?" she demanded again. "If I'm going to tramp to the end of the earth with someone, I'm going to know his name at least." This time her knuckles stayed on her waist.

He shrugged and turned that closed face to her. "Wyndham." He sounded like he was suffocating. And he stepped off purposefully.

Strange patches of white on the shaded sides of hills or under the few trees that lived. Leah reached out to touch one. "My God, it's snow . . . in July."

He didn't stop at the sound of her voice and she struggled after him. Glade Wyndham. Was that really his name? Would a CIA agent tell you his real name? He probably had dozens. Why would the FBI have to pay the CIA for information? But the CIA was after them, too. No matter how many answers she dragged out of him, they only confused her more.

Glade Wyndham, if that's who he was, was two men in the same body. The one capable of the patience it took to get her up there at all and to drag along an unnecessary cat. The other, swift, cruel, and secretive. She never knew which would surface next.

There were signs even here, burned in wood anywhere

that the trail branched, with arrows and names like WALL LAKE, TRAPPERS PEAK, TWIN LAKES, BIG MARVINE, BIG FISH LAKE. It sounded as if they were in Texas.

Glade turned from the trail and stomped up a hillock and over it to disappear from sight.

Leah gasped at the thought and followed, bent double now under her load, watching her ankles turn between the springy grass clumps, feeling something warm ooze about her toes.

When she'd labored to the top of the hill, she looked out upon a small pond so shallow and clear that she could see the rocks and mud at its bottom. A grove of dead trees behind it and a flat shelf of rock the size of a dining room table beside it.

Glade Wyndham leaned over the rock with his maps spread out and his pack propped against it.

Leah winced down the hill and crawled onto the sun-warmed rock.

Goodyear crept toward them, his tongue as well as his stomach dragging on the ground. He too sought the rock and lay out on his side like a dead horse.

Leah unlaced the horrid boots. "You were right last night." She drew off a boot to find the socks pink with blood. "I have misjudged murderers. They're worse than I thought."

He looked up finally. "Hmm?" He focused on her face.

It started as a rumble and at first she didn't know what it was. But then it erupted from deep in his middle and came out laughter. Laughter that softened the lines of his face, lit in his eyes as he threw his head back. Here was a third Glade. A few more, she admitted, and he might become an all-around human being.

If she hadn't been so angry, the startling depth and warmth of his laugh might have been contagious. But she would not laugh with a man who had offered to kill her several times.

Even worse, he couldn't seem to stop. He'd look away and begin to regain control and then look back into her face and lose it.

Leah saw red and tears at the same time. She drew off

the other boot and dangled all four socks stained with her own blood.

This produced only another fit of mirth. Leah dropped the socks and leaped at him, her hands flailing at his head in the abandon of revenge.

He caught her in midair and carried her, kicking, to the pond where he dipped her to her ankles in frigid water. She screamed rage. He dipped her again. "This'll help, believe me," he managed between gasps.

Glade deposited her, dripping bloodied feet and all, back onto the rock. "I'm sorry, Leah, but I haven't had a good belly laugh in ten months. I thank you. I needed that." *Now* he was puffing. He still couldn't look at her. "You were so bedraggled—"

"And you think I like looking like this? Feeling like this? You. . . ." Leah gave up and stretched an unwashed, miserable body back on the rock. "Now I can see how one person can kill another. I could kill you right now."

"Well, for some people it takes provoking." He'd stifled his mirth to a fake coughing. "It looks like we'll stop here for today."

Chapter Seventeen

"TELL me about Clifford." Glade handed her a slice of rye bread smeared with a cheese spread he'd made by adding water to a packet and squishing it between his fingers.

"Clifford?" The spread tasted of cheddar.

"At the travel agency. One of the other nasty men who ruined your life."

"I've got better things to do than provide you with comic relief."

He grinned and gestured at the landscape. "Like what?"

She told him about Clifford. Leah had quit college one year short of her degree to work in a travel agency to help support her mother and sisters after the lawyer's warning that the Harper life-style would have to change. She'd been at the agency almost two years when a promotion became available, and Leah and the rest of the office knew she would get it because of her work record.

Glade wasn't laughing yet. He was boiling water for soup, but there was a faint upturn at the corners of his mouth.

Clifford Averill, a man-boy of twenty with one year of college, no personality, who hadn't been with the agency long enough to build a work record, who was the brunt of office jokes, got Leah's promotion. Clifford Averill was inexplicably on his way up.

"He was the boss' son?"

"He was the only male who had been there longer than two months."

Glade emptied a dried-soup packet into a plastic cup and added hot water. "You sound like sour grapes."

"And you are a spy and a male chauvinist." Who would have thought Lipton's instant chicken and noodle could taste so good?

"Correction. I *was* a spy. Now I'm a criminal." He quaffed the soup as if it weren't boiling hot. "So you quit the travel agency."

"Yes. And then I got into modeling underwear for catalogues."

Now he was laughing.

"I was desperate. We had to pay for Suzie's abortion. She was the youngest, only sixteen when we transferred her to a downtown school. She couldn't handle the adjustment. Then there were hospital bills because the abortion almost killed her." A certain fantasylike unreality about discussing her life with a criminal on the sunny top of a mountain.

They had another cup of soup and some chocolate squares. At least they weren't walking. Leah lay out on the rock, feeling almost human.

She had thought that they were on top of the world already, but another mountain rose from their level on the horizon. He stretched out beside her and caught the direction of her glance.

"According to the map, that's Big Marvine. Sure like to climb it." A wistful note in his voice.

"Count me out!"

"So what did you do after your little sister's abortion?" He was still gazing longingly at Big Marvine.

"I'd left college so Annette and Suzie could have some training after high school. But Annette quit junior college to work as a receptionist to help her fiancé get through med school. I got mad and went to New York."

"To do what?"

"Model more underwear." Leah finally reached the point where she could laugh at herself again.

This seemed to do something to Glade Wyndham, because he leaned over and kissed her. Scratchy beard, warm skin, weather-dry lips. Leah felt it all the way to her bloodstained toes.

"No, not here," he whispered, looking at the lone giant mound on the horizon. "Big Marvine. Now, that would be the place."

"Count me out," Leah repeated and moved away from him. The kiss and her body's reaction to it had caught her by surprise. Her crazy attraction to strength again. And this guy was no proud Jason to shrug off and stop at the first rebuff. Set this man in motion and there'd be no stopping him. And Leah, the fool, had put herself in a position to be alone with him in this wild place. Even she knew that one did not dabble with Glade Wyndham.

The sun offered all the comforts of a sun lamp but without the civilized surroundings. The sky was so clear and intense a blue that it looked solid, the green of the grass so sharp and vivid, the outlines of each rock and tree so distinct. No city haze to deaden colors or blur lines. Leah thought of the fairy tales of her childhood, the enchanted dangerous places and forests. This landscape too was enchanted, haunted—something frightening and hostile in all this beauty. And the last thing she needed in her struggle for independence was to become involved with a powerhouse like the man beside her.

Glade, how long do we have to stay out here?"

"I don't know. We're just buying a little time." He rolled over on his back to stare at the sky. "Any minute now I'm going to make plans for what we'll do next," he said lazily. "It's possible we'll meet other backpackers or a shepherd. If we do, keep quiet and let me do the talking."

"You mean people do this on purpose?"

"Of course. You don't think all this newfangled paraphernalia we're using was invented for a few cowboys or shepherds, do you?" His sun-darkened skin was leathery. Lines ran across a wide square forehead now that the dark tangled hair fell back in repose. With the sun lighting his upturned, relaxed face, his features lost their shadowed brutal look.

They lazed away the afternoon beside the pond in a meadow of tiny buttercups, the yellow-cream heads peeking up and around vibrant green grass clumps. The sounds of bees and flies busy in sunlight, Goodyear's soft snore, the occasional high-pitched hissing of a giant mosquito.

Glade roused himself to cover the places where the boots had worn away her skin with moleskin, a sheet of what looked to be corn-pad material with a sticky side. He cut patches to fit her wounds and insisted she get back into the devil boots to help him set up the tent.

The tent seemed to bewilder him as much as it did her. It was in pieces, like a child's toy, nylon, metal pipe, and string. They assembled it at last under the dead trees behind the pond, and prepared dinner by the rock.

Above them, clouds formed from nothing, fleecy and etched across the intense blue like billowing sheets on a clothesline.

He lit the can under the little stove and put water on to boil, took a flattened plastic bottle from his pack and filled it with water, adding pills to purify it.

"Surely the water's pure up here."

"Not where people come." He tore twigs from the dead

101

trees and built a fire, adding larger pieces he broke by bending around his knee.

And not a minute too soon. The sun set in red and purple swirls behind Big Marvine and, as if waiting in the wings for a cue, the chill wind returned. Buttercups closed, Goodyear came to life, and Leah sought the parka. They poured boiling water over freeze-dried beef Stroganoff and ate it out of the packet. Then bulletlike peas and coffee. Leah heard not a word from her stunned ulcer.

"What really happened ten months ago?" she asked when darkness enclosed them.

He poked a twig at the fire until its tip flared. "I stole something . . . what you call the property." He brought the burning end of the twig up to his face and stared into her eyes across the flame. "I was supposed to photograph it. Instead I bagged it and ran."

"Stole what from whom? Why?" She had a right to know if he had indeed involved her in this dangerous business, even mistakenly.

The twig waved back and forth, making the shadows ripple over the planes of his face and the rock behind him. "Some papers from the oil company where I worked because the agency ordered me to. Okay?"

"Why did you run? Why didn't you just photograph them and put them back?"

"Because I made the mistake of reading them and I couldn't stomach what I read." A hissing sound as he doused the twig in the dregs of his coffee.

Glade Wyndham looked so huge, so strong across the fire, so relaxed in the shadowy wilderness night. Leah resented her reliance on him, the fact that every time an owl hooted or something rustled the grass she wanted to shift to his side of the fire.

"What's a bag job done on a farm?" Could he become so angered by her incessant questioning that he could go off, leave her alone here on the Flat Tops? Could she survive without him?

"I don't know what you're talking about."

"I realize to bag something in your jargon is to steal it . . . but I heard Charlie say something about showing off bag jobs on a farm when I first saw you at Ted's Place."

"Oh, *the* farm. It's a place for field training agents . . . how to climb barbed wire and avoid mine fields and drink a lot . . . kind of thing you can't get out of a textbook at headquarters in Langley. If I hadn't turned renegade I could have retired there as an instructor. I'm not a caseworker, my specialty is breaking and entering, safes—"

"And murder?"

He shrugged. "I took care of a hit man once and there have been others. But that's not my specialty. Sometimes I was just in the right place at the wrong time."

A keening on the wind, far away but eerie, high-pitched, joined by others until it sounded like a chorus of yips that synchronized to a drawn-out yowl wailing mournfully toward their fire. . . .

Leah scooted across dirt and rocks and grass painfully, her rear never leaving the earth or missing a bump. She was now on the same side of the campfire as Glade Wyndham. "What's that?"

The wail of twenty saddened banshees in unison . . .

. . . drowned out by deep-throated male laughter. A hard protective arm drew her in. "You're a funny woman, Leah. You can keep your head while being chased by airplanes and gazing on the disfigured corpse of a tortured woman, but howling coyotes chase you right into the arms of a murderer."

"It's just all this . . . this openness—"

"There're walls even here," and he sounded sadder than the coyotes. "They're getting tighter every day. You just can't see them yet. But the coyotes and deer and elk can—"

"Do coyotes attack people?"

"No, they're waiting for sick ewes or does or tiny lambs . . . for the weak."

"Like you? Like you and Welker wait for people like me? The weak and honest?"

The low laughter drowned out the coyotes again. "No, Leah, I'm honest, too. That's how the whole problem started. If I'd just done my job." He snuggled closer until

one whole side of her warmed without the help of the fire.
"I wish. . . ."

"What?"

He stood suddenly and left her to the cold night. "Nothing, Leah Harper. Nothing."

"But why has it taken everybody ten months to find you?" she persisted, telling herself she didn't mind the rebuff.

"You don't know much about big organizations, do you?" He emptied the last of the coffee on the fire. "They're ponderous machines. But once they do get everything together and rolling, they can come down very heavy on anyone who gets in the way. And you and I, Leah, are in the way."

There is nothing to do at night on the top of the world, no light to read by, nowhere fun to go, no TV. They crawled into their sleeping bags and listened to each other lay awake . . . to the creaking and the rustling and the night wind . . . and then to rain.

Still smelling of singed fur, Goodyear sat on Leah's stomach and washed. Then he curled up on the parka rolled under her head, used her shoulder for a pillow, and purred ferociously into her ear.

Glade stirred restlessly beside her.

She had the feeling they were both thinking of the same thing . . . and she didn't want to. She'd noticed mother nature clicking behind his passionless composure. Maybe it was just her own ego, playing tricks. But Leah wasn't interested. It was too cold, crowded, and uncomfortable. It would just be something to do, a way to use each other. She had been used enough.

Big, dark, mysterious—all the attributes to snare the lonely. Murderer, thief, criminal—what other things would he admit to? What more could he?

Sudden ruthlessness, sudden gentleness, the warmth of his laughter, the cruel grip on her arm, the understanding pauses on the trail, the heat of a kiss. . . .

"Glade? Would you really have killed me at that fishing cabin when you thought I was Sheila?"

"Yes." The flat finality of his clipped words. . . .

Chapter Eighteen

"I'M not much of a cook," Glade apologized.

"Oh, it's delicious." Leah moved to a drier part of the rock. The night's rain had left little puddles. "What is it?"

"It's supposed to be a pancake," he said with disgust.

The pancake was raw dough surrounded by a charcoaled exterior. The metal plate had chilled it to crunchy. She took a gulp of Tang to unstick the dough. "The syrup is . . . sweet," she said encouragingly. He'd mixed purple powder with water to make a raspberry syrup . . . sort of.

"These have to cook one at a time. Ready for another?"

"No, I think this will do it." Leah forced down every last congealed lump and tried to smile. Her ulcer considered shoving it back. She fought it down and worked harder on her smile because she didn't want to hurt his feelings.

The irony of that made the smile real, if bitter. He'd told her last night that he could have taken her life and by morning she worried about hurting his feelings. There was something wrong with women. Or was it just Leah Harper?

"I grew up on a ranch west of here. We camped often but we didn't have all these fancy directions on foil packets. Pork and beans in a can, steak skewered on a stick over the fire. We slept in the open or pulled ponchos over us if it rained. But we couldn't have carried it on our backs. We had packhorses."

Leah stared at him. "You were a cowboy?"

"Mostly just a boy." If Leah hadn't known better, she'd have said there was a hint of shyness in his grin, the way his eyes dropped to the little stove.

"Here in Colorado? Can't we go to your people at the ranch?"

"When my father died, he willed me an education and my older brother got the ranch. Until last summer I hadn't been back for twelve, fifteen years."

"Well, your brother then. . . ."

"Cal sold out . . . to an oil company."

Glade ate five pancakes while Goodyear watched the tiny transparent animals in the shallow pond. Some looked like corkscrews, others like cockroaches, still others like beetles. They didn't swim. They squiggled through the water.

"The pond freezes to the bottom in winter. Those little creatures probably live their lifetimes in one summer." He poured coffee and added pointedly, "Not everyone can look forward to a long life span."

She'd never dared so much coffee but it was warming and smelled like roasting nuts on the cold air. Only the afternoons were livable up here. "And you think your days are numbered?"

"And yours if I don't think of something." He sat on the rock and "thought" the whole blessed day, staring at the curve of Big Marvine.

Leah decided he was a boob man and tried not to go crazy with boredom. Mother nature clicked all around her but didn't disturb Glade Wyndham. It must have been her imagination the day before.

By afternoon she was pacing through the buttercups despite her sore feet. Glade sat motionless with the tip of his thumb stuck between his teeth. Goodyear batted lazily at a grass frond, rolled over on his back with his tail and hind legs angled up the side of the rock and the lush buff of his oversized stomach exposed to the sun. He resumed his nap unaware of how uncomfortable and ridiculous he looked.

Leah stretched out beside him and stroked the proffered underside, dozed to the tune of his fantastic purr—and awoke to find Glade Wyndham staring through her. . . .

The rigid mask had slipped, leaving a look of helplessness on the tanned face . . . tumbled curls over a wrinkled brow . . . firm mouth gone slack with . . . remorse? Fear?

106

For a moment, before he focused and realized she stared back, before face and body tightened to withdraw into the strong male, Leah had the insane desire to comfort him.

They both blinked. "Well, have you thought of a way to save our necks?" she asked, reaching for Goodyear in her confusion. But the cat had left her side to sit aloof by the pond and watch them.

"When I met you in that restaurant in Oak Creek, I was supposed to meet a reporter for the Denver *Post*. He didn't show." Glade stretched and stood to find a stone at the pond's edge. "It was just me then. It didn't matter so much." He skipped the stone across the water and picked up another. "You've complicated everything."

"Why a reporter?"

"The only thing I could think of to do with the papers —and I thought all winter—is to turn them over to the press. But I don't know how to do that and save our hides, too. There are too many very talented people after us."

"Couldn't your brother—"

"I want to keep Cal out of this. They've probably got him well covered by now, anyway." Another rock skipped across the pond's surface and Goodyear crouched.

"I still don't see. . . . Why do you want to get the papers to the press?"

"Have you ever seen a pile of mine tailings?"

"I don't even know what they are."

"It's what's left after the earth has been disemboweled. I've seen it in thousands of places, piles of mine tailings over a hundred years old, some here in Colorado. And do you know what?" Dark eyes looked through her. "There isn't even a weed growing on them. After all this time." He returned to his thinking position on the rock and to his silent mood.

Leah walked to the top of the hill and looked back at the pond where the man and the cat sat like statues.

Glade had grown up on a ranch with his brother, Cal, had become a mining engineer and a CIA agent, had stolen the property and run out on both jobs. The property was so important that Welker was willing to pay a high price for it and involve Leah, that Charlie would see Glade had a fatal accident, and the goons would kill anyone who got in the way of their search for Glade, including Sheila and presumably Leah. And oil shale . . . and weeds didn't grow on mine tailings. . . .

Leah shrugged and wandered back down the hill.

"Swords," Glade announced over a freeze-dried pork chop at dinner. "Maybe he can get us out of this." He looked hopeful for a moment and then shook his head. "No, that's too long a shot even for this."

"Who's Swords?"

"That hit man I took care of?" He pointed his fork at her. Leah backed away. "He was about to take care of Swords. He seemed pretty grateful at the time."

"Is he powerful enough to get around the FBI and the CIA and—"

"He's powerful enough that it'd be hard to even get in touch with him. Still, he's better than nothing. . . ."

Leah awoke in the green nylon tent and would have jerked upright if there had been room. "What's that?"

"Sheep," Glade answered irritably.

The sounds were distant, a few bells and many complaining ba-a-as. It sounded like a restaurant full of indigestion.

"Shepherd's just moving them in. No fire this morning. We'll eat and break camp."

"Where will we go? Have you thought of anything?"

"We'll walk out of here. I want to get to a telephone." His fist struck at the nylon roof. "The property has to get to the newspapers. I'll try again. It's all I can do."

"That's fine for the property but what about us?"

"I'll keep working on that, Leah. Maybe Swords will. . . . I'll have to work on it."

They had plastic bacon chips in their Styrofoam eggs and broke camp. Glade had everything on their backs in record time.

They started toward Big Marvine. Three nights of sleeping on the ground had not rested her sore muscles and all the old aches were soon back. But his fear and worry that catastrophe was closing in on them kept her moving.

They crossed rolling hills and as they crested one they saw the sheep they'd been hearing since dawn. It looked as if white fluff balls had been scattered across the green, as if someone had blown the fur tops from giant dandelions. The sheep grazed near two small bright lakes.

Glade and Leah angled away to skirt the lakes on the far side and soon the lakes and sheep were lost from sight.

"Where was the shepherd?"

"He's around."

"Do you think he saw us?"

"They don't miss much." He stopped to point out a hoof track in a damp patch of dirt. "Elk."

"Why don't we see any wild animals? Here we are in that great wilderness I've heard so much about. . . ."

"They won't show themselves to us. We're the enemy." His boots were suddenly smeared with Siamese. Goodyear purred, rolled, rubbed, nudged, and then tried to climb Glade's pant leg.

"What's the matter, fella?" he asked gently, picking up the cat. "Can't take a little hike? You're in worse shape than your mistress."

"If I remember right, you once told me I had a great body."

"Yeah, like a stick with arms."

More elk tracks as they neared the base of Big Marvine. "Hunters come up here in the fall, slaughter only the biggest, healthiest, best of the herds. People. The enemy."

"You're one to talk. You kill people."

"I've never killed for sport, Leah."

"Then for what, the government?"

He shrugged and walked on.

At the base of Big Marvine they snacked on dry granola and water. Leah lay back with her head on a soft part of her pack. The only good thing about hiking was that it felt wonderful when it stopped. Streaky clouds scudded before a wind that was not apparent below. They were early today.

He let her rest for a surprisingly long time while he broke twigs between his fingers, threw pebbles to crack like bullets against a log, scratched an ecstatic cat, looked often at the huge mound that rose behind them.

"Let's have lunch on top of Big Marvine," he said suddenly, hurling a pebble so far that it cleared the log and Leah couldn't hear it land.

"You go ahead. I'll wait for you down here."

"Cheese, rye, sausage, Maalox . . . you're about out of Maalox." He put the lunch into a nylon stuff sack and tied it to his belt.

"That's because of your cooking. Leave the Maalox with me."

"No Big Marvine. No lunch." He lifted her from the ground so fast, she felt dizzy.

"I thought you were in a hurry to get to a telephone."

"It'll take days to walk out of here. One afternoon won't matter that much."

"The shepherd will see us."

"He's seen us by now. They see everything. They don't have much else to do. Besides we're just a couple of backpackers." He strapped the canteen and two rolled plastic bundles over his shoulder.

"What are those?"

"Ponchos. In case it rains. You don't have to carry anything."

"Rain!" Leah sat down again.

"Just a precaution. Come on."

"Only if you answer some questions first." Anything to get out of climbing that damn mountain.

He rolled his eyes toward the clouds, shifted his weight from one foot to another, sighed, and finally said, "Okay. What?"

"Did you kill on orders from the CIA?"

"Leah, I was not an assassin like the fictional James Bond. Once in a great while I would get into a situation that I couldn't have gotten out of if I hadn't killed someone. My job was much less exciting than James Bond's, too. In fact, it was rarely exciting at all. Next question."

"This property that has to get to the press—this information—you're not trying to start another Watergate or Pentagon Papers or . . . anything. Are you?"

His brow lowered to shadow his eyes. "What?"

"Look, I'm not brilliant, but I'm not completely uninformed."

"I don't know what you're talking about." His voice went flat and secretive. She sensed he was thinking hard.

"If the CIA and the FBI and an oil company are after these papers. And you have to get this information to the press. The government doesn't want you to . . . *How big is this thing?*"

"It's big, Leah." He shifted his weight again and looked away. "I don't know how far up it goes, but. . . ."

She hoped he wouldn't go on, because she didn't want another Watergate and she didn't want to climb Big Marvine.

"I worked for this oil company," he said finally. "I was placed there by the agency."

"An American oil company?"

"Yes."

"And your brother sold your ranch to an oil company. Oil shale?"

He nodded, his expression haunted. "I worked on a study with many other people. We looked into the possibilities of mining shale, strip, open pit. . . ."

"But the CIA wanted more information than what you had access to in your work?"

"There was a deal going. Between the government and the company."

"But you worked for the government."

"There are many forms of 'the government,' Leah, separate, distinct, and suspicious of each other. It was a CYA sort of thing . . . it had to be. But I'd been out here, saw what was happening . . . what could happen. It was the first time I'd been home in years. If shale—"

"CYA' More bureaucratic alphabet soup?"

"It means, cover your ass. It's the dominant survival technique in organizations of any size, in and out of government. Leah, do you really want to know more?"

"No." She felt sick.

She climbed Big Marvine with him.

Chapter Nineteen

THEY wore the hoods of their wind-shirts so that the shepherd couldn't determine the color of their hair, although Leah was sure he was too far away to see them. She could just make out his tiny horse grazing beside a white tent.

The trail zigzagged constantly to get up the steep and completely open side of Big Marvine. Leah stopped looking down at about the fourth switchback. She decided Glade wanted to climb it only to keep her too winded to ask questions.

Goodyear had followed them a short way, but when Glade made it clear he wouldn't carry him, the cat returned to the bottom. Leah would have loved to go with him but her companion looked so stony she was afraid to say so.

She'd made little sense of what she'd learned. If she thought it all through carefully, she might be able to piece this story together. But Leah had taken in enough to know that—if he wasn't lying—that story might be more than she had any desire to tangle with. He was planning to expose another scandal and everyone was out to stop him. The murderer-spy had become a man with a mission and even more confusing.

By the tenth switchback, she began to hate him for making her climb, for taking her away from the civilized world, for being in such good shape that the climb didn't bother him, for involving her in this ridiculous situation of government and information and oil companies, and finally for existing.

She lost count of the switchbacks, stopped often to rest, was afraid to look down, afraid to look up.

Glade waited tight-lipped and impatient when she stopped to rest, spoke only to warn her of treacherous places in the path and then with curt civility. Another mood change. Because he'd told her too much?

At the end of the trail he stood with his hands on his hips, his breathing deep but even and Leah lying at his feet.

She didn't smoke, drink, overeat. She'd been in the habit of rigorous calisthenics since her modeling days, but she was not ready for the Rocky Mountains.

And they were still not on top of Big Marvine. The path disappeared but the terrain sloped upward past a line of scrubby pine bushes, all grotesquely bent over in the same direction by the wind, and farther on, a jumble of broken rocks on the skyline.

"This is as far . . . as I can go. I don't want . . . lunch. I'll wait here."

"You've come this far, damn it." He spoke through clenched teeth that contrasted with several days' growth of black beard. He looked like a wolf. His canine teeth seemed to have grown on the way up Big Marvine. "You're going to the top."

"Why? So you can push me off?"

"Don't tempt me." The rough hand on her arm again as he pulled her up. "Trust a woman to spoil the one good day I've had in months."

They passed the line of scrub pine and headed for the rocky summit.

"If you start crying, I'll—"

"You'll what? Kill me?" Leah said sweetly. "Because I got you into a situation you couldn't get out of otherwise?"

He didn't answer, but pulled her along faster.

They ate lunch at the very top of Big Marvine, just as he'd said they would. The wind that had been blowing the clouds across the sky was with them now.

Leah drank the last of the Maalox and wolfed sausage, cheese, and rye as if she'd eaten nothing for days. She sat, as once before, between his legs with her back resting against his chest and one kidney against his gun. His body protected her from the cruelty of the wind but not from the razor rocks on which she sat.

The view was staggering, vaster than the one from their first camp on the rim. But she still couldn't see the third person on the Flat Tops, the shepherd, too tiny and insignificant a being to show up on the incredible panorama that finally reduced Leah to a need for confession.

She babbled to her sheltering spy about her mother and the view became comfortably distorted through tears.

"Christ." The hard voice produced warm breath on the part in her hair. "And you found her?"

"I was just coming in to tell her that I'd lost another job. My mother was so fastidious . . . she took her clothes off before she got into the tub to slit her wrists. What I remember most is my own scream. It bumped off the tile and came back at me . . ."

"I thought you were in New York modeling underwear."

"I'd quit that and gone to work as a secretary at a publisher's. But secretaries stayed secretaries in that company. Annette and Suzie kept complaining I wasn't doing my fair share so I transferred to the Chicago branch of the same publisher. I was still a secretary but we agreed to take turns living with Mother for one year each and that would give us two years off."

The twin lakes looked like mere puddles. Clouds rimmed the sky white all around them, spilled like thin milk over flat-topped monsters in the distance.

"And then Suzie married Ed. That left two of us. And then Annette married Doctor Ralph. And Leah had Mother all to herself. I was fired from the publisher's because typing and filing bore me and they finally noticed it. I took a job as a sales clerk at a boutique—"

"And were fired because that bored you, too."

"It went out of business. I was just going to break the news to my mother when I found her . . . dead."

"So far your life does not sound like a roaring success." There was no sympathy in his voice.

"I keep wondering how much farther down I can get. I did until I met you, that is."

"Well, now you can get down a mountain."

Before leaving the summit, they peered over the other side into a canyon lost in clouds. The sheer drop turned Leah's stomach. Something shiny under a corner of rock caught her eye and she bent to pick it up. "Coors Beer," the label said. A strange thing to find at the top and the end of the world.

"What did you expect? The Ten Commandments?" He reached out to take the can from her. But it dropped to the ground between them as a new sound in the air came to them both at once.

"What is it? A plane?" she asked as they stumbled down the rocks and raced for the grotesque pine shelter.

"Helicopter."

"After us?"

"I'm not taking any chances."

Leah lay flat on her stomach and wiggled into a depression under curved branches. Glade crawled in behind her and they lay horizontal to the view and to the line of pine bush. She could just see the twin lakes over his dark head . . . and the military-looking helicopter as it cleared the side of Big Marvine.

It flew low over the plateau, circled the lakes, and angled gradually away toward the rim on which they'd camped that first night. Milk-thin clouds seeped in a slow tumble toward the helicopter. They could no longer hear its sound.

Leah felt Glade's body tense against her side as the copter turned and flew back toward them.

"What if they find our packs?"

"We've had it."

The helicopter, resembling a dragonfly in the distance, settled finally in the air . . . and then descended, landing beside the white tent of the shepherd. The miniature horse bucked and pulled at an invisible tether. Glade Wyndham made a nasty choking sound in his throat.

"Is there another way off this mountain?" she asked.

"No. We'll have to wait." The fist next to her shoulder tightened until the black hairs on his fingers stood erect.

Now that she was out of the direct sunlight, the mountain's chill crept through her wind-shirt.

Two minuscule people moved from the stilled helicopter to the tent and then off toward the white specks of sheep.

"Maybe the shepherd didn't see us," she said through chattering teeth.

"Not likely, but just hope, Leah. Hope hard."

The two people disappeared. "Maybe the helicopter just came to bring the shepherd some food."

"Anybody with an ounce of sense or knowledge about mountains wouldn't have brought a chopper in here now." He put an arm across her chest and snuggled his warmth close against her. "It'll rain soon . . . at least fog. They won't be able to get it off the ground if they don't move fast. They'll be trapped up here. But so will we."

The horse had settled down. Clouds trickled closer to the sheep. Leah thought of Sheila and the burning Volks. Her troubles with work and family suddenly seemed petty. "Glade, all those thing I said about my life. . . ."

"I know." He nuzzled his hot face under her chin and kissed her neck. "You've had rough luck. Meeting me didn't make it any better. I'm sorry." He slid sideways to lie on top of her and his weight and heat stopped her trembling. "You feel like a piece of ice."

"I keep dreaming of that parka at the bottom of the mountain. What if Goodyear didn't go back to the packs?"

"He won't go near the shepherd because shepherds have sheep dogs." He relaxed again and flattened her body into the depression in the earth.

She drew heat from him but felt the strangeness again at being here with this man at all. "Don't call me Leah Harper anymore and. . . ." She meant to add, "Don't kill me," but his lips stopped her.

The horse and the helicopter stood motionless in the sun below, but milky mist shrouded the sheep and slithered toward the lakes.

"Your moods change so abruptly, it's hard to trust you."

Her legs, on either side of his, still felt the cold. Pine needles pricked through her jeans into her knees.

He chuckled and his ribs pressed against her. "What do you bet someone in Langley is saying that same thing about now?" He slid his arms under her, cradling her head in the palm of one hand, drawing back to look at her face. "You like your murderers to fit into the common mold, don't you?"

At the word "murderer" Leah squirmed beneath him but he settled more heavily, driving the hard earth into her back. When he turned sideways to glance at the plateau, she could see the pulse in his neck, feel his hardness against her leg. Leah was altogether too warm now.

He turned back with a slow, not particularly warm smile. "Leah, I had great and wonderful plans for Big Marvine, but I'm afraid it's time to go."

She couldn't believe how quickly the cold moved in when he moved off. "Why?"

"Look."

The plateau was gone . . . white with cloud . . . but no helicopter . . . no tent. . . .

"This may be our last chance." He pulled her out into the wind and drew her so tightly against him she thought she'd crack. Then he released her.

"Run, Leah," he said gently. "Like you've never run before."

Chapter Twenty

MILK-clouds leaked over the top of Big Marvine when they reached the head of the trail. Misty fingerlets lapped at their boots while sun still glared in their faces. Leah had never imagined clouds rising up the side of a mountain, had long taken it for granted that clouds lowered from the sky. But as they started down the trail they were soon muffled in chill, damp gray.

Glade Wyndham loomed darkly ahead in the suffocating murk.

"We can't possibly make it down in this. I can't see."

"It's the only way. The fog will provide cover. Feel for the trail with each step. It's a godsend for us, after all, Leah."

The godsend laced her eyelashes with tiny drops, made her sinuses drain. It swirled white in some places and formed dark writhing shadow-shapes of things that weren't there in others. Leah saw a horse and rider, distinctly, coming up the path, the horse's head bobbing as it walked, but horse and rider evaporated as they neared.

The reality of her aloneness had never been more apparent. She felt cut off and floating. The jarring of injured toes against boots as she jolted downward, the ache in her knees, and the fear of walking off into oblivion kept her panic just under control.

Her mother's dependence on her father had been disastrous. Her sisters acted like willing and pale appendages to their mates. And Leah had set out for Colorado to prove her own independence. But her vow to rely on no one but herself evaporated in the mist shrouding Big Marvine, like the phantom horse and rider. Her spy bobbed ahead like a shadowed safety buoy and when he stopped suddenly, turned and kissed her, she wanted to cry.

The fog encrusting his beard was wet on her face. "I think we're going to make it." His whisper was jubilant. "We're almost down. Be quiet now, sound carries on fog."

With this warning, Leah realized how much she could hear . . . a tree creaking below, sheep bleating far away. The sounds of their boots and breathing seemed loud enough to give away their position to anyone within miles.

The air smelled of moss and rotting wood and damp earth.

At the bottom of Big Marvine, the fog had thinned enough to let them find their things. Goodyear lay under the flap of Glade's pack and was allowed to ride that way as they skirted the base of the mountain. The fog lifted higher, and they caught a glimpse of the helicopter and the shepherd's camp, and then all was hidden in a slow soaking drizzle that promised to last the day.

Leah followed Glade for hours through the rain and hoped they weren't getting lost. Her companion looked grotesquely humpbacked with the poncho covering the great lump of his backpack.

A grove of live pine sheltered their tent that night and Leah awoke once to find the rain had stopped and Glade talking in his sleep. A few incomprehensible phrases in what sounded like Spanish with a guttural German accent.

Sun warmed their breakfast rock the next morning. Leah gulped hot coffee gratefully. "I don't want to know anything about it, but do you know you speak Spanish in your sleep?"

He glanced up from the little stove with one of those brutal heart-stopping looks. "I have recurring nightmares."

"In Spanish?"

"Chile." He pronounced it Chee-lay.

"Chile! When they—"

"I worked for a copper company before Allende threw it out. But I stayed on for my other employer, melted in. People of Chile have little or no Indian blood, an American can infiltrate almost—"

"Allende! Glade, you shouldn't be telling me this. I mean, it was in the papers about . . . I don't want to know."

He sighed and brought out the bottle of whiskey from his pack. She hadn't seen it since that day in the pickup. "Have you ever stopped to think, Leah Harper"—he gulped from the neck of the bottle and shuddered—"what can happen when nobody wants to know?"

He no longer looked like the savior she'd followed through fog and rain the day before. The gilt was tarnished, worn. They were both dirty and rumpled. She had no mirror to look at herself, but she could see the hopelessness on his unshaven face . . . and drinking whiskey for breakfast was somehow like a last act. He'd seemed so triumphant coming down Big Marvine.

If he gave up now, she would have to depend on herself as she had once brashly set out to prove she could.

Birds sang to the morning. A squirrel, pumping its oversized tail, chittering its indignation at their presence from the safety of a tree limb. Wild columbine turned enormous blossoms to the sun, raindrops still glistening on delicately shaded lavender.

Leah had another cup of coffee. "Do you know where we are . . . exactly?"

"Yeah." Glade took another drink of whiskey. "We're lost."

The sun warmed Leah and dried the columbine. Still they sat. Still he drank.

She threw her cup to the ground. He didn't look up from the spot of earth he seemed to be trying to dig into with his eyes.

Leah slid off her rock and grabbed the bottle from his hand. That got his attention, but he still had a faraway expression. "What's the matter?"

"Here we are lost and the whole world is after us and you sit drinking your breakfast." She capped the bottle. "That's what's the matter."

"According to the map, if we walk west long enough, we'll come to a marked trail."

"Oh." Leah took the bottle back to the rock with her. If she had felt threatened at being alone in the wilds with an admittedly violent man, she felt more so with a drinking one. If his moods were unpredictable when he was sober. . . . "Well, liquor won't help us find that trail or get out of here, will it?"

"No, ma'am." He pushed himself to his feet and walked toward Leah and the bottle, the faraway look gone, his focus steady on hers. "But it might help me get through another day in a very long ordeal."

Leah felt an awful but tantalizing prickle and couldn't lower her eyes as he pried her fingers from the whiskey. "Drinking won't help you get the papers to the press, to—"

"What do you know about that?" He raised the bottle to his lips and his eyes turned cruel. "You're in the middle of

120

something important and all you can think of is your own little problems, whine about men because they beat you out of a job, feel sorry for yourself when you could get involved in something"—he waved the whiskey in front of her—"something more important than Leah Harper."

"You're going to walk out on me, aren't you?" Jason had asked, rage etching the lines of his face. "Because you're afraid to really get involved, right?" Jason had towered over her. "Selfish is what you are, Leah. So go . . . sit around and feel sorry for yourself and be secretly glad that you didn't give anything away. Go back to nursing your ulcer, flitting from one job or man to another so you can claim failure. Anything important happen to you"—Jason had been drinking, too—"you wouldn't be around it long enough to know. You're like a bee starving in a field full of flowers because it can't decide which flower to molest first." Mutt, the soft-eyed dog, always whimpered, cried when they fought.

Glade Wyndham emptied the whiskey bottle. "They're going to rip up a whole section of beauty that outshines even you, but you're still back with your sucker of a sister's abortion." His laughter was hollow now as it had been when she first heard it.

"Glade. . . ." She tried to sound soothing, reasonable.

"Why aren't you afraid of me anymore, Leah?" The bottle dashed to splinter against the rock beside her. "I think I liked you better when you were afraid of me."

Leah slid backward off the rock, putting it between them, looked away from the hard stare. "Because I don't . . . really believe you can be all those things you say you are." She held her voice steady but her mouth was dry.

"Then you're a fool." He moved around the rock.

"You can be so kind and gentle at times. . . ." She backed to a tree and then slid around it, leaving pine branches to whip back at him. Given the nature of this beast, how had she put it off this long? Could she stop it now?

"She doesn't want to get involved, our Leah," he whispered and advanced with her to the next tree. "Because it's disturbing. She might have to give up something. You're a fake, Leah."

The treacherous, breathless urge to submit . . . the tickly sensation. Leah watched him draw closer . . . it was the size of him, the darkness, the mystery that froze her like fear froze a rabbit . . . it was. . . .

"Oh, God. Glade!" Leah swiveled around the tree to run but was caught by the belt and swung back against him. "Glade, it's just the whiskey. Please . . ."

"I should never have brought a woman along. . . ." The detached, impersonal voice, the rough beard painful on her sun- and wind-scarred skin.

"I'm not just a woman. . . ." She sank to the ground under his weight.

He blocked out the sun.

Leah found that she was still afraid of this man. And that struggle was useless. And that he was not necessarily kind and not necessarily gentle.

Chapter Twenty-one

LEAH hunched over the cat on her lap. Goodyear poked a chilly wet nose into her cheek as if in sympathy. But there was only cold-blue dislike in the slanted eyes. Still . . . Leah found such comfort in the crackling plush coat. She could almost leave her hand print in it.

"Did I hurt you?" . . . the flat voice behind her.

"Yes . . . no . . ." Leah closed her eyes and kneaded Siamese fur with the fingers of both hands. The spurty purring promised love and loyalty. Claws pricked her bare skin as they constricted, let go as they relaxed in a repeated feline rhythm.

"Then what's the matter?"

Goodyear sprang from her lap, yawned, and stretched, as if to say, "That was nice, but I can take it or leave it."

"I don't understand you," Leah answered them both.

"Neither do I." He sat beside her. "You're ashamed then?"

"No . . . yes . . . I don't know."

"You needn't be," he said with that finality of tone. "There wasn't a thing you could have done about it."

"I don't like being helpless."

"You sure could have fooled me." He plucked a grass stalk and put it between his lips like a cigarette. The bitter-spicy stench of whiskey clung to them both. But she realized he wasn't drunk now, if he had ever been.

"And I'm not a fake."

"Oh, hell, Leah, you'd been asking for that for three days. And it's not exactly like it was hermetically sealed or—"

"Why, you overblown . . . egocentric male. . . ." She turned to the hard face and saw dark eyes laughing at her. "I hate you . . . I . . . ."

"No, you don't." He ran the grass stalk to tickle along her leg. "You just want to."

"You're a bully, and a . . ." Her voice broke. She really didn't hate him. Why, for God's sake? "I don't understand you." She tried to push his hand away but it came back to knead her hair and scalp as she had the cat's. She cried until he pulled her in against him.

"You're not helpless. It's just that you need me now," he said soothingly. "There's no shame in needing." He ran dry scratchy fingers over her ribs where her blouse hung open. "You're a city girl thrown into a situation that frightens you." His hands, his movements were smooth, catlike, caressing.

"I'm not just *a* woman. I'm me," she demanded uselessly. "And . . . and I'm thirty years old."

The rich, full laughter of the other Glade warmed her through. "And barely ripe . . . poor Leah." He slid her forward until her back touched the grass and her shoulders were cradled in his arm. "Poor Leah," he said gently and hid the glare of the sun once again.

123

Leah couldn't have said which Glade she feared or enjoyed more. But the gentle Glade was somehow more dangerous. . . .

They walked, demon-driven, the rest of that day and the next. They walked in the rain, seldom speaking and never touching . . . except once when they leaned against each other laughing at a miserable dripping Goodyear, who'd just returned from a necessary trip into the trees.

"Why does he stay with us?" Leah took him in under her poncho.

"Where else can he go? He's domesticated. This place is as bizzare to him as it is to you."

Leah awoke feeling filthy in her sleeping bag and hearing more than the normal sounds of morning in the forest. She heard a helicopter, and farther off, the harsh barking of excited dogs.

Her spy slept peacefully. How had he ever escaped dangerous situations when he slept so well? "Glade!" She pummeled his chest. "I think they've found us."

He came awake slowly and then tried to sit up suddenly when he realized what he was hearing. They peered through the tent opening at a calm sun-filled forest. But the sounds were not far away.

They packed quickly, stuffed a reluctant Goodyear into Glade's pack. Quietly, Glade and Leah climbed to the top of the low mountain on which they'd camped to discover a meadow stretching below on the other side. A jeep trail crossed it. The helicopter stood with blades stilled. A pickup and several jeeps parked by a large tent. Five men stood around a pack of leashed dogs.

One of the men was the grinning Charlie, who had asked her if she was Sheila her first day in Colorado.

Another, Leah had seen at Ted's Place, too. He'd been eating a hamburger as he crawled into a pickup full of caged dogs. Now he held something out for them to sniff.

"Is that your sweat shirt?" Glade whispered.

"I think so . . . yes. What'll we do?"

"Walk quietly in the other direction until we can run."

He turned and slipped through the trees and then returned when she didn't follow him. "Come on."

"Those men aren't goons, right? They're CIA." It was now or never.

"Yes, but let's not talk about it here."

"You go. I've slowed you down long enough." One more day with this man and she'd really be lost.

"What are you saying?"

"They want the property and you. I don't have the property and I don't know where it is. This isn't the group that killed Sheila."

"Well, no. They wouldn't dare. . . . Welker knows about you. But . . ." He studied the group below. "We may have a chance. . . ."

"No. Go. And with my blessing. I'll give you as much time as I can. Now hurry."

"I don't like this."

"It's the only way and you know it. Get your whatever-it-is to the press and . . . good luck."

"Please come with me."

"Glade, they're not even bloodhounds. Just a bunch of nondescript—"

"They treed me a week ago."

"I'll give myself up before they get the chance." She took a deep breath and hardened her voice. "I'm probably in as much danger from you as I am from them."

He still stared at the men and dogs on the meadow. He shook his head slowly. "I don't trust them, Leah."

"Look, here's my one chance to get out of this." And away from Glade Wyndham? "When they realize I have nothing to tell them, they'll let me get on a plane and away from Colorado and the goons. And you'll move faster and easier without me."

"You don't know them. What if they don't believe you?"

"Glade, I can't take any more of this running, or being filthy, or . . . in the open all the time." Where the wilderness screamed her vulnerability back at her at every step. "I have to get back to my own world." Where there were walls and people and reason. Where she wouldn't need a strong man to look after her. "Your world is too dangerous."

"And my future too dim?" Bitterness, disappointment in his voice? It was hard to tell which.

She nodded and clamped her teeth so that her chin wouldn't tremble.

"You're sure?" All expression, emotion gone now.

"I just want out," she whispered and closed her eyes.

"Good-bye, Leah Harper." He tucked a strand of hair behind her ear. "I think you're making a mistake but . . . good luck."

Glade Wyndham disappeared through the trees with a half-hearted wave. The last thing she saw was two cobalt-cold eyes peeping from under the flap of his backpack.

She'd forgotten the cat again! Leah shrugged. The man and the cat had more in common with each other than they did with her. But she would miss them.

Leah sat down to watch the scene below through tears. The enormity of her sense of loss did not surprise her, but it did take her breath away. "That's okay, Leah. You've had losses before and you recovered. You've just got to disentangle yourself from this mess." They would be better off without her. And she couldn't afford them.

The canines had had a good sniff of her sweat shirt. Their handler released them and all four took off importantly . . . but in four different directions.

Charlie doubled over and slapped his thigh. His companions looked grim. The handler mouthed curses and the dogs returned for another sniff.

Leah giggled silently, cried silently, and finally hiccuped loudly. But the dogs made such a racket, no one on the meadow heard her. She could smell herself but then maybe the wind was in the wrong direction.

The dogs were released again. And spurted different ways again. But one of them, on the far side of the tent, began to howl. Everyone raced across the meadow away from Leah.

She laughed and cried so hard that her empty, ulcerous stomach gurgled warning. But there was no one to hear.

Everyone stood looking up a far tree that the dogs were trying to climb.

Finally, one of the men climbed the tree after a boost from a companion's shoulder.

Leah crept back into the trees to answer a call from her bladder, delayed by an overwrought breaking of camp. When she came back, the group below was returning, Charlie clutching his ribs. The dogs walked subdued, heads hanging in shame.

Charlie disappeared into the tent and came out with a can that gleamed golden in the sun. He pop-topped it and drank between spasms of laughter.

Leah rummaged through her pack and found a packet of cheddar cheese spread. She dug it out with her dirty index finger and had breakfast. "Mother," she whispered to the piny air, "wherever you are, you wouldn't believe this."

The helicopter took off eventually in one direction, the dogs in another. Charlie stayed on the ground, drinking beer. Leah ate cheddar until it was gone.

She had not made a mistake this time. Her mistake had been to blindly follow him to begin with. She had her own life to get on with.

The dogs returned before the helicopter, but without Glade and Goodyear. She was relieved. The sun rose higher. Charlie was on his fifth round at least.

The handler released the dogs so they could urinate. One of them raised his leg directly below Leah and looked up at her. She could have sworn he'd seen her. But he trotted back to camp.

There was a snorting sound behind her and Leah turned to stare into the eyes of a great bull elk. He was startled to panic with pupils dilated and antlers mossy with fur. He was so unexpected, so fine a creature that she sat entranced, almost hypnotized. With all the barking in the meadow, why that elk wasn't miles away in another direction, she'd never know. Leah blinked.

The elk blinked.

The dog had stopped in the clearing to bark for his four-legged friends who came racing toward him. Then the entire pack turned on Leah and the majestic animal behind her.

Leah Harper stood as crashing flight sounded at her back.

She left her pack where it lay and walked slowly down the mountain toward the dogs. Men raced across the meadow. The helicopter sounded in the distance. Leah hoped Charlie and the handler got to her before the dogs recovered from their surprise.

Chapter Twenty-two

LEAH sat on a canvas stool drinking coffee and feeling embarrassed about her unwashed condition.

One of the grim-faced men handed her a cheese sandwich and sat on the edge of a cot facing her. "I'm Peter Bradley." He smiled and it made him handsome, even if his name probably wasn't Peter Bradley. His rumpled white shirt was rolled to the elbows and open three or four buttons down the front to show off the brown hair on his chest. "There are a few holes in your story, Miss Harper. For instance, how did you know we were with the government and looking for this man you say left you this morning?"

"He told me you were CIA men."

"When? You say he left you before you came upon our camp."

"We'd seen the helicopter when we were on Big Marvine."

"Uhm. Now, there's miles of wilderness here. How did you happen to find us?"

"I didn't find you. I sort of . . . stumbled across you. I heard the dogs and the helicopter—"

"That's handy, that helicopter. This man you call Glade Wyndham dragged you around the Rockies for a week and then just left you alone in the wilderness this morning. Why?"

"I've told you . . . or them." She motioned toward the two men who were going through her backpack.

"Tell us again." His eyes warmed, inviting confidences.

"He said that he had something to do and that I slowed him down. He said if I walked west long enough I'd find a marked trail."

"Seems kind of cold-blooded, doesn't it? To bring you all that way and just leave you?"

"I . . . guess so."

"And yet you're protecting him—"

"No!"

Peter Bradley squeezed his lower lip between his thumb and forefinger. The helicopter and dogs had left again and it was quiet. Now and then a slight clank sounded as her belongings were spread out on a long table. Charlie lounged in the tent opening with his beer can and his grin. A fly landed on her cheese sandwich. Leah was growing tired of cheese.

"Why did you go with him?"

"I told you. He made me go at first and then after we found Sheila . . . I felt threatened too, so I stayed with him."

"Why did you feel threatened?"

"Sheila was in *my* car."

"And yet you walked boldly into this camp this afternoon."

"Trap" . . . the very air breathed it. Leah tried not to blink. "He said goons did that to Sheila. I thought you were a different bunch because you had the helicopter."

"But some days ago you hid from our search plane . . . left your sweat shirt—"

"I didn't know it was you then."

"But you knew this afternoon. You didn't suspect your goons, whoever they may be, could have had a helicopter, so you just walked in—after walking haphazardly for miles since early this morning—across miles of wilderness

129

and just happened to stumble in here." Something about him resembled a less formal, less staged Joseph Welker.

"I heard the dogs."

He lit a cigarette and walked to the folding table. The size of the tent, the long table and cots, the map pinned to a board—it all reminded Leah of a Civil War movie. This could have been Grant's command tent, except for the modern vehicles outside and the stacks of food coolers lining the walls.

Peter Bradley held the stack of paper money from her billfold under her nose as if asking her to smell it. "A lot of cash to be carrying around on a camping trip."

"I told you Joseph Welker paid me to meet Glade and tell him about the goons and that the FBI was willing to—"

"Would you like to talk to Joseph Welker?"

Even the men at the table stopped rifling her things to hear her answer.

"No. I just want a ride back to civilization . . . and to catch the first plane east out of Colorado."

He seemed surprised. "Why don't you want to talk to Welker?"

"Because he got me into this in the first place."

"You left your pack with all this money on the side of a mountain to walk in here." He waved the cash at her again.

"I don't know why I did that. I guess I was tired of carrying it. I'd been walking all day."

Bradley stepped on his cigarette butt and turned to Charlie. "What do you think?"

"I think she's lying," Charlie said softly and his grin pulled the corners of his eyelids down so far that it almost closed them.

Peter Bradley stood over her. "There were two sets of boot prints next to your pack. He stood there with you and looked at this camp, didn't he? Your Glade Wyndham? He said that we weren't goons, that we were government. And that was this afternoon, wasn't it, not this morning? And he's not far away, is he?" His hand lifted her chin so that she looked up at him. "He hasn't been leaving this area all day, has he? Just since you walked in here. In other words, he used you as a decoy, didn't he?"

Leah let herself blink back tears that weren't there. "Yes."

She couldn't have planned it better if she'd made it up herself. Their search would narrow and Glade, who'd left her in the morning, would be well out of it.

But the exhausting questioning went on and it was mostly the same questions. Leah wondered if she hadn't made a mistake, after all. She didn't feel any safer with them than with Glade. Afternoon dimmed to evening. The helicopter and dogs returned. Delicious smells came from the fire that flickered light through the tent's walls. Leah thought she'd fall off her canvas stool if this didn't stop soon.

"Did he make love to you out there?"

"What?" Leah snapped alert. The first new question in hours.

"Did he screw you?" Charlie conjugated fuzzily. He was trying to light a lantern hanging from the tent rigging.

"Is that why you protected him? Why tears came to your eyes when you talked of taking the first plane east? Did he love and then leave you?" Peter Bradley gestured melodramatically with his prepackaged martini. It was still in its pop-top can.

They were treating her like some kind of criminal. "No."

"No, what?"

"That's not why I want to leave Colorado. Do they put olives in the can and everything?"

"Would you like one?"

"No, thanks."

"What *do* you want from us, Leah?"

"Dinner."

He shook his head and then he rubbed it. But Leah had dinner. Steak and roasted ears of sweet corn and baked potatoes and a tossed salad and fresh—not freeze-dried. Government people ate well even in the rough, she observed.

"How do you feel now?" Bradley sat beside her at the

131

long table and poured her a mug of coffee.

"If I had a bath and a real bed I'd be in heaven."

"Where was he going from here?" Bradley asked as he offered cream and sugar.

Leah sighed. It was to begin again. Would the interrogation last the night? "He didn't say."

"Did he have the papers on him?"

"I told you I didn't see any papers."

When she fell asleep at the table, they poured her more coffee. Charlie sat across from her. His bright-yellow shirt kept blurring in front of her eyes and his grin would warp unpleasantly. The lantern hissed and smelled of kerosene. Anyone passing it slung giant shadows up the tent walls.

Charlie left with the dogs and handlers and another lantern. She was so fogged and fuzzy she couldn't tell how long he was gone, but when he return, Bradley looked up. "Anything?"

"No. You?"

"Nothing."

"When are you going to let me have a try?" Charlie's look made Leah's stomach contract. "He's getting farther away all the time."

"Not yet, for Christsake!"

Leah did not get a bath and a real bed that night. She slept in her dirty sleeping bag on a cot and she couldn't even stay awake long enough to worry about Charlie.

The horrible thrashing of the helicopter blades and the wild flapping of the tent wall by her face awakened her the next morning. She was handed a plate heaped with steaming scrambled eggs and strips of thick succulent bacon with a sweet roll balanced on top and a mug of coffee.

Leah took them out into the sun and sat Indian fashion on the ground. It wouldn't take many meals like this and the one she'd had the night before to slow down the human search party. She smiled to herself and then wished she could share the delicious moist eggs with Glade and the strange fat cat who would eat anything but Styrofoam.

Her eyes roamed the pine-crowded slopes across the meadow. Where were they? How were they?

"Miss him, don't you?" Jolly Charlie sat beside her.

Leah wiped her cheek and tried to hide her face in the coffee mug.

"Yeah, old Glade always got around the honeys, he did." Charlie's hair looked as if it had been cut around a mixing bowl. Then after the bowl was removed the barber had chopped out a section for each ear. "Pretty good on the sauce, too. Used to have some good times with old Glade. Never thought he'd sell out, but if there's money in it—lots of money—makes it hard to resist for anyone, huh?" The friendly tone, the boyish haircut, the perfect teeth that never seemed to disappear even when he talked —were meant to be disarming.

But Leah, who could be snowed by nature, had been suffocated by people for thirty years. "Does he really think I'm that naïve?" she wondered.

Peter Bradley came out of the tent with one of his sober companions and leaned over to grasp Charlie's shoulder. "Take it easy now."

"I don't know what you're talking about."

"Yes, you do." Peter glanced at Leah. "Yes, you do." He walked to a jeep with his friend and they roared off without looking back.

"Where are they going?"

"Into town. He doesn't want to be responsible. Too high up . . . you know." And Charlie's grin turned sly.

"Responsible for what?" Leah sensed warning to her nerve ends. Trouble.

"Well, we're going to play a game. He doesn't like games." He looked at her through grin-slatted eyes and slapped his knee. "I'm glad you wouldn't do it his way. You know that?" He pushed himself to his feet and walked away to return with his mug and the coffeepot. He refilled her cup and sat cozily beside her. "My way's a lot more fun than his."

"What game?" Leah tasted egg.

"You can't blame old Pete . . . all those congressional investigations, Welker on his tail, you know."

"*What* game?" Leah set down her cup and drew up her knees to encircle them with her arms.

133

"I call it the 'to tell the truth game.' Or the 'hang in there game.' If you don't, it'll just kill you." And Charlie slapped his knee.

Chapter Twenty-three

LEAH clung to the rope ladder with blotched fingers. Rough fibers wore at her skin, burning, searing. She kept her eyes clamped shut and saw red behind her lids.

The sounds she made, the grunting whimpers, were carried away on swirling air stirred by the giant blades above her and drowned in the bludgeoning noise of the helicopter.

A long-forgotten nightmare surfaced . . . the dream of a little girl who clutched a swinging rope hanging from the rigging of a sailing vessel in a storm . . . and gigantic waves would toss the vessel and tip it and make her swing far, far out on the end of the rope, sometimes touching freezing black water with her feet and then the ship would lean the other way and the child-Leah would be brought back at heart-stopping speed to crash against the wooden side of the vessel and just before she hit she'd awake screaming. . . .

It was the sickening uplift in her stomach that brought memory of the child's nightmare, the cramping in her lower abdomen, the cringing, tingling constriction of her uterus, the tightened terror of muscles. The woman-Leah was reexperiencing all these sensations now. And now she was awake with no wooden vessel to stop her far-flung flight through the air as the ladder swung in broad . . . swooping . . . nauseating arches each time the helicopter turned or jagged or increased its speed.

Leah pressed her forehead against the scratchy rung between her hands and tried to keep her body rigid so that the ladder would stay with her feet. She'd wound her arms through the rope sides between rungs and they cut into the inside of her elbows even through the layers of wool clothing Charlie had dressed her in.

"Mustn't let you die of exposure," Charlie had said. "In case you want to tell us somthing when you come back."

One of the last things she'd seen before she'd closed her eyes, was Charlie doubled over in mirth below her and jagged treetops whizzing dangerously near.

"Do try to come back now," Charlie had said. . . .

They couldn't kill her. It was her government, too. They'd just scare her a little and then stop this in hopes that she'd tell them something.

She tried to think of something else but Charlie's game was working too well. She had to concentrate on holding onto the ladder with hands frozen by panic and protesting with strain. She didn't dare open her eyes, yet she dreaded crashing into a tree or a rocky mountaintop. She fought for breath. The air, disturbed by the copter's blades and her swooping, dizzying flight, came thick and crushing and too much one minute. It seemed to be sucked away from her the next so that she existed in a vacuum. Her hair whipped about her face as if intent upon smothering her.

Leah clung helplessly to her tether. They'd driven her to it by setting the dogs on her. Her whimpers turned into involuntary groans she could feel but couldn't hear, as icy shudders ran through her body.

And then her tether jerked crazily. "Mother!" she screamed on gorged air. Her boots lost the swinging ladder.

All of Leah's weight pulled at sore hands, arms, and shoulders. As her feet swung out, her head snapped back and her eyes opened involuntarily.

The gray beast of the helicopter with sled-runner feet swung past her vision to be replaced by a frothy-edged cloud. The pain in her neck revived her and slowly, with an effort that dragged on her jaw muscles and drew her lips apart, she forced her head back. Looking down to try to catch the gyrating ladder with her feet, she saw a mountaintop and far below that a small puddle of water.

As her feet groped frantically for a rung, the copter hesitated in midair and began to descend. The puddle grew to a lake of cold blue—as cold a blue as Goodyear's eyes.

"That bath you wanted last night?" Charlie had said. "We'll throw that in for chuckles, okay?"

"Oh, God," she thought. "He couldn't have meant that lake." But her progress toward it continued. The azure color changed subtly to cold green as the lake grew larger and nearer. She stared at it, dangling by her arms, until the whirling blades rippled its surface.

The end of the ladder slapped against a boot and she found a rung with one foot and then the other, but the child of the nightmare screamed inside Leah as the bottom rung dipped thrashing water. The smell of fish and wet weeds and rot churned on the air around her.

Leah screamed aloud and tried to climb the unsteady ladder toward the gray monster above. "Mother!"

The rope in front of her face seemed to whine. Between the rungs she could see a yellow jeep parked on the bank and Charlie watching her through field glasses.

Water seeped through her boots to her feet, swirled around her calves, and found her knees. It was as cruel and icy as its color. Leah stopped climbing and whimpered in terror. She watched an angry lake reach for her waist. Numbing cold washed through her body, threatening to stop her heartbeat.

And then even Leah's whimpers died. She stared in silent paralysis at the man on shore as agitated water whipped around her chest. He would just have them dunk her to the neck to frighten her. He wouldn't let them . . . she gulped air and closed her eyes as the searing cold enclosed her neck . . . and then her head. Leah was submerged.

The shock of the cold on bare skin forced the reservoir of air from her lungs into her throat. Long hair swept like slimy seaweed across her eyes. The lake tugged at it as it lifted, ruffled it out, then billowed it back against her. The helicopter sounded a muffled pounding under water.

Her body demanded air. A warning, low-pitched buzzing in her ears. . . . She wanted to scramble up the ladder, but her hands had a helpless frozen hold she couldn't break. Her torso began the tortured hideous dance of suffocation.

Leah didn't realize that she and the ladder were rising until air hit her in the face. Her mouth and nose were suddenly gorged with it. Wind, whipped up by the helicopter and blown through her wet clothing and hair, was more chilling than anything underwater. But Leah was almost past caring.

Waves chopped at her boots as she was dangled toward Charlie. Through her hair and the water streaming down her face, she caught a glimpse of another jeep coming to a stop beside his.

The helicopter brought her to shore, where Charlie was pulling blankets from the jeep and mouthing shouts at two other men.

He had to pry her fingers loose one at a time from the ladder as the copter hovered above, still sending wind chill through her sopping clothing.

Charlie's grin was gone, his eyes snapped fury. Someone caught her from behind as the last finger came loose.

Limp and without feeling, Leah was carried to the blankets. The helicopter moved away. As the sound of it died, she heard, ". . . will hear about this!"

Leah looked up into the face of Joseph Welker.

"Well, she wouldn't cooperate," Charlie answered.

They stripped off her wet clothing and wrapped her in blankets and shouted threats and insults at each other.

"She's ours. . . ."

"Don't say another word to this man, Miss Harper," Welker ordered.

Leah was not about to say a word to anybody. She didn't know if she could even move. She could breathe, swallow, and blink. She didn't try anything else.

"I wasn't going to kill her."

"Pneumonia kills people. So does exposure. She looks to be in shock."

Welker carried her to his jeep, cuddled her on his lap

137

all the way back to the camp in the meadow while Brian Kruger drove. Leah couldn't feel the blankets against her skin.

Brian laid her on a cot in the "command" tent and dressed the open wounds on her palms. "This will hurt," he apologized in his soft voice.

But it didn't hurt.

He smeared something on her forehead and then held her up to pour hot broth down her throat.

Joseph Welker commandeered her backpack and all that had been in it, checked through her billfold, and added it to the pile. He wrapped her in dry blankets, then carried her off to the jeep once more, throwing a last threat to a sullen Charlie over his shoulder.

Leah trembled and knew she was finally warming. She slept cradled in the arms of the FBI and awoke only momentarily when she was transferred to the back seat of a sedan. She had no idea how long she slept or how far they traveled but when the car stopped, it was night. Leah was feeling again. She hurt.

They carried her into a building she couldn't see clearly and up a flight of stairs.

"Bring her stuff into Number Five and get some brandy," Welker snapped at a woman under a light bulb in the narrow hallway, and whisked Leah into a room that smelled of paint.

He set her down in a deep soft chair next to a moss-rock fireplace that took up most of one wall and then knelt to build a fire. Brian pulled on a handle at the base of an oversized couch and drew it out into a king-sized bed.

Welker looked over his shoulder as the woman brought in Leah's luggage. "We found the blue Vega," he explained. "And I've been worried sick about you ever since. This is Julie."

Brian spread blankets on the bed. Julie poured brandy into a glass and handed it to her. Leah pushed it away with a mottled bandaged hand.

"Look, honey, it'll do you good."

"No." Leah found her voice squeaky but was relieved

it still worked. So had her arm when she'd refused the drink. She commanded her toe to wiggle under the blanket. It did.

"Do you want a doctor, Miss Harper?" Welker stood over her anxiously. She sensed he didn't want her to.

"No. I want a poached-egg-on-milk-toast and a cup of hot chocolate."

"Yuk." Julie grimaced and drank the brandy herself. She left the room to return with an armload of groceries.

A fancy kitchenette made up one corner of the room. Julie loaded the refrigerator and started an egg to poaching while she made coffee for the rest of them. She was middle-aged and full-bosomed, wearing a smart pantsuit. Her short hair fluffed softly toward her face. The whole effect was very attractive.

"I managed to cook it but don't mind if I can't watch you eat it." Julie handed the plate to Leah with a kind smile and a penetrating glance.

The fire, roaring up the chimney draft, was three times as big as any Glade had built. Brian disappeared between curtains to talk to someone outside on a balcony. Leah ate slowly and carefully. It was difficult to balance the plate and keep the blankets around her.

When Brian returned through sliding-glass doors, wind billowed the curtains into the room and brought the smell of rain.

"Where am I?" she asked finally, pushing lank, stringy hair from her face and handing the plate to Julie.

"Steamboat Springs. This is a skiing condominium complex." Welker sat on the rock shelf that stretched in front of the fireplace. "Feel better?"

"Did you find Sheila?"

"Yes." Pain struggled to surface on his face. "I'm afraid she's. . . ."

"We found her, too. But we couldn't get her out of the Volks fast enough."

"You were there?" He sat up. "Did you see who did it?"

"No. We heard a scream and a car drive away. The Volks exploded, but Glade carried her out before it went up completely. She died anyway."

"Did she say anything?"

"She said she didn't want to die."

The pain was back, in eyes framed by old-fashioned horn-rims. The wrinkles deepened on his face and above his collar. There were too many of them for his age. He reached for her hand on the blanket. "I'm very sorry about what happened today, believe me. It was against any regulations in existence. I'll see that something is done about it. Shelia's death is an indication of how important it is that we find Glade quickly. You can see that."

"I don't know where he's heading or what he intends to do with the property or if he has it with him." She drew her hand away from his. "I do know that I've taken all the questioning I can handle for one day."

"But you must be debriefed before time erases anything or—"

"I have nothing to tell you."

"You may not realize what you know."

"I want to be alone. And now."

"She's been through a lot, Joe," Julie reminded him. "I'll move in here for the night and—"

"No. Alone. Or I'll never say another word to any of you."

Welker, Julie, and Brian fought it out among them. Leah refused any offer of companionship. Finally they left her staring grimly at the fire.

Leah uncurled one stiff leg and then the other. She stood. The blankets dropped to the floor. She grabbed the mantel. When she was steady, she tried a few steps and then bent carefully toward the handle of her beauty case. She hadn't thought to ever see this luggage again.

In the bathroom she avoided the mirror and turned on the shower. She stood under it to wash her hair—three sessions with the shampoo and one with conditioner—gritting her teeth against the ache of muscles in her neck, arms, and shoulders. Wrapping her hair in a towel, Leah took bath oil from her case, ran the tub full of hot water, and removed wet bandages from her hands.

She scrubbed and soaked, her mind a blank. That finished, she went to work on her complexion by feel,

140

with her back to the mirror. Leah sat on the stool lid to file broken nails down to her finger ends, thinking only of what she was doing and nothing else.

Finally, she faced the mirror. Her skin had lost the blotchy look. Sun and windburn had turned into an even tan except for the red scar of a rope burn slashed across her forehead. The eyes under it looked vacant. The shadows under them looked bruised and the lips rigid.

She combed out wet hair and bent closer to the mirror. A tiny spark reflected on one side of the part. Leah reached up to pluck out a short hair and examined it under the light. It was the color of silver and it was stiff and wiry. The stony face in the mirror did not react.

She found her robe, added a log to the fire, and sat on the rock shelf to brush out her hair in the heat. A nervous shudder ran completely through her and was gone. A minute later there was another. Leah tried to ignore them.

When her hair was dry she peered between the curtains to the balcony and saw a flare of light as someone lit a cigarette. She checked the door to the hall and found it locked . . . from the outside. She was a prisoner.

Leah warmed some milk in the kitchenette and drank it with a piece of dry bread while the shudder spasms repeated themselves at shorter and shorter intervals.

Finally, there was nothing more to do but sit and stare into the leaping flames. Leah doubled over and hid her face in her hands . . . shadowed eyes and tousled black curls behind her eyelids . . . the pulsating roar of a helicopter inside her head. . . .

Chapter Twenty-four

"HOW did you find him? I mean, how did he act while you were with him?"

"Unpredictable." Leah sat stiffly on the couch that had been a bed until a few hours ago. It felt strange to be wearing a dress.

"What do you mean by that?" Joseph Welker exchanged a glance with Brian Kruger. Julie sat on the other end of the couch writing down what little Leah was saying.

"One minute he's"—Leah shrugged—"and then . . . he. . . ." She shrugged again. Even that hurt her neck.

"You do think he's mentally stable." Welker paused in his pacing. He didn't look as if he'd slept much, either. "Don't you?"

"I . . . guess so."

"And he just laughed when you gave him my message in Oak Creek?"

"Yes." Leah had told him everything she'd told the men in the meadow. She had little to conceal—but Joseph Welker pinned down what she did have quickly.

"That means it isn't money he wants. He wants the information exposed, doesn't he?" He sat down and removed his glasses to rub his eyes. "Damn! He's going to try to get it to the newspapers. I should have known. That could make him a very dangerous man." He exchanged a glance with Brian that made Leah uneasy. "I wish I could talk to him. He's making an awful mistake. Did he tell you what the property was?"

"No." Her palms were bleeding again, oozing from cracks and scrapes in skin that tore from its healing process each time she used her hands.

"Let me get something to bandage those up again," Brian said and left the room. He had a baby face under thin hair and soft eyes that followed Joseph Welker's every move like Mutt's had followed Jason's.

Julie seemed to be a general fetch-it girl and secretary. But all three of them were here for one reason . . . to work on Leah Harper. Their tactics were different from Charlie's but the object was the same—find Glade Wyndham.

"Hapless little crusade, I'll bet you anything," Welker mumbled as he pulled a Colorado road map from his jacket pocket. When Brian returned to wrap gauze around Leah's hands, Joe Welker sat in a chair to study the map. "He must have let something slip. You were alone with him for days."

He rose and started pacing again. "While in the Flat Tops, you were with him every minute?"

"Yes. From the time we left Oak Creek."

"He couldn't have slipped off and retrieved something without your knowing it?"

"No. And how did you know we were up there anyway?"

"We didn't. We were following the gentlemen you encountered yesterday."

"How did they know?"

"One of them overheard a camper in a restaurant in Meeker say he'd seen a man, a woman, and a giant Siamese head up the trail to the primitive area at night. When I got word of this, I thought it was Sheila with him because I thought she had the cat. It seemed to have an attachment for that Volkswagen of yours and hopped in when we opened the door. Sheila was to be a foil to get the danger off your trail and the cat was an added advantage."

"Then why did she follow me to Oak Creek? She should have gone in the other direction."

"That was the plan at first. She was to follow you from Walden and come straight to Steamboat after assuring herself that you turned off at Oak Creek."

The sliding-glass doors were open and the heavy scent

of sun on rain-soaked pine needles came to Leah, bringing memories that she didn't want.

"But she didn't show up here. She called me from Oak Creek that night and said she'd seen you being followed and put herself in the way, hoping to draw the danger off. Apparently she succeeded. She died to save you. Help us?"

"He's trying to shift the blame for Sheila to me," she thought. Did he really believe Sheila died because of her, not because of a fool order from him?

"If it had been me, Mr. Welker, in that Volkswagen? Who would have been blamed for my death?"

"Your government needs your help, Leah Harper."

"My government just dangled me from a helicopter!" Her hands tightened around gauze.

"Is that all your government's done for you?" Julie whispered from the other end of the couch.

"Oh, no. It's taxed me silly instead of those who have all the money and it's used me and lied to me, sent people like Glade Wyndham to places like Chile to commit murder in my name . . ."

"So he told you about that." Joseph Welker stared at the ceiling. "Leah, did you have to explain to your government why you left Chicago and came to Colorado? Did you have to present your papers at armed checkpoints all along the route or at state lines? Have you ever been visited by secret police in the middle of the night?" He stopped the incessant pacing to whirl around dramatically and face her. "Have enemy soldiers ever attacked your home or molested you? Leah, is there really any other country in this world in which you would rather live the rest of your life—not visit—but live, work, marry? Is there?"

Leah blinked. "No."

"Then, can you really claim that your government has done nothing for you?"

"It's my country, too. It's my government. You work for me! And the CIA has no right—"

"Would you feel safer in a country—given today's world—that had no CIA or FBI?"

"No . . . but—"

"All right. I'll grant you that Charlie, in his fervor, made a ghastly mistake yesterday, for which he will pay. But Glade Wyndham is also making a mistake and it's up to you and to me to persuade him otherwise, Miss Harper. This country you own as yours so fondly can only take so much and it has had enough of scandal and insecurity—"

"It can take the truth, Mr. Welker," she spat out quickly so that she could finish the sentence.

"Do you know for a fact that what Glade wants to make public is the truth?"

"I don't know anything for a fact because I'm given none. I am expected to take you on faith because of who you are, presumably. I'm expected to make grandiose judgments on your word for things and on the basis of emotional patriotism and then risk my life because someone else decides it's necessary. . . . Don't ask me to make decisions on something I don't know anything about!"

"All right, I'll tell you what I know. We'll take a walk and let you get some fresh air. But first let's have lunch."

Juie heated canned soup in the kitchenette.

Welker studied the map while they ate. "He's heading generally west . . . now why?"

"Heard any more from Meeker?" Brian asked, with the expression of respect he reserved for Joseph Welker.

"No. Everybody's got Meeker covered. Goons'll pick him up for sure if he gets anywhere near."

"What's Meeker?" Leah said.

"His brother's ranch is outside a town called Meeker. Take a look at the map, Leah. Starting at Ted's Place where you first saw him, I've drawn a line following his course. He's moved haphazardly, but generally west. Did he mention any names of the towns you see west of the Flat Tops, like Grand Junction or Craig?"

She studied the map. If she and Glade had continued down the road from Oak Creek instead of taking the turnoff to Trapper's Lake and the Flat Tops, they would have ended up in Meeker . . . where goons and everyone else awaited them. She hoped Glade hadn't continued in that direction when he left her. He'd been dangerously close the way it was. Had he abandoned Goodyear?

"Miss Harper? You're not listening."

"Hum? Oh. No, he didn't mention any towns. There aren't many that far west, are there?" Most of the towns seemed to be bunched along the eastern approach to the mountains. "Maybe he's heading for Utah."

"Did he mention Utah?"

"No. But there's a lot of open country between here and Utah to hide something in. Why do you need a town?"

"You could be right. We've searched that ranch he lived on. He didn't have the papers with him when Charlie picked him up. Well, let's take that walk."

Leah slipped into her tennis shoes. "I'm not up to much of a hike but it would be nice to get out in the sun."

"We'll just stroll." He held the door for her and Brian went on ahead.

From the number of doors in the short hall upstairs and the identical hall below, Leah guessed that there were eight apartments in the building, four above and four below.

She slid on her sunglasses the minute they stepped outside. Other buildings in the complex lined up beneath the ridge to their left, white stucco with wooden trim and balconies painted brown. Stacks of cut firewood were piled in the corner of each balcony. Concrete steps led to a sparsely populated parking lot on top of the ridge. Brian waited for them there, looking silly in coat and tie.

The sun was high and warm, the air thin on oxygen and rich with odors of pine and earth. With all her aches, Leah felt good to be out again. "It's funny, after all that time in the wilderness when I dreamed of bathtubs and soft beds and luxury . . ." she thought aloud.

"Well, you can hardly claim we've housed you in squalor." He pointed the way to Brian who turned to walk a good twenty yards ahead of them along the crest of the ridge.

"No. That apartment is luxurious enough, but . . . empty. I hated that trudge through the Flat Tops while I was there but—"

"Maybe it was the company you had that brings back

146

fond memories, Leah. For all his mistreatment of you, you have a soft spot for Glade Wyndham, don't you?" Welker walked leisurely beside her with his hands in his pockets. "I've known Glade for some years." He smiled down at her and shook his head. "He could make the dungeons of a castle half flooded with water seem romantic—"

"Romantic! He's a beast."

"Some women find beasts romantic and Glade's been known to switch tactics to suit the occasion. He knows his way around women."

"That's what Charlie said."

"If he didn't have those papers on him when Charlie picked him up, he either got to them later or is on his way to them now. He'll have to get to a telephone to contact a reporter. Did he mention any names? You must have talked about something all that time."

Leah sighed. He was determined to ruin her stroll. "We walked mostly. He wasn't talkative. He asked me about my life so that I wouldn't ask him about his." She owed Welker nothing but trouble. She wouldn't tell him about Norton and the Denver *Post*.

In front of them Brian's head kept turning from side to side as if he scanned the area for snipers, reminding Leah of secret servicemen guarding the President on television. She looked over her shoulder to see another man doing the same thing behind them, keeping pace, a cigarette hanging from his lips. Didn't they notice how they stood out in their conservative suits in an area like this?

"You're hot, Leah," Welker said, noting her glances. "We'll protect you. But you must help us do that, you know. Those men are guarding your life . . . as Sheila did."

"From who?"

"Everyone after Glade will soon know, if they don't already, that you spent a week in the wilderness alone with him. There are leaks in any camp."

They walked along a path through a line of scrub bush to a patch of trees.

"Now, I want to know—"

"Mr. Welker, you were going to give *me* information. Remember? Are you working with Charlie and his friends? Or against them? What do those goons want with Glade? Why do you think I can be of any further use to you? Why are Charlie and Bradley operating in Colorado at all? I want to know everything about Glade. I want to know everything period . . . or I want to know nothing and go back to Chicago. You have a choice."

To her chagrin, Joseph Welker began to answer her questions. They weren't going to let her go back to Chicago. "Glade and his older brother, Cal, were raised on their father's ranch some miles out of Meeker, Colorado. Glade was used to isolated living, hard work, being bused long miles to school. A hardy family background, conservative in political and social outlook. . . ."

Welker's voice descended into an impersonal steady monotone as if he were reciting from memory a written dossier on Glade Wyndham. The thought struck Leah as chilling.

"As I said, life was rugged and the men of the family were big and stolid. Unfortunately, the mother was frail and died when Glade was twelve of what the doctor termed exhaustion. The older brother married and brought his young wife home to care for the bruisers. She took two years of it and left. She also left behind another Wyndham . . . a baby boy, Glade's nephew Jerry. Glade was fifteen at the time." He stopped his ambling and looked at Leah squarely. "This seems to have affected Glade's opinion of women . . . permanently.

"Glade was an excellent student. His father paid fully for a college education and while Glade was off studying to become a mining engineer, a neighbor accidentally backed over the father with a wagonload of hay. It killed him. The brother got the ranch. Glade was free and set up with an education. He dated women and enjoyed them but carefully avoided long-standing attachments while in college and ever since. He has a preference for blondes and next comes redheads, brunettes, and whatever else man and nature can concoct. He—"

"What about his other job?"

"He was recruited in college and spent most of his time abroad after that." Welker rarely mentioned the CIA by name.

"Working at two jobs."

"Yes. About ten months ago, he unexplainably rifled his company's safe and disappeared with some papers. He also withdrew all his money from a bank account."

"Why was he working for an American company in the U.S. ten months ago?"

"That company hired mining engineers. What could be simpler?"

"But why was a CIA agent working for this company in the United States?" Leah insisted. Welker could be as evasive as a politician.

"That, I'm afraid, Miss Harper, is not in my domain."

"It isn't theirs either, is it? And Colorado certainly shouldn't be."

"It's understandable, though. Glade is their renegade. Of course, they want to clean up their own affairs."

"The FBI and CIA are after the same man and the same papers but they're not even working together. Seems a little inefficient, doesn't it?"

"I have orders to get to him first, to save his life and to retrieve the papers."

"And the goons?"

"We think they have orders to stop him outright. They already know what the papers contain."

"You mean you don't? You don't even know what you're after?"

"Unlike you, Miss Harper, I do take some things on faith. I'm reliably informed that the contents of those papers are a matter for investigation by the bureau, that untold harm would be done to the nation if they were made public before this investigation . . . they were stolen, remember, from a large and respected company—"

"Which sends out hoods to kill ex-employees."

"That I find deplorable also and am trying my best to see that they don't succeed. But men in Glade's line of work have been considered fair game, whenever caught, since time immemorial."

At a break in the trees, Brian stopped them with a raised hand. Another mountain rose before them, wide swaths slashed through its trees for winter skiers. A stilled chair lift angled up its side and another lift sat idle in the distance. To the side and beyond the ski runs, the jade-green valley led away to Oak Creek with its river snaking through herds of grazing cattle and an occasional brown haystack shaped like a soggy loaf of bread.

"We'll turn back here, I think." They started for the condominium complex, slowly. "Now I've told you a great deal, Miss Harper. Will you help us? I want to know what's in those papers. I want to find Glade Wyndham before any harm can come to him. If I could just talk to him. Why did he steal the papers to begin with?"

"I don't know where he is or where he's going." Leah felt suddenly exhausted. Her tennis shoes shuffled stones loose from the earth. If she told him just a little, would he let her go? "He was ordered by the CIA to photograph those papers and return them to the safe. Instead he took them and ran. They have something to do with oil shale . . . a deal between the government and the oil company. That is all I know, Mr. Welker. Please let me go back to Chicago."

"A deal . . . you're sure?" They walked in silence back to the parking lot. "A deal?" He stood staring at the peaked aluminum roofs of Steamboat Springs. "This makes it all the more imperative that I talk to him. If we could just flush him. I'm afraid I can't send you back to Chicago just yet. But I will take you out to dinner tonight," he added thoughtfully.

That night they dined at the Iron Horse, a group of connecting railroad cars lined up behind a motel. It had mirrors along one wall and windows along the other. A narrow aisle parted a single row of tables on each side. The damage to the carpeting matched that in her apartment in the complex . . . ski boots.

Their waiter was a male ski bum working to exist through summer. Leah had seen the type during two expensive weekends away from New York when she'd dabbled in skiing at a Vermont lodge . . . young, unattached, year-round tan, perfect teeth, handsome . . . a ski bum was a ski bum east or west apparently. But from her glimpse of the dizzying slopes and their incredible lengths that afternoon she figured the bums had a lot more fun in the West.

Leah refused a cocktail. She ordered eggs Benedict to Julie's disgust. Sitting between Welker and Brian, she could see Welker in the mirror opposite.

"You have to be careful of cholesterol," Julie pointed out as Leah broke a yolk.

"Replace that gauze after you bathe tonight," Brian offered through a mouthful of sirloin.

"He's got to run out of cash soon," Welker said over lobster. "He'll have to go somewhere and we've got his brother covered. He emptied one bank account ten months ago. The only way anyone found him was that we were all waiting for him to dip into the other one."

"That's why it took ten months?" Leah tried a sip of wine on her ulcer.

"Yes. He was living in a rented cabin in a place called Rustic. It's in the canyon between Ted's Place and Cameron Pass, where you met him in that fishing cabin. Eventually he wrote a rent check on that secret account."

"Secret account?"

"He thought it was secret. Actually there are few secrets from Uncle Sam . . . but Glade had been out of the country for ten years." Welker was sipping his third martini with his second glass of wine. Face on, he looked relaxed. In the mirror opposite he looked drunk.

Leah, of the sober set, felt it was high time she took advantage of someone else. "You have access to bank accounts?"

"The law reads that banks must photograph checks for over a certain amount. It's a way to trace money leaving the country. But it's such a hassle, banks just photograph all checks. Retrieval is a problem, but it can be done."

Leah couldn't finish her eggs Benedict and had trouble sleeping that night. She couldn't rid herself of the mental image of shadowed eyes, the rich sound of deep laughter, the . . . she knew she'd been wise to leave him, but as usual she'd run to the wrong place.

The condominium was as poorly built as everything else in this age and she heard sounds from the next apartment through the walls. She was on her way to the bathroom when Brian shouted from the hall, "He's here! He's got it."

In the bathroom, Leah heard Joseph Welker on the other side of the wall ask, "Is it complete, college organizations, bank . . ." and a flushing toilet drowned out the rest.

Leah walked through the bed-sitting room to the sliding-glass door and opened it slightly. The screen was kept locked but the door opened for ventilation because there was no other window. The balcony guard was just opening the sliding door next to hers.

"What's going on?" he asked between puffs on his cigarette.

"The Harper file is in," Welker answered with satisfaction. "Have we got anything?"

"Well, we had trouble at the bank," a strange voice answered. "But I think we've got most of it."

As the balcony guard listened at the open door next to her, Leah listened at her own to a detailed rundown of her life.

Leah Harper listened to the Harper file and felt naked. Innocent transactions, pastimes, and family life sounded sinister, even criminal, when recited by the new voice. Her father's death, the family removal to a poorer section of town, Leah's employment record, men she had dated, even Jason, Suzie's abortion. Everything was there.

"And then she went to the Hagstard Publishing Company."

"Publishers?" Welker exploded in the next room. "Wyndham's spent a week in the wilderness with a publisher's representative? This is worse than I thought. Everybody's after renegade agents' memoirs these days. And with the property, too? Jesus God!"

"She hasn't worked for them for two years—"

"What do you want to bet?" It sounded like he threw

something against a wall. "How about college organizations, anything there?"

"Nothing remotely subversive." The strange voice went on to her mother's suicide.

"Who found her?"

"The subject. No foul play indicated. Clear case—"

"Maybe we can work on that. Guilt . . . her own mother. Have you completed the bank work?"

"Yes. It's all here. A Chicago and a New York bank."

"The mother's death . . . go over it again."

Leah repeated the horror of her mother's death with them.

"That and the publisher. Work on them and get going."

"I just got here. I need sleep."

"Sleep on the plane. We'll get you to Denver. Can you imagine Glade Wyndham's memoirs published? And the Enveco papers?"

Leah slid through the opening in the sliding-glass doors and hit the screen. Her hair stuck to it and pulled as her body slid to the floor, a buzzing in her ears, fresh salt-tainted blood shooting up her throat and through half-parted lips.

Chapter Twenty-five

LEAH was being carried. She could feel the jerky movement of someone else's walk. A small low building . . . brick and lighted windows.

A sign painted on window-glass . . . PLEASE REMOVE SKI BOOTS AT THE DOOR.

Leah was in the building, in front of a desk under a round glaring light.

"You should have taken her directly to the emergency

room and called first," someone said disapprovingly.

Soon there were other glaring lights overhead.

"Ulcer. Bleeding. I must ask you all to leave. This could be serious. No stress . . . no questions."

Leah awoke in a strange white room, in a strange white bed. A woman leaned over her.

"There, I thought you were coming around," she said cheerfully. "Are you hungry? You've slept so long. How about a nice poached-egg-on-milk-toast?"

The woman fed it to her by slow patient spoonfuls. "There now, you can sleep some more. I can see you're still tired. Rest is the best thing for you."

An oblong pill with the texture of plastic slipped onto Leah's tongue followed by the edge of a paper cup with water. "Don't worry now, my dear. You're fine. The bleeding has stopped. Just rest. Ulcer shouldn't worry, should it? Nothing too bad, you just overdid, didn't you? You must be careful to take care of yourself with your problem."

"Look, I don't care if you're Lieutenant Columbo. She stays another day." The young doctor's wire-rims glared back at Welker's horn-rims.

Welker snapped the wallet closed on his intimidating badge and replaced it in an inside breast pocket. "Listen, there is . . ." he began patiently but was interrupted by Brian Kruger's rush through the door.

"We've got him! They just picked him up."

"Who?"

"The State Patrol. They grabbed Wyndham out of a telephone booth in Craig. We'll have to spring him." Brian and Joseph Welker disappeared.

The doctor turned to Leah. "I don't know what kind of trouble you're in. But I've won you and your stomach another twenty-four hours."

Leah smiled at him through a drug-induced haze.

"You're not in serious condition, miraculously, and you've lived with that ulcer since you were a child. But sleep while you can and try to keep your life under better control from now on. If you let your nerves and people like the man who just left get ahead of you, you'll end up right back in a hospital."

When she was alone, Leah gazed sleepily through metal-paned windows on the steeply slanted roofs of Steamboat Springs, Colorado . . . the giant green mountain behind them with ski trails slashed through its trees . . . an intense deep clear sky. . . .

Leah drew a relaxed sigh, curled up in a fetal position, and slept.

The next evening Leah had finally shaken off the hospital "drug cure." It had left her with a headache and she knew an angry ulcer better than to risk aspirin. She sat once again in front of the roaring fire behind locked doors in the FBI-provided condominium. She'd eaten and relaxed in a hot oil bath, but still the drug hangover throbbed in her head.

Rain pelted the roof and the balcony outside. She hoped old "cigarette-face" was getting soaked. He'd been stationed outside her door at the hospital, too. Wind lashed air through the pines so violently she could hear them moan over the crackling of the fire.

She warmed milk and poured it into a mug, thinking of the phone call she'd made that morning from the hospital. And that memory made her seek one of the doctor's tranquilizers. And taking the pill made her angry because she knew they were powerful and she'd have another hangover to get used to when it wore off.

There had been a telephone sitting on the table next to her hospital bed. She was alone, relaxed to the point of euphoria, felt daring, mischievous, silly. . . . Leah was high. With every poached egg came a pill in that plate . . . they'd begun to add up in her bloodstream.

Leah had picked up the receiver with a giggle and started with surprise when someone asked who she wished to call.

She gave Annette's number in Chicago and was almost jolted sober when the call went through and her sister answered.

"Leah? I've been worried sick. You've been gone so

long. You haven't written or phoned. . . ." Annette scolded on in her fussy way and Leah wept silently at the normal family sound of it. "And then when those men came around asking questions, I could have died. We thought you were in horrible trouble. They were so secretive. You are all right, aren't you?"

"What men?"

"Well, you remember when Greg Henshaw was getting a security clearance to work at the atomic plant? When we lived in the old house in the suburbs and those men came and asked Mother and Dad all about him? That kind of thing. Are you working in a secret job of some kind?" Annette sounded relieved at the thought.

"Something like that. Don't worry. I'm fine." Leah suddenly yearned for another pill. She mustn't involve her family, must keep them calm and unquestioning. "How's Suzie?"

"Oh, that's another reason I'm glad you called. Suzie's in the hospital. Leah, she lost the baby two days ago. But she's okay, just depressed. She'll be so relieved to know you're all right. I've got the boys staying here and Ed's coming over to dinner tonight."

"You're sure she's okay?"

"Yes. Ralph talked to her doctor. It was just one of those births that wasn't meant to be. The baby wouldn't have been right. But she's blue. I wish you were here, Leah. After Mother dying the way she did and now Suzie . . . I really miss your commonsense way of getting things back to normal. But we'll cope. Promise you'll call again or write soon? So we won't worry about you, too."

"I promise." Leah had choked back tears.

And now she shook her head over the mug of warm milk and added a log to the fire. Who else had been questioned about Leah Harper?

This was the first time Annette had ever praised Leah for common sense. It was so unexpected she couldn't help thinking of it. She'd always thought her family considered her nervous and flighty and too independent. Poor Suzie. Leah, the oldest sister, should be there coping now.

"Oh, hell, she's got a husband. He should be coping."

But would Ed be sympathetic enough to see his wife through this?

"What would Annette think of my common sense if she knew of the situation I'm in now?"

And Glade had been caught. His mission had been so important to him. Leah didn't understand him or his mission but her disappointment over his failure was deep, surprising. She'd counted on his success because he'd wanted it. How many people had he killed?

She jerked around as the lock clicked in the door. Julie stuck her head in. "Brought you a present. More eggs and that bottle of Maalox you wanted and"—she had a sack under one arm and something under the other that Leah couldn't see until she'd kicked the door closed and turned; it was an angry round ball of Siamese—"and an old friend of yours." Julie dropped Goodyear on the rug. He had a spot of cream on his nose.

"We sprung him, too. You wouldn't believe what-all that animal has just eaten."

Leah sat very still as the blimp surveyed the room, his eyes scanning over her as if she were a chair. He sniffed the carpet, peeked under the couch, upset the basket, and pounced on a wadded-up Kleenex that rolled to the floor. Patches of scorched hair on the underside of his tail had fallen out, leaving funny pink holes of skin in the lush cocoa-brown.

Finally, Goodyear came to rub the side of his neck against Leah's leg, his toenails kneading the carpet, his motor in overdrive.

"Hello, fat cat. Long time no—" Her voice broke.

He let her hand caress him from ears to the end of his tail twice and then, still purring, he jumped to the rock shelf in front of the fire, licked a paw, and rubbed the cream off his nose.

"That cat needs a muffler." Julie put the eggs in the refrigerator. "And probably a bicarbonate of soda." She set a liquor bottle beside the Maalox on the counter. "And how are you feeling? You look awfully pale."

"Will I be allowed to see him?"

She came over to place a hand on Leah's forehead. "See Glade? Do you want to?"

"Yes."

"Then of course you can see him." Julie knelt to look into her face with that sweet warm smile. "Hey, we're not the Gestapo, you know. Those doors are locked for your own protection." She patted Leah's hand and watched Goodyear wash behind his ears. "He's talking with Joe right now. But I'll get him up here when they're done. Shouldn't be long."

When Julie left, Leah took a resisting Siamese onto her lap because she needed him . . . even if he didn't need her.

She was sitting this way with her face buried in fur that still smelled of campfires when the key sounded in the lock once more.

Glade Wyndham stepped into the room.

"Remove those clothes and bathe. I'll wash them with the rest of your stuff—yuk! Maybe I'll burn them." Julie's voice from the hall. The door closed. The key turned in the lock.

Glade stood just inside the room staring at Leah, surprise and shock in widened eyes and tensed body. Leah watched as suspicion dawned on his face.

"Didn't they tell you I was here?" She couldn't believe it.

"No, they didn't." He looked like a bank robber. His beard had achieved wonders since she'd seen him last, and the man under it looked weighted with exhaustion.

Goodyear jumped back onto the ledge and took his comforting warmth with him.

"Glade. . . ."

"Got a razor?" he cut her off and glanced into the bathroom beside him.

Leah stood and tightened the belt on the robe that was all that covered her. She passed him to find her razor in the beauty case on the vanity beside the sink. "Careful, that razor's only accustomed to legs."

Leah went back to the fire and tried to stop shaking. Why should he trust her? She'd left him. But it hurt.

"Leah?" Julie's voice in the hall. And she actually knocked on the door.

Leah leaned against it. "What?"

"Can you hand me his clothes? I'm washer lady tonight," Julie whispered.

Leah gathered up the pile of clothes on the bathroom floor and handed them out.

"Look in the frig. He's probably hungry." Julie locked the door in Leah's face.

A thick T-bone sat beside the eggs in the refrigerator. She set the broiler under the oven to heat.

When Glade emerged, clean-shaven and slightly scarred (there had been no shaving cream), he wore only a towel. "Nice setup." His eyes steady, his tone oily with contempt. He picked up the bottle of scotch Julie had left on the counter, glanced about the apartment with its Mediterranean furniture, and looked even more suspicious.

Leah put the steak under the broiler and plugged in the percolator. She broke eggs to scramble. "What the hell's going on anyway?" she asked flippantly. He mustn't know how glad she was to see him.

He ran his fingers along the back of the framed picture above the fireplace, picked up the lamp, and looked under its base. "You tell me."

He peeked under the rim of the counter.

Glade stood beside her to reach above them for a glass. He poured a scotch, found ice, and leaned against the refrigerator to watch her turn the steak.

"Cozy. All the comforts of home." He raised his glass, his eyes roaming her bathrobe with intended insolence.

She let her eyes do the same with him and turned away with a giggle. "Tell me, where do you keep your gun now?"

"What have *you* been drinking?"

"Tranquilizers. I just got out of the hospital this afternoon. My ulcer erupted." Her giggle died half born, like Suzie's baby. Even the doctor's drugs failed her now.

Glade sat across from her in the tiny cubicle to have steak and eggs with his scotch. "I think you should know, if you don't already," he said around a mouthful, "that this room is well, if amateurishly, bugged."

"I can't think why." Leah went to the refrigerator to get him some more ice and tried again. "The walls are so thin you could hear an elk fart at twenty paces."

His suspicion broke into a brief smile. "Why else do you think we're in here together?"

"Can't imagine. There are more towels if you're cold." She tried to look away from the ugly scar that slashed diagonally across his abdomen, an old scar with a strange dip at its base, tried not to think of how he might have gotten it.

Leah expected the listening troops to march in and haul one of them off to another apartment, now that they'd admitted aloud their knowledge of the bugs. But Glade cleaned up his plate in peace.

"What's that?" He reached across the table to touch her forehead.

"Rope burn." She turned her palms up on the table and stared at them. They were finally healing after very special help at the hospital. "Your . . . friend Charlie put me on a rope ladder under a helicopter and dunked me into a lake. And then your friend Welker rescued me. He protects me by locking the doors on the outside and grilling my family on my life history and examining photographs of my bank checks. You were right, you know." Leah looked up from her hands through tears. "I shouldn't have given myself up. I should have gone with you. And I don't care who hears that."

He closed his eyes for a moment and then placed a finger on her lips. When he'd refilled his scotch, he drew her in to the couch. The fire flared as he poked it and added another log. Glade sat beside her, cradled her in one arm. "I'm sorry about my friends, Leah."

"I wish I'd never met you." But she nestled against him. "I wish you hadn't, too."

They sat quietly, waiting for someone to separate them. They couldn't really talk, so they watched Goodyear drag the greasy steak bone across the carpet to the rock shelf. He held it down with one paw and turned his head from side to side to gnaw at fat and gristle. Leah looked from the cat to the man. They were so similar, so cold, ruthless, independent. Is that what drew her? Their independence?

Rain continued its onslaught of the balcony, hissed on the fire when stray drops found their way down the chimney.

"Does this place come with a bed?" Glade said finally when the FBI still had not appeared.

"You're sitting on it. Pulls out to a king size. Why?" Leah turned into the cozy but hard cradle and touched the cleft in his chin.

Glade Wyndham kissed her ear and then whispered in it, "Thought I'd show you where I keep my gun."

Chapter Twenty-six

GLADE sat on the end of the couch by the sliding-glass doors, long legs stretched out and crossed at the ankles. Morning light gleamed on inky curls.

Julie had done a yeoman job on his clothes. Leah could smell the bleach across the room. Once-dark denims and navy shirt were now faded to the light blue of current fad.

"You can't be the same man I let in here last night." Julie settled beside him with her notebook.

Glade stared her down with a macho look and continued to poke contentedly at his teeth with a toothpick. Leah hid a grin behind her mug of hot chocolate.

When Joseph Welker sat on the rock shelf, the Siamese next to him was on his feet with his back arched in one leap. A hiss and a few dancing steps sideways brought Goodyear to the floor. He jumped to Glade's lap and curled up to stare daggers at the FBI.

"Cat doesn't like you, Joe." Glade turned to Julie and

opened the notebook for her. "Better write that down."

Welker's glance was patient and level. "Have you decided? You've had all night."

"Couldn't think last night. Too tired." He smiled at Leah.

Julie bent closer to her notebook. She had her face straightened out again before she sat back.

"Look, we both want the same thing. This matter should be investigated and the bureau is the legal vehicle to do that investigation. The newspapers and the publishers"—Welker paused to glance at Leah—"will get their story and a much more complete one when this matter is thoroughly investigated—"

"Or buried deep in a file somewhere so that no one is embarrassed by it," Glade finished the sentence for him.

"Is that what you're worried about? What if I give you my word that won't happen?"

"Your word doesn't go high enough and you know it. Your word would get lost in a paper shuffle."

"You've endangered your own life and that of Miss Harper long enough." Joseph Welker stood in a TV lawyer's stance with his hands behind his back, staring at the ceiling, rolling to the balls of his feet and then back onto his heels. "What if I got you the word of someone higher up? Someone like—"

"Swords," Glade interrupted and tightened his lips until they turned white.

"Swords! Harry Swords? Well, I hardly think we need go that—"

"Harry Swords and Pete Bradshaw or no deal."

Welker paced, thought, finally shrugged. "I'll try."

Their eyes locked. "And safe transport to neutral ground."

"That, too, with cash to tide you through the investigation and any troubles it might cause. Well?"

Glade stroked the cat thoughtfully. The room seemed to hold its breath. He looked up at Welker. "Then . . . I'd listen, anyway."

"Good. That's all I ask. I'll get on it right away." Joe Welker left the room in a rush.

Glade shook his head slowly and sighed. "Babes."

"What?" Julie finished her scribbling and looked up.

"Shouldn't mess around in the woods," Glade whispered so softly that Leah barely heard it. He laughed and his arm slipped off the back of the couch as his hand found the back of Julie's neck.

The next thing Leah knew, she'd spilled chocolate down her front and Julie had slid sideways, her eyes closed and her mouth open.

Goodyear hit the floor and Glade Wyndham was across the room to take Leah in his arms. "How many at the doors?"

"You didn't kill her, did you?" Leah whispered back.

"No. How many?" His arms tightened brutally.

"There's always one on the balcony. I suppose Brian is in the hall. I don't know of any others."

Glade rummaged through a drawer in the kitchenette and then moved to the balcony doors. "Goodyear stuck to me like glue after we left you," he said aloud, easing the glass door open. "I'll bet you're glad to have him back."

"Yes." Leah knew they were making conversation for the bugs and realized with astonishment that he was making an escape.

She bent to touch Julie and heard mesh give as he cut the screen. So did the man on the balcony. Shoes sounded on boards just as Glade withdrew his hand from the slit, slid the screen open about two feet, and stepped back so that the drapes hid him from view.

The guard peered through the opening at Leah, and as he noticed Julie on the couch, he unbuttoned his suit coat.

Leah had a brief glimpse of a holster under his arm, of Glade's hand flying out to grab his hair and draw him into the room as the other hand chopped down on his neck.

Julie murmured. The guard lay sprawled half in the room and half on the balcony. Glade reached under him to remove the weapon from its holster, stepped over the guard, and disappeared. Leah blinked. He hadn't even offered to take her along.

He hadn't even looked back.

"Welcome to the United States of America," Leah said shakily as Julie opened her eyes.

Joseph Welker surveyed the room, thunder on his face. Goodyear sniffed the inert guard. Leah brought Julie a scotch and water.

Brian leaped over the balcony rail outside and back into the room. "No Wyndham. But I saw another guy I didn't like the looks of."

"Why? Why!" Welker boomed for the tenth time and resumed his pacing.

Brian dragged the guard into the room and closed the screen, the glass door, and the drapes. "Joe, I think the goons are here." The baby face had paled.

Leah had cream of potato soup that night. Julie fried chicken for the rest of them in Leah's kitchenette. They'd spent the day together, the revived guard guarding the balcony from inside the room, Brian making short forays outside to keep an eye on the suspected goons, Welker making an occasional trip to the apartment next door to use the phone or answer the ring heard clearly through paper walls.

Julie and Leah were washing the dinner dishes when the CIA arrived, Peter Bradley from the meadow and Charlie from the helicopter and a third man who filled the crowded room to suffocation . . . and who looked a lot like Glade Wyndham . . . but who was not.

"What is this, an armed camp?" Peter Bradley looked at the guard with drawn gun at the drapes. "There's a couple of shadows outside that I sure hope are yours, Welker." He carried a rolled newspaper.

"Goons." Joe Welker caught Julie's eye and pointed at the percolator. "Knowing you guys, I'd half hoped they had connections with you, Bradshaw."

"Not our style." Bradshaw, who had told Leah he was Bradley, sat on the couch and motioned for the man who had to be Glade's brother to sit beside him. "You got trouble." He turned to Charlie. "Go out and keep an eye open. And Charlie, that's all you do."

"Go with him, Brian," Welker ordered.

Charlie grinned at Leah as he passed.

"Is this how he's paying for what he did to me?" she thought and wanted out. Goons or no.

"This is Joe Welker, FBI, Cal." Bradshaw folded and unfolded the newspaper. "Cal Wyndham."

"How do you do, Mr. Wyndham." Welker shook hands with Glade's brother formally, then took his favorite seat on the rock shelf.

"Understand my brother's in some kind of trouble." Cal Wyndham's dark curls were shorter than Glade's and tighter to his head, with speckles of gray among them. He was an inch or two shorter, somewhat fuller around the middle, and his voice and eyes were softer than his brother's. Good humor had permanently pressed lines in the ingrained tan of his face. As much as he resembled Glade, Cal didn't look like the kind of man who would run off and leave a woman without even a farewell as his brother had that morning.

"Where is Glade, anyway?" Bradshaw asked.

"Gone. Slit the screen and took off this morning."

"You mean you had him and you let him go?" Bradshaw slapped his leg with the newspaper. "Why are the goons hanging around then?"

"Apparently they think he's still here."

Cal Wyndham grinned. "Never was any stopping that boy."

Bradshaw ignored him. "Then why did you let us come all this way for—"

"I thought perhaps we could join forces. We'll never get him in time, working against each other."

"You got your orders and I got mine." Peter Bradshaw removed his tie and stuck it in his pocket. "And I doubt they're the same, Joe."

"My orders are to get the papers."

"So are mine. But it's what's done with them and the thief that's different and you know it." Bradshaw scratched his chin and settled back against the couch. "Of course, if you need reinforcements, I could call in someone from the Denver office."

"We have our own Denver office," Welker snapped.

"What papers?" Cal asked.

"Your brother has stolen some papers from his company's safe, Mr. Wyndham."

"That doesn't sound like Glade, but then I haven't seen much of him lately." Cal leaned forward to pet Goodyear, who was sniffing his cowboy boots. "He could have come to me if he needed money. He knew that, too. You sure he stole something?" he asked suspiciously.

"He's admitted it, Mr. Wyndham. I had Pete bring you here in hopes that you could talk to him. But. . . ." Welker shrugged.

"Seen this?" Peter Bradshaw handed Welker the newspaper, avoiding Leah's eyes as he took a cup of coffee from her.

But Cal gave her an appreciative smile as she leaned over to pour for him. "You boys travel in style, don't you?"

"I'm sorry. This is Miss Harper. Your brother's current."

"Well, *he* always did travel in style. Do you think my brother stole something, Miss Harper?"

"Not for money. And I'm not his current anything. Cream?"

"You think Glade leaked this?" Welker looked at Bradshaw and flicked a finger at the newspaper.

"No. They lifted that out of the Washington *Post* and it's all speculative. But this is sure a bad time to have Wyndham on the loose. How the hell did you let him go?"

"Never mind that now. What'll we do? We've still got Leah Harper. Maybe he'll come back for her . . . or. . . ."

Bradshaw looked directly at Leah for the first time. "You don't know Wyndham, Joe. The world's full of blondes."

"I can't think how that story got started," a cold voice said drily from the doorway to the hall. "I'm not all that fussy about hair."

Glade Wyndham closed the door and walked into the room. He was alone and he carried Leah's nail file in his hand.

Chapter Twenty-seven

THE guard turned his gun in Glade's direction.

Welker and Bradshaw jumped to their feet and simultaneously started a barrage of questions.

Glade greeted his brother and sat on the floor next to him, ignoring the guard and everyone else. He began to discuss the fine points of Goodyear's size and coat with Cal. The cat was on Cal's lap, trying to chew off one of the buttons on his plaid shirt.

Leah retreated to the kitchenette, where Julie had dropped the percolator when Glade made his silly dramatic entrance. In intervals between mopping up coffee grounds with paper towels, Leah peered at the men and seethed at the one she'd been so glad to see because he appeared not to notice her. He'd noticed her last night.

"Don't you know there are men out there waiting to kill you?"

"Can't be pure Siamese with that heavy bone structure and weight."

"Where's Brian and Charlie?"

"Why did you sneak out of here?"

"They tell me you stole some papers from your company, little brother."

"Why did you come back?"

"Leah"—Julie, on her hands and knees, looked up from the floor—"do you have any idea what's going on? I mean, off the cuff?"

"There's goons out there, Wyndham. . . ."

Welker shoved the newspaper between Glade and his brother. "And what's this all about?"

Glade read it through slowly. "Looks like things are

rolling without me, doesn't it?" he said softly and then looked up with a smile. "I'm here to make you a deal, gentlemen."

Leah stood, startled and disappointed, a stained paper towel dripping coffee through her fingers. After all he had put her through and himself as well for what Welker had called a hapless little crusade. . . .

"'What do you mean . . . deal?" Bradshaw reached under his coat. "What do we need with a deal now that we've got you?" he asked, pointing his gun at Glade.

Cal Wyndham's face turned as hard and watchful as his brother's. "Put that thing away. What are you all, a bunch of John Waynes?"

"But you don't have the papers, do you, Pete?" Glade asked in a whisper.

The phone range next door and Julie left to answer it.

"How do you plan to deal with the CIA and the FBI all at one time, Wyndham?"

"Jesus God, Peter, can't you at least hear what the man has to say?" Welker exploded.

"Stay out of this, Joe. He is, after all, our man."

"He's in our territory. And so are you."

"Joe?" Julie called from the doorway. "It's Swords. He wants to talk to Glade."

"Swords! What the hell's he doing in on this?" Bradshaw slapped his forehead and backed into his corner of the couch.

"I'm making my deal with him, too," Glade said quietly and walked to the door.

Cal and Leah were left alone with the guard, listening to voices in the next apartment, without quite being able to untangle the words, and listening to Goodyear purr.

"He sounds like a pump I had once." Cal smiled at her.

Leah leaned her head back in the chair and considered taking a tranquilizer. The conversation next door went on and on.

Cal Wyndham kept looking over his shoulder to the silent guard by the drapes and shifting his position uneasily. "Ought to be weapons-control legislation for government employees."

Leah had to laugh. "I agree. Would you like a drink?"

He followed her to the sink to select from the assortment of bottles that had wandered in before dinner. "How long have you known my brother?"

"Off and on for about two weeks. But I don't really know him."

"I thought I did. But I never thought he'd steal anything."

"And I never thought he'd make a deal. Shows how little one person knows another, doesn't it?" she said bitterly.

"Always had it figured that he worked for the government secretlike while he was doing his other work." He looked down into her face questioningly.

"He did until ten months ago when he stole those papers. He was supposed to photograph them for the CIA, but instead he took them."

"But why?"

"He didn't like what was in them. He decided finally to turn them over to the press . . . some kind of scandal involving oil shale."

"Shale?" He combed his fingers through the tight curls in a gesture reminiscent of his brother and added water to the whiskey in his glass. "I wonder if it has anything to do with . . . did he tell you I sold my ranch?"

"Yes."

"Glade got real sore about it, thought I should save it for Jerry. He's my son. He's in medical school in Denver," Cal said proudly. "Jerry was miffed, too. Not that he wanted to be a rancher but him and his uncle had fits about mining shale. But I had to sell out. I'd 'a been surrounded by shale operations and tons of people and no water. I'm still living in the buildings but I sold the cattle. I thought Glade'd be glad I sold to the company he worked for—"

"What company is it?"

"Enveco."

"The Environmental Energy Corporation." Leah thought of the credit card in her purse and the serene heron and . . . Sheila. "Hard to believe somehow. . . ."

"People that make up advertising slogans don't have nothing to do with the people that decide what to do. They're just hired from the outside to tell the public what they think it wants to hear."

Still the low murmur of male voices on the other side of the wall, with an occasional heated outburst.

Leah resumed her seat by the fire and picked up the newspaper that Welker had left on the rock shelf. It was a copy of the Denver *Post*. OIL SHALE SWINDLE RUMORED, the headline read and below that, ANOTHER RIP-OFF SUSPECTED. . . .

The *Washington Post* reported today that widespread rumors of collusion between government and industry to defraud the American public in the leasing of public lands, rich in oil shale deposits, may have some basis in truth. Industry bidding on these lands fell off when studies showed the economic waste and geographic destruction involved in mining shale and when Arab-American relations eased. Rising tensions in the Middle East have revived interest in the bidding, sources say. *Post* reporters claim to have information suggesting the leak of bidding information so that a few of the larger oil companies can gain control of these lands.

When asked for comment, White House press secretary Norm Walters said, "Of course, we're looking into this. But I must say how disappointed I am in the *Washington Post*. After the fine work it did on the Watergate coverup, to insist upon raking the gutters for fresh scandal just to keep up its subscription lists . . . well, I'm just disappointed, that's all."

"Instead of putting our dollars into research to harness the sun and wind," says prominent environmentalist Dr. Paul W. Wingless, ". . . it looks as though we are once again being forced to decide whether to ruin the seas in offshore oil drilling or ruin the land in mining oil shale. Either way is suicidal and it will eventually be necessary to do both if we are to retain our reliance on an oil-based economy. And all because of major industries organized around the exploitation of a fast-depleting oil source. Shall we put off the dislocation and crisis of switching now when it is painful until later when it will be catastrophic?" asks Dr. Wingless.

"I can't make that kind of a decision," Leah sputtered to a surprised Cal.

They both jumped when Brian burst into the room. "We've lost the goons. Can't see them anywhere. You seen anything?"

The guard flipped his cigarette butt into the fireplace. "No."

"Well there's a window broken downstairs. Where's Joe?"

"Next door with Glade Wyndham and everybody else."

"Wyndham? Who brought him in? We didn't see—"

"Came in by himself. Probably through your broken window. He's on the phone to Swords. . . ."

But Brian was on his way out, swearing softly.

Goodyear stretched and sharpened his claws on the couch. He disappeared into the kitchenette and it wasn't long before something crashed to the floor. The guard and his gun swung around.

"Take it easy. It's just the cat." Leah didn't know who was more dangerous, the FBI or the goons. But she, too, was uneasy at the thought of Sheila's murderers in the building.

In the kitchenette, Leah found the wastebasket overturned and chicken bones all over the floor. Goodyear disappeared into the bathroom with what was left of a wing.

"Damn you, blimp, I'm tired of cleaning up floors!" But Leah was doing just that when the men returned.

"I don't like this, Swords or not," Pete Bradshaw snapped.

"What's this, Joe? Have you got Leah working as cleaning woman now?"

Leah gave him a dirty look, threw the last handful of

bones at the basket, and stood to wash her hands at the sink.

He reached around her to pick up the scotch bottle. "Stay cool," he said under his breath and moved away.

"When do we leave?" Joe Welker asked.

"Tomorrow. And I go alone." Glade took a tray of ice from the refrigerator.

"No deal, Wyndham," Bradshaw said threateningly. At least he'd put his gun away.

"Glade, you can't expect us to let you go off alone. Be reasonable." Welker reached into the cupboard for a glass. "And why wait till tomorrow?"

Leah went back to her chair by the fireplace, thoroughly sick of them all. What did he mean—stay cool?

"Okay, I'll take Leah and Goodyear Harper and go tonight. They're getting to seem like family anyway."

"No deal," Bradshaw said again. "They're on your side."

"Goodyear is on Goodyear's side. Leah never knows what side she's on." Glade sat on the arm of her chair. "Do you, Leah?"

She balled her fists, refusing to look at him.

"There, you see?" He laughed and the ice tinkled in his drink. "She'll be my hostage, to make sure there's no cross."

"Who'll be our hostage?"

"You can keep Cal."

Leah and Cal looked at each other in astonishment.

"You take Brian and Charlie with you, too. That way everybody's interests are covered," Bradshaw said.

"Not in the same car. They follow behind. Leah and I haven't had a chance for a good talk in days."

"We're not that stupid. You'd just lose them."

"Any car you guys scare up will be well provided with a homing device, anyway. . . ."

"No deal."

"Then no papers," Glade said with flat finality.

"You can't take Miss Harper," Welker said. "She's just out of the hospital."

"That's your doing. Her ulcer behaves beautifully when

172

she's with me. Do you want to go with me, Leah?"

Leah looked around the crowded room. . . . Joseph Welker had his Harper file, Bradley-Bradshaw had his Charlie. What other little surprises did they have? "I don't want to stay here."

Brian appeared at the door. "Joe?"

"Are they in the building?"

"No sign of them anywhere. But I found this downstairs." He held up a gun.

"I left it there. I lifted it off him this morning." Glade nodded toward the guard at the drapes. "How many goons were there?"

"We saw two."

"You'll find one about ten yards off the balcony to the right under a bush near two boulders about this high. The other one is under a white Ford at the back of the parking lot." Glade reached down to sweep the Siamese off the floor with one hand. "I didn't get the license number."

"How do you know?"

"Because that's where I left them."

Welker got back to business. "How long will it take to get the papers?"

"Two, three days."

"Days!"

"I had ten months to hide them, you know."

"Then we all start tonight."

"We don't all start. Leah and I go alone. Charlie and Brian follow in another car. That's my last offer. You can meet us at the end of the trip and I'll deliver."

"Meet you where?"

"I'll call you here and let you know when we're halfway there."

"How stupid do you expect us to be?" Pete Bradshaw unbuttoned his shirt. Now he looked like Peter Bradley once more.

Brian and Charlie came in wearing identical expressions. "What are we going to do with two stiffs, Joe?" Brian asked quietly.

Welker turned to Glade. "You killed them?"

Leah drew in her breath, felt blood rushing hot to her face.

"That was for Sheila, whoever *she* was." Glade walked to the sink to refill his scotch while everyone in the room stared at him.

"See what happens," Welker said to Bradshaw, finally breaking the long silence, "when you turn these creeps loose in the U.S.?"

"Good point, Joe, good point." Glade raised his glass to Charlie and his voice turned low and silky, "What are we going to do about Leah's little ride under the helicopter, I wonder?"

Charlie's grin looked stuck.

Chapter Twenty-eight

LEAH wore her blue jeans again. She sat in the front seat of the white Ford that had been sitting at the back of the parking lot with a body under it.

Glade Wyndham and Joseph Welker argued in low voices outside.

She rolled down her window and gulped at the freshness of night. She was tired but it felt good to be out of that stuffy crowded apartment. The bargaining had gone on forever. Welker had been loath to let Leah go. It must be after midnight.

Both backpacks sat propped against the backseat. Where was he taking her now? Why? And he'd murdered again . . . just when she'd begun to think he was more to her than a Jason or. . . .

Glade slid in beside her. Welker handed an envelope in through the door. "The rest when you deliver. And I'd better get that call or we'll turn every cop in the state out to find you."

"Don't forget the cat." Julie dumped Goodyear onto Glade's lap. He crawled to the seat between them and eyed Leah without love.

Glade started the engine and drove out of the parking lot onto the service road. Car lights flared across them from behind like searchlights as Brian and Charlie turned to follow.

"What am I doing here? You don't need me." The lump in her throat was threatening to outdo the pain in her stomach.

"Well, I couldn't leave you with them, Leah. After what they'd already done to you. Use your head."

"I suppose I'm safer with you?"

"I hope so. But there were at least four men in that car that took off and left Sheila in a Volkswagen about to explode." He handed her the envelope. It was filled with crisp bills.

"So you can be bought."

"That's to pay you back for the money I borrowed from your wallet this morning while you were in the bathroom."

Leah put the envelope in her purse and took out a Kleenex. "What did you do?" she whispered. "Sneak up behind those men and stick a knife in their backs? Or crush their heads with rocks or put a silencer on that gun and—"

"Do you really want to know?" The deadly tone he'd used at Pair-O-Dice Cabins.

She turned away so that she couldn't see the look that went with that tone. "No."

They rode in strained silence, except for Leah's little sniffs as she tried to stop weary tears. The service road came to the highway, the car still alight with the headlights close behind. Glade turned toward Steamboat Springs.

"Killing is wrong." She stared straight ahead and saw nothing.

"Will you stop sniveling!" The car braked abruptly and Goodyear, who had been leaning over to sniff the radio dials on the dash, tumbled to the floor. "Getting killed isn't all that fun either. Ask Sheila."

Just as Goodyear began his leap back to the seat, Glade accelerated and the cat was back on the floor. Leah picked him up.

"Let's stop arguing." He glanced into the mirror on the windshield and pressed the gas pedal again. "We're upsetting the cat."

"Upsetting the cat! What do you think I am? A little over two weeks ago I found my mother dead in her own blood. I came to Colorado to make a new start and I get beaten and tied to a bed, drug all over the great out-of-doors for days on end, hung from a helicopter and dunked in a frigid lake, have my entire life drug up and put in a file, my family harassed clear back in Chicago, end up in a hospital, and *let's not upset the cat?*"

Leah struck Glade on the side of the head.

The white Ford swerved into the other lane. The oncoming headlights blurred together as both cars screeched brakes. They missed each other by a breathless half inch and the white Ford swerved back onto its side of the road slowing so suddenly that the car behind braked with an answering screech.

Leah didn't know whether to cry or to shake. Finally, she did both and saw the night lights of Steamboat Springs' main thoroughfare through a mist.

"You know," Glade said thoughtfully, "if you'd come loose like that more often, your ulcer might not bother you so much." And he began to laugh, that rich, full laugh that Leah would hear in her dreams till the day she died.

She swung out again with such force that the Siamese flew into the back seat to escape the fracas. But Glade was ready for her and caught her wrist. Laughing harder, he turned the Ford around a corner so abruptly that Leah fell against him.

They were on a side street. Glade checked the rear-view mirror and swerved onto another street and she was thrown against the door.

They crossed the main thoroughfare again.

"What are you doing? Are you crazy?" Leah was

thrown back against her tormentor. "Stop!" The car swerved and she was back on the door. "Glade!" The car slowed, turned another corner, speeded up. . . .

Leah closed her eyes. Glade was still laughing. She couldn't look at him or share his excitement. Goodyear landed suddenly on her shoulder, clinging with every toenail he owned.

The white Ford stopped. Leah opened her eyes.

"Grab the cat and your purse. I'll get the packs," he ordered.

The overhead light came on as he opened his door, went out as he slammed it, came on again as he opened her door.

Leah stepped out on shaking legs, surprised to find her purse in her hand and the Siamese under her arm. "I am at the end of my rope, mentally, physically, emotionally. . . ." She found herself pushed down behind a smelly garbage can in an alley. "Not that you'd understand the emotionally and—"

"Be quiet, will you?"

"And I can't go traipsing after you up some mountain."

He patted the top of her head. "From here on in, you can ride all the way."

"But we're leaving the car—"

"I know. Come on, this way." He took off at a run between two houses.

Somewhere a dog barked and then another. Goodyear hissed and tried to swivel out of her hold. "Wait. The cat. . . ." Leah slung her purse onto her shoulder by its strap and used both hands to subdue the animal.

They crossed another street and ran between houses again.

"Why do we need the packs if we're not walking?"

"You'll see." He raced ahead of her to the next street and up a dark sidewalk, stopping beside a pickup truck that even in the night shadow looked ready for the crusher. Unlocking the door in the small camper shell on the back, he threw the packs inside and then pushed Leah into the cab.

"Are we stealing trucks now?"

"No." The entire cab shook when he'd finally coaxed the engine to start. "I bought it today with your money."

A darkened Enveco heron hovered on one leg above a gas station closed for the night. If it hadn't been for the corner streetlight she wouldn't have noticed it at all. It brought back the memory of a yellow Volkswagen exploding in an innocent mountain meadow. "Do all big companies hire goons?"

"No, these guys are probably just for hire by anyone for specific jobs."

"Like the advertisers," Leah thought.

YAMPA RIVER, a sign said as they crossed a bridge, and the truck was soon on a highway heading west and leaving Steamboat Springs behind.

"I take it you're not going through with the deal, after all." Leah had to shout over the tortured rumble of the old truck. "That's something."

"What makes you think that?"

"Why else go to all the trouble to lose Charlie and Brian?"

"I don't like them. Try to catch some sleep while you can." Goodyear slept curled between them. But Leah couldn't manage it. The man next to her was too tense. His very stiffness screamed warning.

"We're not out of danger, are we?"

"No, we're not." His head kept turning from the road ahead to the little round mirror outside his window.

Night pressed in on the truck. Clouds hid most of the stars. The air around Leah exuded oil and dirt and uneasiness.

"If we're not going to get the papers, where are we going?" Wouldn't it be wonderful if they were heading for an airport and a plane that would take them to some luxurious hideout in Hawaii or. . . .

"But we *are* going to get the papers, Leah."

"This is the direction they expect you to go. Welker's been following you on a map with a line moving west across Colorado."

"Everybody is about two bites from our tail." They

slowed. A car passed from behind. "They have been for quite a while."

They crossed the Yampa River again. She couldn't see it in the dark but she heard it briefly as they passed over the bridge. It sounded angry.

"Are those papers worth all this? Are they? I mean, swindles are getting to be a way of life. Are you trying to be some kind of hero?" Leah pushed away the sudden image of the two women passing her so quickly as she screamed about her mother on the front steps in Chicago.

"I'll be unsung, dead or alive. Does that make you happy?"

Some miles later a town appeared. CRAIG, the sign read.

"Breakfast time." He pulled the rattling truck over. It was an all-night truck stop. Semis bordered the street on either side.

The Dr. Pepper clock above the coffeepots said it was a quarter of two in the morning. A sign on the cash register informed them, OUR CREDIT MANAGER IS HELEN WAIT. IF YOU WANT CREDIT, GO TO HELL'N WAIT.

A short man in a khaki jacket and a welcoming smile bustled up to them. "Hey, buddy, what's up? You're late. I been in and out of this place three times," he said to Glade and then turned to Leah. "So this is the chick I outfitted for you, huh?"

Glade scanned the room nervously. "Ben. . . ."

"You guys aren't just in from the trail. You smell too good." Ben seemed almost to bounce with energy or excitement. "Hey, am I finally going to get in on the action?"

"More than you'll like if you don't keep your voice down. Leah, this is Ben."

"Ah, the man with the exquisite bachelor's pad. I think I have your boots somewhere."

Glade nudged Leah into a corner booth. "Order me something big with eggs in it." He slipped an arm around the considerable breadth of his friend's shoulders and hustled him down a narrow hall to the men's room.

The waitress curled her lip when Leah asked for her poached-egg-on-milk-toast. A Coors Beer sign blinked

179

faulty neon in the window. A heavy man, looking wrinkled and No-Dozed, belched on his stool at the counter, picked up a tall thermos, and walked to the cash register.

Smoke hung in a spaced-out cloud just below the lights in the ceiling. The smell of bacon grease, beer, and cigarettes mingled unpleasantly.

Leah was wondering if she should have ordered for Ben, when he emerged from the hall, looking subdued. He left the diner without even glancing at her.

Glade leaned against a wall in the narrow hall, a phone to his ear, his denim jacket two shades darker than the tight bleached-out jeans. His shoulders blocked the hall, his expression and stance were rigid with that intensity he wore like clothing when his problem gripped him. For an instant Leah wanted him with an intensity of her own. She inhaled stagnant air and looked away.

When Leah looked back to the hall, Glade was disappearing into the men's room at the back of it. When he emerged he made another call.

They ate quickly. The blood from his rare steak mingled with egg yolk and grease from the hash-brown potatoes that automatically came with eggs in Colorado.

"Who'd you call?"

"Welker. Always keep my promises." He dipped toast into the mess on his plate.

Leah swallowed and looked elsewhere. "So you're going to deal."

"He's got my brother. But he's very unhappy about our losing our companions."

"Ben left."

"Yeah." He stared her down over the rim of his coffee cup, daring her to ask about Ben. His knees pressed painfully against hers under the table.

"If we're not running off, why are you taking me?"

"I might need your help. If I have to have somebody at my back, you're still the best bet I could come up with at short notice."

"I'm no help in dangerous situations and you know it. I can't—"

"What is it with you?" he snapped. "It's always I can't.

You don't know what you can do till you have to. I've been out of the country a lot, but the word liberation means revolution. So I was curious. . . ."

He mopped up the last of the yuk on his plate with the last of his toast. "When I got back to the States, I expected something new. But I got, instead, 'Glade, I'm tired.' 'Glade, I'm scared,' 'Glade, I can't' " He smiled and Leah knew he was waiting for a slap or a kick, bracing for a challenge he could easily overpower and that he might well have gotten.

But the door opened just then and two men entered. Leah froze halfway between a grimace of protest and a false smile. One of the men was pasty-faced, the other dark. Both looked tired and sour. But they noticed Leah and then Glade while trying not to apppear to notice anyone. They couldn't quite hide their surprise. Neither was a truckdriver, nor a lineman, nor a cowboy coming in the wee hours to sober up on diner coffee.

"That's interesting. If you're done, I think we'd better go. But leisurely, naturally," Leah said.

Chapter Twenty-nine

GLADE WYNDHAM had picked up his cue without hesitation, wrapped the fat and bone of his steak in a napkin, finished his coffee over quiet small talk, and signaled for the check.

Goodyear roused for a steak breakfast as Glade pulled the truck out into the street. "Okay, what spooked you? I saw them when I paid the bill."

"They didn't fit. Any more than Welker and aides fit in Steamboat Springs. Any more than you do. CIA agents are supposed to be medium height and unnoticeable. You can be spotted a mile away. And you were, Glade, just now. So was I."

"I was hired as deep cover. Nobody intended I branch out. What about them? What was it exactly about—"

"Intuition."

"Oh, Jesus!" But he checked the outside mirror.

"Listen, pig, I've lived in cities all my life. And there are some people you work hard to avoid and you pretend not to notice."

"They wore suits, is that it?"

"And their eyes. They looked like yours."

"Their eyes?" He sighed and shook his head.

"Yes, eyes. Those men have killed. And city stuck out all over them. And the highway patrol picked you up in Craig. And they noticed us as if they'd just peeked into the Wyndham and Harper files. And they tried so hard not to show it. And for an instant they looked as if they couldn't believe their luck. What more do you want?"

The creep was laughing. She was too tired and scared to hit him.

"I want to pull this truck over and. . . . However. . . ." He leaned across her to open the glove compartment. This time, instead of a bottle, he brought out a gun and laid it on her lap. "I want you at my back. One for you, one for me." He pulled out another.

"One more crack about women and I might use it on you." She left the nasty thing lying on her lap without touching it.

"Why is it whenever I'm with you I wonder how I got there? Why I went in the first place? How do I let myself get into these—"

"You said you wanted to come along. I had a hell of a time convincing Welker to let you. If he wasn't so hot for those papers he wouldn't have let me talk him into it."

"What I meant was I wanted to get out of that apartment and away from them."

"Poor Leah, you're always getting away from something, only to get into something worse." And he laughed.

"Why not have Ben at your back? He lookes more capable."

"I have other plans for him. Besides I want you to see something. Leah, don't you really know why you wanted to come along?"

"No." But Leah was afraid she did know.

Glade reached across the cat to put his hand on her knee. Goodyear bit his wrist.

Leah stood at the back of the truck, shivering in her windbreaker. She stuck her hands in her pockets, felt the grisly cold of metal in one of them, and took that hand out again. A constant whishing sound somewhere near. . . . She could smell water.

Glade shoved an oblong yellow object toward her. "Gas cylinder for the boat. Here, take it."

"What boat?" she said suspiciously and experienced that sinking feeling she'd known before when around him. The cylinder was slippery and heavy.

"This boat." He drew a large bundle from the camper shell, balanced it on his shoulder, and started around the truck. "Come on."

"What do we do with a boat?"

"Ride in it. I told you, you wouldn't have to walk, didn't I?" He moved ahead of her as if his burden was heavy.

She'd expected a lake. But it was a river. And even at night it had a strange color.

Dropping the bundle, he stood on the bank and looked down at the water. "Shit!" He kicked a tall grass clump with his toe. "Leah, this river's twice the size it was when I went down it last fall. And I'm no river rat. There isn't time to train you, either. I'm afraid we're going to have to fake it and pray."

The river answered him with a sinister whoosh. It should have looked inky in the dark before dawn, but it had a funny creamy color that might have been tan in daylight. It didn't smell of fish or reed. It smelled of earth and . . . decay? Death?

"I'm not going on that river. And if you think Goodyear will, you don't know cats. He'll be climbing our heads." She turned to see the gas cylinder inflate the heavy

183

bundle into a rubber boat that would look small and flimsy on a river that appeared to be a good hundred feet wide. "Cats hate water."

"I suppose ex-underwear models do, too." He grabbed her wrist and pulled her back to the truck. "I'm worried about Goodyear, too. We'll be in the middle of the river where he can't jump out of the boat. But I couldn't leave him back there. They wouldn't have cared for him when they didn't need him anymore." His concern for the cat was the only emotionally warm thing about him.

"You are crazy, Glade Wyndham."

By dawn they had stuffed the contents of the backpacks and her purse into rubberized duffel bags, along with the provisions he'd bought in Steamboat Springs with her money. They had changed into tennis shoes and he'd moved the truck back down the road and off into the trees. Leah was still protesting.

Goodyear sniffed at the boat suspiciously.

Glade threw her a life jacket and strapped one on himself. He'd lashed the four duffel bags in the center of the boat with a series of ropes and he now added a fifth to the top of the pile. It was empty. "This is for Goodyear."

He handed her a small metal case and put an identical one in his pocket. "There are matches in this and the case will keep them dry. If you get thrown out of the boat and can get to shore, you can build a fire to keep warm. Here's your paddle. I'll explain. . . ."

"Glade, I don't want to go on that river." Just the thought filled her with terror. "I'll wait for you in the truck."

"I'm not coming back here. There's no going back on the Yampa River. It won't be long before Charlie and your friends at the restaurant in Craig find that truck anyway."

"But we lost Charlie."

"Nobody loses Charlie for long." He grabbed Goodyear and stuffed him into the top duffel, drawing it up so that only a small air hole remained. The bag bucked and pitched as if it were filled with ten cats.

Just as a sharp pain stabbed her middle so hard that she doubled over where she stood, a car motor rumbled on the road behind them. The pain released Leah in time for her to glimpse headlights bobbing through the trees and hear the vehicle bottom out on a chuckhole.

Glade had the boat in the water and sat on the bank, holding it with his feet. "Get in front, fast!"

The boat wobbled threateningly as she stepped into the cramped space and practically capsized when he jumped in behind.

"Dear God, what am I doing here?" she thought and leaned back against the gear as the river caught them. The floor of the boat buckled and warped as if trying to heave her out. There was nothing to hold onto except the paddle, which wouldn't do her much good if she and it ended up in the water alone.

"Turn back, Wyndham!" Brian ran along the shore, his suit jacket flapping, his city shoes slipping on the rocks. Behind him, Charlie stood on the bank and raised both arms to steady the aim of the weapon in his hand.

"Duck!" Glade yelled and Leah slipped sideways along the duffels at her back, but not before a cracking echoed across the river and water spewed several inches from the opposite shore.

"He's bluffing . . . shooting high." Glade's voice came muffled behind her. "They can't risk me till they've got the papers." And then only seconds later, "You can sit up now. We're out of range, anyway."

Brian and Charlie were tiny in the distance. Leah turned to face what lay ahead and tried to force down sickness.

The funny-colored river whispered derision. Trees slipped by rapidly in the dingy dawn light. A fine spray wetted her face. It came over the rim in front of her and soon dampened her hair, too, began to bead her lashes. The floor of the boat was cold through her jeans. *And there was nothing to hold onto!*

"I guess we can let the cat out for a while," Glade said. "He can't jump ashore here."

Goodyear put two front feet on her shoulder, his whiskers brushed her cheek. "Yowl!" he roared in her ear. Leah almost dropped the paddle. He slithered down her front, digging in his toenails, until he could sit on her lap and glare slit-eyed up into her face, his ears laid back.

She unclamped a fear-frozen hand from the paddle to pet his head. His fur was already damp. "I'm sorry, blimp. I didn't mean to get you into anything like this. I told you two strays were no good for each other. This wasn't my idea. I crave hot baths, flush toilets, central heating, a roof over my head, and warm food like some people crave cigarettes and cocktails."

Goodyear hissed and jumped to the pile of rubber duffels.

Glade laughed. "Listen, city girl, there's no time to feel sorry for yourself. I was going to give you a quick lesson on river running, but our friends interrupted us. Now, pay attention. If we're not both going in the drink, you have to help get us down this river." He went on in a steady patient drone for a half-hour, explaining what to do in an emergency, repeating himself endlessly, trying to instill confidence in his boatmate—but he only increased her fear.

Goodyear hissed and yowled and paced the unsteady boat. A line of living trees stood to their knees in water. A piece of sod that had broken loose from the river's edge floated by like a small lost island. It rocked gently as it passed, dandelions still in bright bloom amid the grass on its undulating surface. Leah watched it sink.

"This river's in flood," Glade interrupted his discourse long enough to explain, and there were nasty undertones in the way he said it.

Leah drew her knees up to her chin and hugged them.

"Rapids. Straddle the left side of the boat as if you were riding a horse bareback. Tuck one foot under the rim of the pontoon where it meets the floor. The other under the boat in the water. Grip the paddle—"

"But I'll get wet."

"You're going to be wet anyway. The point is not to drown," he suggested dryly.

The sun rose behind clouds offering no warmth. Breeze rippled the water and blew chill through her damp clothes.

Her muscles felt cramped and stiff already.

Birds called good mornings to each other across the river.

Goodyear crawled into his duffel voluntarily, moaning evil-sounding cat curses at his human companions.

The current rippled down the river's center, leaving foam-flecked eddies to slip around and back on themselves on each side.

A cow, stiff and bloated, turned in a slow grotesque death circle near the right bank. Her legs extended as if she had been stuffed with metal rods to make her stand up in a museum display case, but had tipped over.

The boat nosed toward the cow and the foul, putrid stench of decay, the odor gaining new dimensions when water-soaked.

Glade barked an order and they paddled back to the main current.

"Leah, pay attention. I asked, what do you do if thrown from the boat and get ashore?" he went on as if the cow had never been.

Thrown from the boat . . . panic sent nasty tingles through her body.

Leah reached into her jacket pocket and drew out the gun. She twisted around and rested it on Goodyear's duffel, bent down to sight along the barrel and aimed for the space between his eyebrows. "*Get me out of here!*"

His eyes went dead.

"I mean it, Glade Wyndham!"

"Leah," he said softly, "there is no way out. For once in your life you're committed, whether you like it or not."

She meant merely to force him to pull to the safety of the shore but she shivered just them, and the cold finger clamped around the cold trigger jerked.

Chapter Thirty

"ANOTHER lesson learned," he said calmly. But the index finger that reached out to move the barrel of the gun aside trembled. "You pulled the trigger only far enough to cock it. Let me show you." He took the metal monstrosity from her carefully. "Do you really hate me that much?" Surprise and a fleeting hurt look on his face.

"I hate . . . I hate danger." Leah was crying and didn't care. She'd almost killed someone. She'd almost killed *him*.

Her gun, in his hand, came right up to her nose. "Leah, it is now cocked. See the hammer? If I pull the trigger the rest of the way, it will fire. Never point this revolver at anyone . . . unless you mean to kill him. And be sure to pull the trigger all the way back." He aimed the barrel toward the sky and eased the hammer gently into place with his thumb. "But you don't want to kill me. You need me now because there is no way off this river except in this boat. There are rapids ahead. You can't get down this river alone and neither can I. We're both committed." He put the gun in her hand.

She replaced it in her pocket and looked away.

"Your aim was dead center and steady there for a minute. Don't forget how you did that." He loosened the strings on a duffel and brought out a large plastic bottle. "Here, I bought three bottles and emptied them into this. It's Maalox."

She took a long sip. And then another. "Why? Why do we have to do this . . . river thing anyway?"

"The papers are here . . . downstream."

"Damn the papers! You're just going to make a deal.

188

And after all you've put us through."

"We could get down this river in two days. I've given us three to allow for difficulties. We meet the CIA and the FBI at a place called Split Mountain Ramp in Utah. It's a place to haul boats off the river. Now, if we make that rendezvous and Swords keeps his word, there's a chance that we'll both get out of this with our hides."

"And if this Swords doesn't keep his word? What do we rendezvous with then? Death? And what makes you think the goons won't be at Split Mountain Ramp?"

He just shrugged and looked away.

She was still twisted around to face him when the river began a low murmur behind her; the boat slipped faster through the water. Glade looked beyond her, reached to pull up the strings on the cat's duffel.

The murmur grew in intensity.

"Okay, here we go. I know you can do it." He gave her a confident smile. "Turn around and climb onto the rim."

Leah turned around and froze. A line of mist above white water . . . and through the mist, the river changed levels as if in an illusion . . . the Yampa wound on past the splayed water ahead, but lower . . . much lower. . . . The murmur was now a roar. Leah tasted Maalox.

The floor of the boat buckled and bulged beneath her. She slid from her giddy, uncertain seat to slip a leg over the inflated pontoon rim and mount it. The water washing over her lap was cold. The mist in her face turned to spray. The boat and river raced faster.

Remembering to grip hard with her knees only at the last minute, she felt the boat rear and her paddle flailed air. A spout of water hit her full in the face. She couldn't see.

Then the boat bucked, trying to throw her as the back came up and they swooped down into chaos, with a lurch that almost knocked her over, almost pushed her stomach up her throat.

When her vision cleared, a rock loomed ahead. Instinctively, Leah paddled to steer away from it. But they caught it on the side with a sickening thud and then a pause while everything but them seemed to be in frantic motion . . . a tortured screech as rubber and rock rubbed together and the boat tore loose, turning slowly around until Leah was going backward and sitting high in the air.

When the boat lowered, she was looking at the rapids that should have been behind her and the roar was diminishing. She turned to find Glade smiling.

"Shall we turn around?" He stuck his paddle into the Yampa and held it still until Leah once again faced forward. "You did pretty good, but . . ." and he began to recite instructions again as she crawled shakily back to the floor of the wallowing boat. It was four inches deep in water.

Glade let a soaked Siamese out of the duffel, found what looked like a bicycle-tire pump in another and pumped out the boat while he talked. Goodyear shook water all over them, then settled down with a clinging hold on the duffel pile. An angry tail switched back and forth, making a slapping noise on wet rubber. The cat was even past moaning.

Leah was too cold and wet to talk, too miserable to comment when rain and wind began to lash at them, but she listened now to what the man behind her said.

And from what he said, she reasoned that they had a choice of dying by being sunk, or washed out of the boat, or ripping the boat on a rock and deflating. But they all added up to drowning.

Soon canyon walls, hundreds of feet high, surrounded them, sheer treeless sandstone monsters the color of the river, their sides pitted with holes and deep caverns cut into their bases. They resembled enemy fortresses in the dismal light of a rainy day.

Raindrops pocked the river and made bumpy ripples bounce under the boat. But it didn't wash the river's grit or its sour smell from her clothes and skin and hair.

The exhaustion of shock and fear, and over twenty-four hours of sleeplessness added weight to the heavy depression of certain doom and the cold, wet discomfort.

As they swept on, the river became angrier, noisier with unexpected twists and shoots through narrow cliff walls. They were up on the rim again and again to fight rock obstacles, or keep the boat from being swept into the low-ceilinged caverns at the base of cliffs.

"You're getting better," Glade would yell encouragingly. "Good girl," he would say and then start the endless process of pumping out.

Goodyear crept in and out of his bag, unable to find a dry hiding place.

The shoreline reverted to trees and rocks. Glade suddenly screamed to paddle for shore. Leah dragged a tired body back onto the rim and forced aching arms to pull at his command.

A giant round earth clod bore down on them in a swirl of white water, pushing a wave in front of it that would surely capsize them. The clod towered over the boat and managed somehow to stand on end.

Terror renewed failing strength. She paddled so hard that their boat hit the bank and swung Glade's end around behind her. With a struggling cat under one arm, he jumped out to anchor them to the shore as the boat bucked with the wave and an entire uprooted tree crashed by so closely she could have touched it with her paddle. The huge root system still embraced a glob of the earth in which the tree had grown . . . an ancient cottonwood, its trunk at least four feet in diameter . . . trailing soggy leaves against the pontoon rim . . . brittle branches splintering and cracking over the river's din.

They stared after it until it disappeared into the rain and murk ahead.

Leah shuddered. If the Yampa could conquer so massive a tree, what chance did they stand in their puny rubber raft?

They gave the cottonwood time to gain distance on them and paddled back to the current. The rain stopped but the wind was still cold through her wet clothes. They pulled over about noon to a patch of sheltered shoreline and he built a fire that smoked until the wood dried. Goodyear took off through the trees and Leah was sure they would never see him again. She stretched out on the damp earth beside the fire and soon the cat returned to huddle close while Glade heated water on his little stove.

"I'm afraid we're down to survival rations," he apologized and offered her hot bouillon and dry granola.

Leah stared into her soup, listening to the roaring sound around the bend where the river would lead them after lunch. She knew the meaning of that sound in every cell of her nervous system . . . and she was committed.

When she finished the bouillon, Goodyear licked at her cup. "Why does he put up with all this? Why doesn't he just run off and leave us?"

"This is why." And her crazy spy brought out a can of Kal Kan Mealtime for Finicky Cats. "He wasn't raised to be a wild animal."

Leah watched in a state of shock as he chipped away at the lid with his pocketknife. "That cat's not finicky!"

Goodyear left her side, crawled onto Glade's lap, rubbed his neck against anything he could reach, and started his soggy motor. Glade emptied the kitty food onto a flat rock and chopped it into bite-size pieces.

"And I get bouillon and cereal. If you ever treated me as good as you do that oversized imbecile of a feline food machine . . . I'd. . . ."

"You'd what?" He moved to her side of the fire, stretched out behind her, and warmed her where the fire didn't. "What?"

"I might . . . just might even shoot somebody for you." She snuggled back against his body heat.

"Wait till we get to Hardings Hole where we'll stay till morning, Leah," he whispered in her ear. "And I'll pay you for all I've put you through today." He kissed her cheek. "With interest."

Glade added wet firewood and the blaze turned to choking smoke. Goodyear licked all the food and half the moss off the rock.

Leah tried to ignore the ominous roaring on the other side of the bend. "Why don't weeds grow on mine tailings?"

"Because a few inches of earth on top are alive, and what's below is dead." He disappeared behind the gorge of smoke from the fire and his voice came through it disembodied. . . . "Mining oil shale will bring tons of death to the surface. It'll wipe out everything for miles, and to process it will rob water from more than Colorado, or Wyoming, or. . . ."

"So drill oil from offshore, in the oceans."

"And leak death to the seas that provide life to an entire planet in one way or another? This river supplied water for people miles away in other states. Shale will have to take water from rivers like this one and so from cattle ranches, citrus groves, truck and grain farms, and cities. The places that provide homes and food can't withstand the demands of shale to provide power."

"So what's the answer?"

"Put the billions required to serve up death in the form of oil into other kinds of energy.

"Can it be done. Really?"

"Most of it. The public may have to choose between an eighth control on an electric blender and suicide. But government and industry are set on keeping a profitable status quo."

"And yet, you're going to deal with that very government."

"I've made an agreement to have something investigated and brought to light before too much damage is done to the Rockies."

Leah remembered the bull elk she'd seen just before she'd entered the CIA camp and wanted to tell him about it. It suddenly seemed important. But she was too tired to word it right. And he was too impatient to get back on the river.

"We've got Little Joe and Big Joe to get through." He kicked dirt on the fire till it died. "And then I promise you rest at Hardings Hole."

Goodyear drew blood from Glade's hand as he was stuffed into his bag.

"Take one thing at a time," Leah told herself. Little Joe wouldn't be as bad as Big Joe and she'd have practice on the little rapids first. But she wished she were back in Chicago with a ten-speed blender.

The Yampa rounded the bend in a rush.

The puny boat met a tumult of flying water that glanced off rocks in every direction.

Glade yelled something behind her that she couldn't hear over the angry clamor.

Leah remembered to clamp her knees tightly on the slimy rim of the boat before it pitched upward and then swooped nose down into a deluge of churning foam.

Something bludgeoned her in the nose. It may have been her paddle. Hair and water left her sightless. When she shot up again, the rubber boat was not between her legs.

Chapter Thirty-one

THE life jacket tried to buoy Leah up. The Yampa tried to pull her under.

It felt as if someone splashed a bucket of water in her face whenever she tried to breathe.

The river took charge of her body, doubling it up and then stretching it out, turning and twisting it through the water, hammering it against slippery rocks that she would cling to, and then breaking her hold easily to hurl her on to the next rock. It was impossible to swim.

She shot into the air, like a salmon trying to swim upstream, and thought she saw the boat bobbing far away before she spun around and water blurred her vision. The next time she could see, she found no boat. Nothing but crashing, swirling white . . . and the image of the dead bloated cow floating stiffly in a foamy eddy. . . . Had it met its death in rapids such as this?

The Yampa sucked her under. Sound faded but her heart pumped terror to her ears in swift measured plops. And then she shot to the surface, only to meet a boulder with the side of her head. The blow turned the white-water world to black . . .

. . . and a little girl swept way out on the end of a rope over a storm-tossed sea, came swooping down in a helpless screaming arc toward oily night water . . . and slammed into the side of a wooden sailing ship.

Pain seared the lining of her stomach and the heavy gun slapped against her hipbone in repetitious agony. Reality and sight returned.

Exhaustion numbed her. Her arms were too weak to grab for rocks; her legs, too heavy to move themselves and flung from side to side.

Leah floated on her face. Her head jerked up to cough and gasp for air. The water was calmer, quieter. A board floated past her watery vision and she dragged a leadened arm up through weighted water to grab for it. It was her paddle.

"If you're thrown from the boat, try to swim ashore and light a fire," he had said.

But the "shore" was rock cliff she couldn't have climbed if she'd had the strength to fight the current to get there.

"Leah! Leah, grab the boat." Something bumped her leg.

She held dully to the paddle and coughed up Yampa.

"Here, heave yourself over the side. Don't give up, Leah."

Slimy cold rubber brushed against her face. "I can't. . . ."

"Yes, you can. Damn helpless woman."

The paddle tore from her grasp. He placed her hands on the rounded pontoon. "Now pull yourself along to the front and crawl up over the rim. If I pull you in here, I'll capsize."

Leah moved hand over hand up the side of the boat even while being swept downstream. But she didn't have the strength to haul herself out of the water. The rim buckled as he lay over the duffels to grab her wrist.

She looked up into two dripping faces. One of them had the decency to look worried.

The other looked like the reincarnation of the devil, with whiskers.

With Glade's help she got her shoulders onto the rim. He gripped the waistband of her jeans and gave her a final hoist. The boat lurched, tipped, and Leah slithered face first into the water on the floor.

She turned over to lay with her head resting on the inflated pontoon, and he washed blood from her face with a sopping handkerchief.

"You're lucky to be alive, lady." His head disappeared and she could hear the pump working. He peered over the duffels and smiled. "Can you feel anything broken?"

"Yes. My spirit."

He laughed and stuck the pump on her side to clear the bilge there.

Leah watched the sky dreamily as it began to drop rain on her face.

"Well, we can't get any wetter." He started to tell her of the first time he'd "ridden" Little Joe, trying to sound casual. But he glanced up from his pumping to survey the river and stiffened.

"What?" She made an effort to raise her head.

"Big Joe. Grab the ropes on the gear and hold on. I'll try to solo this one." The horrible but familiar roar almost drowned out his voice.

Leah wound stony fingers through ropes and closed her eyes as the boat reared.

There hadn't been time to stuff the cat away and he slipped onto her lap from above, digging his claws into her clothing to stay with her, his body rigid. The downward swoop almost pulled her off the ropes and she knew Glade couldn't do it alone. She felt the careening swing as they turned a full circle, and then was amazed to find them through the rapids on smoother water.

"The river's so high now that it slips right over Big Joe," he said with triumph. "Hardings Hole coming up."

Leah stood on the firm sand of Hardings Hole. Her legs were still at sea and Glade had to steady her as they walked up from the beach.

Thunder rumbled and ricocheted off canyon walls. Rain fell like an avalanche. "What's that?" She reached out to touch a blob that appeared suddenly.

"A picnic table. And there's a grill set in concrete for roasting steaks—sorry, I didn't bring any—and that's—"

"You're kidding. People have picnics here?" Theirs had been the only boat on the beach.

"The river and the weather are usually more cooperative. And this, believe it or not, is a ladies." They approach a tiny green building. "Or maybe it's the men's. Anyway, it'll keep the rain off you until I get the gear into the cave. I didn't bring the tent." He shoved her into a foul-smelling outhouse and shut the door.

She used the facilities, listened to the rain, read the graffiti. On the inside of the door someone had scratched "To Be Is to Do—I Ching." Beneath it someone else had lipsticked "To Do Is to Be—Sartre." A later addition in ballpoint said "Do-Be Do-Be Do—Sinatra." The bottom line, again in lipstick, had closed the argument—"I Do Bees—De Sade."

Glade would have agreed with I Ching and Sartre. Committed, he'd said. And she knew she was—to him as well as the river. And this time she couldn't run from either of them. And she knew instinctively that there was no future in this commitment. If the Yampa didn't get them, someone at Split Mountain Ramp would. They'd both have a fatal accident or the goons. . . .

When she could no longer stand her thoughts or the smell, she stepped out into the clean cold water falling from the sky.

Goodyear arched in a puddle under the picnic table, shaking first one prissy foot and then the next in a four-legged imitation of the Charleston. Even his whiskers drooped.

Leah squelched over to the attached bench and sat. Rain washed the blood, clotted on her hair, in pink rivulets down the stringy blond strands lying over her breast. One of her pant legs was split to midthigh. Her ulcer had subsided to a duller but constant pain to keep the one on her temple company.

"You know, cat? All I need right now is the curse?" she said miserably and rubbed her sore head. "And then I'd just have it all."

A high cliff wall showed fuzzily through the rain and ghosts of other picnic tables not far off. Lightning split something apart on the rim high above and brought a wet cat to her lap. Leah snuggled him close and tried to shield him with her arms.

Glade, looking like a sailor in a squall, stomped by with duffels over both shoulders and disappeared around a corner of the cliff. When he came back for her, Leah carried Goodyear.

"He's shaking. Cats are susceptible to pneumonia."

"We'll light a fire for him."

"Fire! There can't be any dry wood for miles."

"All kinds of it in the cave." And he led her around the end of the cliff and up a narrow trail.

It was more of a shallow cavern, one whole side open, a smaller replica of the kind Indians used to build adobe cities in, high on steep canyon walls.

Blackened rocks rested in a ring around the charred remains of a campfire and a heap of twisted sticks and logs sat at the back.

Glade wrapped the trembling cat in a towel and found one for Leah.

She slid out of squashy tennis shoes and stood barefoot on the dry sandy floor while he broke sticks for the fire. When she peeled off her jacket she found it ripped up the back and strangely lightweight.

"Glade, I've lost the revolver," she said with her hand still in the empty pocket.

"Probably at Little Joe. I guess we're down to one." He struck a kitchen match on the boulder next to him.

"Surely no one will follow us down that river. Why do we need guns?"

"I expect our friends'll try to pick us up downstream. After we leave here, there's access to the river at several places if you disregard the law."

"I thought there wasn't any way out."

"Not that we could walk—it'd be too far. Frankly,

we're sitting ducks in that boat if there's someone on shore with a rifle. But if they sink us, they sink the papers. They're buried over there in the corner."

"When you hide something, you go all out." She pulled off her clothes. Her underpants had turned from white to the beige of the river and when she removed them they left a bikini outline of grit—tiny grains of dirt that the river had washed through her clothing. She could feel them everywhere on her drying skin with the tips of her fingers.

Glade dug in the corner with a stick, drew out a package of black pastic, and then stood staring at the wavering shadow Leah cast on the back wall of the cavern while the real Leah stood by the fire behind him toweling the remnants of the Yampa from her body.

She pulled her one change of dry clothing from a duffel and was dressed by the time he had his shirt off.

"On what glorious adventure did you get that?" She made an attempt at her old flippancy and ran a finger down the ugly scar with the funny dip at its base on his abdomen. "What's this, a dueling scar?"

The marvelous laugh rebounded off cavern walls. "Leah, I told you my clandestine life was very dull, didn't I?" He looked over his shoulder as if there were someone to overhear and pulled her close with that steel grip. "Actually, it's a knife wound, a dirty knife wound," he whispered. "That's where they took out my gall bladder in Santiago." And he laughed again when she pushed away. "The indentation at the bottom is from the resulting infection."

She spread out her sleeping bag by the fire.

"You're not the first blonde to fall for that, though."

"Oh, shut up!" She stretched out on her stomach with her face to the wall and watched *his* shadow.

"Leah, I didn't bring you on this trip to break your spirit." His voice turned serious, soft in one of those lightning mood changes.

"Why did you then?"

"I didn't know the river would be like this. And I don't trust Welker. He's a funny guy. And Leah"—he had a way of saying her name, when he wanted to, that made it

sound different from the name she'd heard all her life—
"when I came down before, it was a fantastic experience."

The naked shadow knelt and she could hear him rummaging through a duffel. The shadow bent over her shadow. "I wanted you to see the river and its canyon." He dabbed stinging fluid on the wound at her temple. "I thought . . . maybe you'd see why I have to do this thing with the papers."

"There isn't any oil shale on the Yampa."

"No, but the beauty here and on the Flat Tops will be robbed by shale." He massaged her neck and shoulders and she began to relax.

"There are other places like this but precious few left for a whole country. Have you seen what we've done to the Appalachians?" His hands moved up under her blouse. "All along the eastern slope of the Rockies there's a heavy population center hard pressed for water—"

"All I've seen is water since I got to Colorado."

"But this is an unusual year. And shale will bring whole new populations to the western slop. Those people will need water, too. Shale will take most of it just for processing." His weight moved over onto her buttocks and his hands worked down her back till her skin tingled.

She remembered Mr. Blum from across the street in Chicago. He'd raved about the bleeding-heart conservationist sissies in her mother's kitchen. What would Mr. Blum think of Mr. Wyndham?

"Think of canyons like this one, Leah"—he unhooked her bra—"filled with the debris from shale. Shale is mostly debris, you know, and dumping it into canyons is the best experts have found to do with it because it expands to—"

"I wish they'd do it right now. Then I could climb up out of here."

The warm hands left her back and he moved away.

Leah rolled over and sat up. She told the naked man who hunkered next to the fire about the bull elk she'd seen while waiting to turn herself in to the CIA and again experienced a sense of unreality. How strange to be sitting in a cavern talking of elk to a man who looked like an aborigine with his unruly mop of hair and exposed muscles.

He added wood to the flames. "You imagined it. No elk would get that close to a pack of dogs and a helicopter."

"Well, this one did. And . . . he was the most beautiful thing I've ever seen. His antlers were like trees and had a mosslike coating. He was enormous and his eyes were . . . watery and soft even with the terror in them. I wish you could have seen him . . . because there aren't words to tell you . . . and—"

"And all he asks is a place to live. Is that too much? To live outside the freedom of a zoo? Is it?"

"No. I want him to live"—they were suddenly back together on her sleeping bag—"but people need jobs, too. In Walden—"

"Other forms of energy produce jobs without taking so much clean air or water. That elk belongs to all of us, Leah. But most of all to himself."

Rain fell like a fourth wall to close them in with the fire. The shallow cavern filled with the smell of wood smoke. Goodyear, who looked as if he'd just been rescued from a clothes dryer, crawled onto their crowded bed and stared at them with amazement.

Glade had her half-undressed when a human voice outside yelled, "Up here! This way."

Chapter Thirty-two

GLADE jumped into his jeans, ran through a stream of profanity worthy of Mr. Blum, and zipped his fly with one hand while reaching for his revolver with the other.

If he wasn't trying to wake up, he was pretty fast on his

feet, Leah thought, putting herself back together in a rush.

The man who ran into the cavern stopped with one foot still in the air when he saw them and the revolver. "Oh."

"You startled us." Glade tried to smile.

"I'm sorry. I didn't know anybody else was at the Hole." He stood dripping and confused. "I've got a party coming up to get out of the rain, but we'll set up tents below." He took a step backward.

"No, that's all right. I just brought this for target practice and"—the revolver disappeared—"and you startled us," Glade repeated lamely. "There's plenty of room and it's bad out there."

The intruder still looked nervous and glanced over his shoulder as voices sounded on the trail. "Well, if we can share your fire, you can share our dinner. I'm Dave Randolf. . . ."

"Glade Wyndham." The two men shook hands through the smoke of the fire. "And this is Leah."

"How do you do, Mrs. Wyndham." Dave Randolf looked blessedly normal.

The cavern was suddenly crowded with people. Bleary-eyed with exhaustion, smoke, and suddenly doused desire, she managed to count fourteen, fifteen with Dave. Almost half of them were women and they all stood barely out of the rain staring at Leah and Glade as if they'd just discovered gate-crashers at a party. One expression on fifteen faces. . . .

Some of the men carried rocks, others Styrofoam coolers. One woman balanced three heads of lettuce and several others had round packages wrapped in aluminum foil. The gals wore floppy, dripping hats. Purses hung from their wrists.

"Won't you come in?" Leah said, trying desperately to adjust from Neanderthal back to civilization.

Dave Randolf made embarrassed introductions, while his party dripped the floor to mud. "We were going to barbecue dinner here and wait out the storm."

"Sounds good." Glade found a shirt to cover his gall-bladder scar.

Leah ran her fingers through her hair and realized her

bra was still un-hooked under her blouse.

"But if you—"

"No. That's fine. You're welcome. We just got off the river ourselves." Glade gestured toward the fire and the women moved to it as if they were one to comb out wet hair and apply lipstick while the men dug a pit in the cavern floor, heaped it with wood and rocks, and started another fire. Literally everyone chewed gum.

The ladies left Leah the space of her sleeping bag and regarded her with suspicion. Two Styrofoam coolers yielded pop-top cans of Dr. Pepper.

The level of suspicion in the crowded cavern hit the scarlet-for-danger point when Leah refused the Dr. Pepper and tipped the bottle of Maalox. She felt as if she'd just passed through a time warp.

Glade sat beside her with his pop can and smiled at the circle. "Medicine. My . . . wife has an ulcer and she went in the drink at Little Joe."

The assembly went silent, even to the last man at the pit, and suspicion turned to sympathy. One of the women moved to Leah's sleeping bag. "Did you really? It must have been awful."

"Is that where you got the bump on your nose and your head? I thought we'd all die there. . . ."

"Will you be all right?"

"How did you ever get out of that alive?"

Leah smiled at the general din and had another slug of Maalox. Soon everyone was retelling the hazards and their fears of the Yampa River.

"Mormons," Glade whispered in her ear. He raised his can of Dr. Pepper. "Otherwise this would be Coke or Coors."

The afternoon wore on and about wore Leah out. Pop-top rings littered the cavern floor.

"It's high time you spent a weekend at home with me, says I. (The kids don't even know what he looks like.) 'No,' says the river rat, 'you need to get away. Let me take you on a float trip.' Float!"

"Rayleen, I was down this river three weeks ago and got a sunburn. I can't help the weather," Dave said.

"Shut up, I'm not talking to you. So I had my hair done, bought two new pairs of slacks and . . . well, look at me!" Rayleen was plump and pretty even with her ruined hair. " 'Bring your swim suit,' says he, 'and get a tan while floating through the wonders of the canyon. See the wild animals on shore.' You know what I've seen? Exactly one dead sheep—domestic."

"Yeah, I wanted to take the kids and go to Disneyland."

"And I wanted to go see my folks."

"What kind of a line did you get, Leah?"

"You wouldn't believe me if I told you."

The pit began to give off delicious odors. Leah slept sitting up, for brief intervals.

"I didn't see your boat down on the beach." Dave sat beside Glade.

"I moved it up behind some trees. Didn't want it washed away. The river's so wild."

"I know. I'm worried about getting this herd out safely. Most of them have never run a river. Did you notice that there aren't any commercial trippers out? This time of year they're usually thick."

"I noticed that. What does it mean?" Glade's exhaustion began to show in the straining sound of his throat.

"It means the patrol has closed the river and we didn't get the word. It's probably sitting home in my mailbox right now. Yours, too."

Couples argued. Glade grinned into his Dr. Pepper. Leah longed for peace and rest. Somebody broke out a bag of peanuts and soon shells were added to the pop-top rings on the floor.

"Do you have any children?" the woman who sat next to Leah asked.

"No, we're not . . . I mean we don't."

"I'm Cindy." Cindy had short frosted hair that would have been cute if the Yampa hadn't been at it. Now she looked like an aging bedraggled pixy. "How long have you been married?"

Leah tried to focus. "Glade, how long have we been married?"

"Ahhh . . . three days."

"Hey, they're newlyweds!"

"No wonder we startled you," Dave said and seemed to relax a little.

Rayleen jumped to her feet as Goodyear emerged from behind the dwindling stack of fire wood. "What is *that?*"

"It's just our cat."

"That's a cat? You're taking a cat down the river?"

"See? I told you it was a stupid thing to do," Leah said to Glade, trying to sound married.

Goodyear had licked the plush pile of his fur back to order and apparently felt himself presentable.

Eventually the pit yielded whole cooked chickens, cornbread, and baked potatoes. Rayleen moved around with a bowl of tossed salad.

"For your ulcer." Dave handed her a paper cup of milk. He offered a long prayer thanking God for the food and permitting them to stay alive on the Yampa, while Leah's mouth watered agony.

"To a long happy marriage," Cindy toasted with milk.

"I don't believe this," Leah whispered to Glade.

Before they finished, the rain stopped and they carried their paper plates outside to watch the sun come out.

Leah forgot to eat. The Mormon couples stopped their arguments.

Hundreds of narrow waterfalls cascaded off high canyon rims. Sun lit rainbows in the spray of each one, clear, bright reds and lavenders and pinks and so many. . . . The sound of the brilliant dancing water almost drowned out the river below.

Sandy cliff walls that Leah had seen only through dreary rain came alive with sparkle. The heavy green of pine contrasted wherever possible. And the air had a freshness that gave Leah the tingles. "Now this, this I could say grace for," she thought.

"What does this remind you of?" Dave asked with a sigh.

"Reminds me that my dishwasher's on the fritz at home," Rayleen answered.

Waterfalls and rainbows lasted only minutes and then

vanished without trace. Leah wondered if she'd really seen them.

"Okay, let's all clean up the cave and leave these honeymooners alone," Dave said finally. "We'll set up camp below for the night."

Paper plates and cups made the fire roar. Rayleen disappeared with a sack of litter and Dave stopped on his way out. "There were two guys asking about a man and a woman this morning before we left Deer Lodge Park." He looked from Glade to Leah uneasily. "They described you two."

"What did they look like?" Glade described Brian and Charlie.

"No. They weren't like that. They looked . . . unhealthy somehow. They kept poking around an old pickup down in the trees. They weren't dressed like river boaters or tourists. They're hard to remember . . . one had a lot of hair with some gray in it. The other had his combed back and he had a bigger nose. I can see them but I can't . . . their eyes looked. . . ." Dave sighed and shook his head.

"Looked like what?" Leah flopped onto her sleeping bag.

"Their eyes looked . . . familiar . . . I don't know. . . ." He glanced at Glade. "Just thought I'd mention it." He left quickly.

"He's talking about the goons we saw in the restaurant." Leah stared at the fire.

"I know." Glade brought out the revolver and a bottle of oil and a rag. "I know."

Leah stepped out of the green outhouse and squinted at morning sunlight reflecting off the sandstone wall across the river. She hugged the torn jacket around her, wishing the sun would hurry to the bottom of the canyon.

The trash barrels spilled over in the wake of the Mormons. Goodyear's tail waved on top of one as he upended in trash.

"Listen, fatso, you're heavy enough." She pulled the tail and the cat connected to it emerged with claws extended.

206

Leah carried him down to the beach while he finished off a piece of bacon.

The Mormons sat on two boats with giant pontoon wiener-like tubes on each side, a long oar at each end, pieces of wood lashed between for floors already awash, and piles of gear roped in the center. No wonder they could carry all that food.

Floppy hats and heads bowed over bright orange life jackets as Dave finished a prayer, shouting over the incessant noise of the Yampa. "And, Lord, please safeguard us from the hazards of the river and guide us in safety through Warm Springs. Amen."

"Hi, Leah." Rayleen's smile was cold. "What is Warm Springs?" she asked her husband.

"Just look at the sunshine. Good day. Be thankful for sun," he answered.

The boats bobbed at their tethers like broncos at a rodeo.

"Good luck," Dave said to Leah. "Watch out for suck holes."

The men on shore cast off from the heavy poles in the sand and waded out knee-deep in water to jump onto the pontoons.

The river carried the fifteen Mormons and the last of civilization from her life with a speed that made Leah wince.

"Think we'll ever get back to the United States of America, kitty?" She carried him up the trail to the campground and turned to watch sun light the excited Yampa River, turn its spray to millions of shimmering crystals.

In the cavern Glade Wyndham slept like a baby on his stomach. "Hey, the CIA, FBI, and the entire goon squad are coming up the path with machine guns raised." She dropped the cat on Glde's head. "James Bond, where are you when I need you?"

"I don't think I'd be able to describe those two goons, either," Leah said over a granola and bouillon breakfast.

"You'll know them both when you see them." He appeared tense now that he'd awakened fully.

"What's Warm Springs?" she asked nervously as they carried duffels down to the beach. "Dave mentioned it this morning."

"As I remember, it's a rock slide area that spilled over into the river."

"And a suck hole? Dave said to watch for them, too."

Glade dropped his duffels on the sand and stared at the water. "Leah, I have the feeling that the river will be the least of our worries today."

She sat on the warm sand to retie a tennis shoe. "Where are the papers?"

Glade pulled up his shirt to expose the black plastic packet taped to his chest.

"It doesn't look very thick. What are these papers?"

"A series of letters relieving Enveco of the necessity to put the land back to rights after shale is mined, and tacitly agreeing that this fact shouldn't be publicized. It's impossible anyway."

"Why not just bury the debris back again?"

"By the time oil is extracted, the rock will have expanded and it'll be too much to rebury."

"So they'll dump it in canyons?"

"And leave it in mammoth piles where they found it. Rain will wash the heavy saline content from the exposed rock into rivers. Those rivers will become like the oceans and worse. It'll be very expensive to process the water for human use . . . what water'll be left."

"And the deal with Welker and Swords?"

"An agreement to investigate and make public the contents of these letters."

"And if they don't keep that agreement?"

"Norton, that reporter from the Denver *Post* will be at the campground at Split Mountain Ramp where we get off the river. He'll be camping there with his family. If it looks like a cross I'll give him the high sign. He's a conservationist and has a good friend at the Washington *Post*. Cal's son, Jerry, has a key to a bank box in Denver containing a Xerox copy of these letters plus one of the study we did for Enveco. If I give the sign to Norton, he'll call Jerry and the story will hit both papers simultaneously in three days. So, you see, Leah, it's not like I'm going into this blindly."

He tightened the ropes that held their gear to the beached rubber boat and explained that he, Norton, and his friend Ben had made this trip last fall when Glade had hidden the papers secretly, telling his comrades nothing.

He'd called Norton from Craig before he was picked up by the State Patrol and again from the restaurant there when Leah had seen him making a second phone call.

"Won't they be watching Jerry? They were all watching Cal, I know."

"By the time we hit Split Mountain Ramp everybody will be interested in only us. The dogs will have been called off Jerry."

"Why the three-day delay?"

"To give us time to disappear until things have cooled."

Leah picked up an unwilling Siamese. His fur was hot with sun. The river's roar was soothing, compared to what lay ahead of them.

"What's the matter?" He ran a finger across tears on her cheeks. But more kept coming.

"You big boob." She leaned over Goodyear to kiss hard lips. "They aren't going to let us disappear. Once they've got those papers, even if they don't know about Norton, they aren't going to let you live to tell this story . . . they can't. Where could you hide from the CIA anyway, even if you got out of the country?"

"I hid all winter. I've got friends."

"But they did find you. Welker told me everyone was waiting for you to use your supposedly secret bank account."

"I have a place to go and I'll take you with me." He pulled her back on the hot sand and Goodyear leapt away with a hiss.

"You won't live that long, Glade Wyndham. I probably won't either. If the Yampa doesn't get us, they will . . . and who will care?" She pressed a wet cheek against the scratchy beard. "No one will give up a blender today for air and water tomorrow, you blazing idiot."

Glade Wyndham made love to Leah on the beach of
Hardings Hole . . . leisurely . . . as if death could not be
waiting for them around a bend in the river . . . patiently
. . . as if Split Mountain Ramp was the last thing on his
mind.

The gritty sand semed to cool under the shade of their
bodies, began to feel as silken as satin sheets. . . .

"Leah, you know now, don't you? Why you wanted to
come with me instead of staying with them in Steamboat
Springs?"

The plastic that enveloped the Enveco papers rubbed
stickily against her skin.

Chapter Thirty-three

LEAH carried the doom feeling with her through the first
two rapids, but was soon perfecting her technique for sur-
viving a swollen Yampa.

"If I'm going down, it'll be fighting," she thought and
felt a pride she knew to be foolish.

What else could she do?

But the rhythmical, unmistakable clapping of helicopter
blades over the river's din drowned her newfound courage.

"Keeping track of our progress," Glade yelled behind
her.

"Who?"

"Who knows? It's everybody against Harper and Wyndham right now," he told her exultantly. Why didn't he fear
danger as she did?

Hundreds of feet above them a narrow slice of sky
shimmered between sandstone cliffs, and a noisy bug of
human making clapped warning directly over them. Leah

watched it until it was time to climb back onto the rim as white water churned ahead.

"You're getting the hang of it," Glade said when it was over.

Leah had time to let a snarling cat out of the duffel before he said, "Mantle Ranch, coming up."

The helicopter moved on and disappeared. The river widened, slowed, and quieted.

"This spread runs in and out of the canyon for miles. There's access by road here. Keep quiet now and pray that we can slip through."

Sun burned through her blouse and tangled wet hair, raised color and detail from the vegetation and rocks on shore and lent glitter to sky and water.

Two giant birds, funeral gray with black necks and formal white collars shot from the shoreline to walk across the water. Making a honking clatter, they spread magnificent wings, then lifted to join the sky.

"Canada geese," Glade whispered and she heard the click of his revolver.

"You're not going to shoot them?" She turned to meet a hard level stare.

"Not them. We didn't scare them up." He pointed ahead.

A helicopter, similar to the one that had dangled her into a mountain lake, sat in tall grass. Several men were running toward a boat like theirs on the edge of the river.

Brian and Charlie were in the boat and another man pushed them off.

Leah saw Brian raise a paddle and Charlie raise a rifle.

"Stop, Wyndham, or we'll stop you," Peter Bradshaw yelled from the shore.

"If you want the papers you'd better pray we get to Split Mountain Ramp!" Glade's paddle propelled them faster. But no shot was fired.

They rounded a bend in the river and Glade said, "Up on the rim and paddle like hell!"

Leah did as she was told and the Yampa responded by closing in its cliffs to narrow the water and speed up its mad rush. But it wasn't long before it stretched out again and their pursuers appeared behind.

"Damn fools," Glade muttered. "I wonder if either of them know how to run a river."

Leah was soon in the abyss of another angry rapids and then helping to pump out a wallowing boat. She watched with satisfaction as the boat behind her struggled through white water.

Brian and Charlie made it, though, following doggedly. Charlie had exchanged his rifle for a paddle.

"They can't risk drowning the papers—or me in case I haven't got them yet," Glade explained and then said softly, "Leah, there's a suck hole ahead. Don't panic, but we've got to paddle to the right . . . and we've got to start now."

She was on the gritty sun-scorched rim and paddling when she saw the low spume of water ahead, grayish below and thinning to white spray above. It didn't look that hazardous but she'd learned to respect the quiet warning in his voice.

Her wrists felt weak and her heart raced. She forgot the boat behind her as she fought the Yampa River.

They cleared the spume by several feet and she looked back to see a boulder the size of a house on the other side of it. The river glanced off the top, causing the spume and creating a hole in the water below . . . a deep hole with water rushing down in swirling vortexes on each side.

If they'd been torn from the main current and sucked into the hole they would probably have capsized or been pushed up against the face of the exposed rock and trapped there while the water spewing over from above filled the boat. To paddle out of the hole, they'd have had to paddle uphill as well as against the swirling vortex-created currents.

She watched for the boat behind them to try out a suck hole, but the Yampa made one of its unpredictable turns and she lost sight of it.

"If that doesn't get them, Warm Springs will." Glade's voice was casual.

The Yampa moved on . . . slowly one minute with side canyons and forests, furiously the next and shooting them between narrow cliffs. The river was as unpredictable as her spy and Leah lived from one minute to the next. She didn't think about a future she couldn't believe existed but gritted her teeth for the next challenge, proud to be alive when they had endured an obstacle.

A sign slipped by on the shoreline, brown with white lettering, WARM SPRINGS. She glanced over her shoulder to see Glade drawing duffel strings around the cat's whiskers, heard the mighty clamor of a river gone crazy somewhere ahead, felt the excitement under the boat.

The Yampa swung in a wide curve and spilled into a canyon of sun-dazzled spray.

A great heap of rocks lay in a jumble on one side, narrowing the channel of the gorged river to forty feet or less. Leah looked down on Warm Springs as the river took a sudden fall to reach it.

Needing reassurance, she glanced quickly back at Glade. He sat astride the other side of the boat, his paddle raised, his lips pulled back from his teeth, his eyes eloquent with anticipation.

The Yampa bellowed anger at being throttled through the narrow chasm and the boat rushed toward the fury of spray as the river speeded up to get through the narrows and out to the freedom of a flooded riverbed.

Water hurtled against boulders and shot into the air, it flew like projectiles off the cliff face. The front of the boat lifted as if mounting a roller coaster.

The downward swoop lifted her hair from her shoulders and she took a deep breath before an avalanche of water cascaded in heavy lumps from above, splashed up from beneath and flew at her from all sides.

"Wouldn't it be wonderful if I'd never come to Colorado?" And the Yampa jerked her outside leg off the rim and up into her face. Her knee slammed into her chin and she bit her tongue.

They hung up for an instant, tilting sideways, then the boat slipped off and she was paddling again. But her partner wasn't keeping up his end of the deal and they glanced off the side of a rock, swung around and rebounded off the cliff wall.

Leah ducked to escape the cliff's overhang that would have bashed her brains into the Yampa and fell headlong into the boat, clinging to the ropes and her paddle as the boat crashed into the cliff again.

Sun, rocks, spray, and cliff face revolved in confusion. All the thrills of a man-made carnival gone crazy and coming at her at once.

Swoop . . . dive . . . swirl . . . nausea. . . . She saw a moment of sky. Whirl . . . buck . . . bend. . . .

Leah saw a spit of land and choked out, "To the right!" But she could feel no help from behind as the tail of the boat tried to tear away downstream. Using every last ounce of strength, Leah fought to meet the shore and get off the demon river. Below the spit, sheer cliff walls closed in on both sides. If they didn't beach now, they'd lose the chance. Couldn't he see that?

Terror gave her muscles a final lift and the boat hit the spit so hard she fell forward on her face and over onto the shore. Grabbing the rim before the boat slid back into the water and skidding backward on her rear, Leah pulled it up onto the rocks and out of the tumult. She reached to free the drawstrings on a rollicking duffel bag and then realized that she had beached the craft alone.

Glade Wyndham was not in the boat.

Chapter Thirty-four

GOODYEAR squirmed out of a duffel that was half full of water and fell off the pontoon to the rocks below. He lay with his mouth open and his sides thumping quick short breaths.

Leah had no time to help him. A bright orange life

jacket had caught on a high rock at the bottom of the rapids.

Glade lay with his face hanging over into the water, his arms outstretched, shirt sleeves billowing as if he were bloated. The river washed over him, rolling him from side to side and finally rolling his body off the rock.

Leah grabbed her paddle and ran along the shore as he started to float downstream. She screamed his name and saw him raise his head and gasp for air, his nose streaming blood.

Stumbling over smooth, slippery-wet rocks she raced to the end of the beach where a slice of tall sandstone-cliff wall cut into the river. She had to reach him before he was swept past that point or she never would.

She waded in to her waist and found the next step a drop off. She backed away from it, her body reeling with the force of water released at last from the rapids.

"Glade!" Leah leaned forward and stretched out the paddle as far as she dared.

Glade flailed water, went under and bobbed to the surface, dark eyes molded a round, blank stare.

Another orange life jacket appeared behind him. Charlie wasn't grinning any more. He bounced off the rock that had caught Glade and shot into the air, his mouth forming a circle, his limbs waving in the mist.

Glade closed a hand on the paddle, but his weight pulled Leah off her feet and the two of them were hurtled against the side of the jutting cliff wall.

Charlie swept past and disappeared around the edge of the wall.

Leah found footing and dug in her heels, holding the paddle with one hand and pushing backward on sandstone with the other, as the water tried to pull him away to follow Charlie downstream.

Brian, clinging to his overturned boat, shot out of the rapids. "He . . . lp," he cried to Leah. Then he too was gone.

Glade lunged forward until his hands gripped shore and she pulled him in.

She rolled him over on the rocks above the water and

stuffed wads of wet Kleenex from her pocket into his bleeding nostrils.

Leah drank long from the bottle of chalky Maalox and then capped it.

The supine cat beside her finally stirred to roll over and hump and retch, as he had so long ago before a plane had chased them all under the bushes. Leah felt suddenly as if she'd known the cat and the man all her life. What had happened to Leah Harper that these two could command a piece of her independence, could insinuate themselves into her dreams, her plan for living? Why had this waited to happen to her until it was too late? Life seemed very precious now.

Hot sun began to dry her clothes. She sat with knees pulled tight to her chest and watched the man pace up and down the rocky shore, hugging himself and shaking.

Leah giggled and couldn't stop it before it turned to laughter.

Glade stopped to stare murder. "Will you tell me what is so goddamned funny?" The low deadly voice lost its effect when shaken with tremble spasms.

"You." And she laughed again and walked down to him. "You were scared . . . you . . . the great big he-man spy. Death scares you, too." She ducked his sideswipe and, still laughing, sat helplessly on the rocks.

"Well, what the *hell* did you expect?" He resumed his pacing. "I came up under the boat twice . . . there's no air under there . . . and almost drowned . . . and what do I get? A laugh!"

"Oh, you want sympathy . . . that's good. Like I got at Little Joe?"

Glade lifted her to her feet and she buried her face in his wet shirt, wound her arms around him. His body shuddered against her.

"I saved your big, dumb life. For what, I don't know. For the Yampa or the goons or Welker or Bradshaw? Why did I bother?"

"Leah, we've still got a chance. This isn't Russia or. . . . There are going to be too many groups vying with each other at Split Mountain Ramp for anybody to quietly do away with us. That's why I set it up that way."

"I just don't trust anyone anymore." She tightened her arms and wished that her dark-browed protector hadn't revealed his fear.

They were back on the river, Glade using a piece of driftwood for the paddle he had lost at Warm Springs.

"What's the next surprise?" Leah marveled at how well her ulcer was withstanding the shocks of the river.

"Nothing like Warm Springs. But there is Echo Park coming up. There's access to the river there, too."

She sat rigid and silent and tried not to think.

"You're upset, aren't you? Because I can be afraid. Leah, what do you want from a mere mortal? Everybody knows fear. You want perfection."

"But you've always been so steely. And if we've got danger ahead. . . ."

"You'd feel better if you had your murderer back." Resignation in the cold monotone.

"Yes . . . no. . . . Oh, I'm just scared."

"Yet you were angry when I killed two goons. What do you think I'm going to do if we meet up with some more of them, try to talk them out of it? Those men at the condominium were skulking around with silencers just waiting to pick me off."

"Then how did you kill them?" She turned to the grim lips over the cleft in his chin where the beard didn't grow, the massive brows, the wide square forehead under dark tumbled curls and thought sudenly, "I've never wanted to live this badly in my life."

He relaxed a little. "I crept up—"

"No." Leah reach a hand over the duffels and past the Siamese. "I really don't want to know how you killed . . . I really . . . didn't want to love you either. . . ."

He took her hand. "You want a fairy-tale lover. Strong and competent and too gentle to defend himself. You sound like the rest of the country."

"I just don't believe in killing."

They managed the next rapids like a professional team,

but then it wasn't Warm Springs. While they were still pumping out, a voice hailed them ahead. Brian waved from a rock near shore.

As they paddled toward him, Brian stood up, looking bedraggled and anxious. He put his hands in the air. "I'm not armed."

"I am," Glade said coolly. "Where's Charlie?"

"I lost him." He ran fingers through thin, wet hair, and when he climbed into the boat, he almost swamped them.

They proceeded down the river with each man sitting on opposite sides of the rim behind her, but the extra passenger put Leah higher in the air.

"I . . . never knew a river could be like this. Thanks for picking me up."

And Leah wondered why they had. Everyone seemed to be the enemy now.

"You really did a job on those goons," Brian said with awe and not too comfortably.

"Echo Park is coming up soon," Glade countered. "Does your boss plan to meet us there? Or Bradshaw?"

"I think so, but they don't want to kill you, Glade, honest."

"Then why not wait till I get to Split Mountain Ramp? What's the goddamned hurry?"

"They're afraid the goons'll get to you first. We got word that there were more than the two you took care of and. . . ."

"And everybody wants to be in on the kill. Bradshaw and Welker don't trust each other."

"Listen, Wyndham, the bureau wants to help you. If you'd only listen to Joe. You don't want to end up with the agency and Bradshaw alone—"

"Where's Swords?"

"He's flying in."

"He'd better be."

And then they passed Charlie. He floated in a slow death circle in an eddy near the shore, face down and unresisting, his hair streaked with foam. Leah swallowed and looked away. The Yampa had given her retribution. It was not a pleasant feeling.

"Leah, there's a paddle coming up on your side. Grab it," Glade said calmly as if Charlie's body did not exist.

Cottonwoods and sandbars appeared around a curve in the river.

"You've got to trust the bureau," Brian continued his argument.

"Echo Park," Glade announced softly.

A mountain rose in the middle of the river with sun glaring down on it so hard it almost made sound. A looming formation of sandstone and across from it a haven of grass and giant trees in a long valley. Leah heard birds singing and longed to beach the boat there forever in peace and rest and off the rampage of water.

But she changed her mind when they skirted a sandbar and the river turned at the base of the barren mountain.

A truck parked along the shore of Echo Park and in the water next to it an empty rubber boat. . . She turned to warn Glade just as Brian said, "The bureau is your only chance. You can't trust the agen—" He stopped with a surprised jerk as a cracking sound echoed back from the sandstone mountain. A small . . . reddish hole appeared in the middle of his face. His knees rose to hide the hole as he tipped off the pontoon rim and disappeared.

"Paddle!" Glade screamed at her. "Keep your body moving back and forth."

Leah wanted only to scrunch up in the bottom of the boat, close her eyes, and hope to ride it out. But the weapon that made that hole in Brian's face could deflate the boat and put a hole in her easily. She thought of Sheila and paddled any which way, bobbed forward and back, and they moved like a car gone wild with a drunken driver along the edge of Echo Park.

One second she was looking at a swirl of sky with sandstone mountain jutting into it, and the next—murky river and black rubber. "A bullet would be a faster way to die than drowning," she thought and heard the clapping of helicopter blades over the sound of her heart and the Yampa. Brian's friends had arrived too late.

The helicopter lowered behind cottonwoods and two

men with long weapons broke from the trees and ran toward the boat tethered to the shore.

"Now, straight ahead and balls out!" Glade commanded. "Pray for rapids so they'll have to paddle instead of aim. The cavalry has saved us only for the moment."

Where the sandstone mountain ended, another river joined them and they swooped ahead on the force of the combined waters.

"Where's Goodyear?"

"Our feline crawled into the bag when Brian left us. Faster, Leah, they're gaining. Be prepared for dodging tactics again when I yell."

They zoomed ahead. The river and Glade's strong arms sent them on so fast, Leah felt her paddle wasn't contributing much.

"I didn't want to love you either," a voice announced behind her. "And I wish I'd never gotten you into this."

"Can't you shoot back?"

"I don't have the range they do."

The river dropped in a whoosh with the familiar roller-coaster feeling but without the rapids and Leah heard the rifle's snap.

"Leah, are you hit?"

"No."

"A bullet just slammed into the bag behind you. Move from side to side this time, keep your head low, and dodge!"

Her spine prickled, waiting for the searing bullet. She rocked back and forth and river and sky and trees whirled in front of her.

"Suck hole ahead," he yelled. "Guide to the left!"

Aching muscles paddled on adrenaline, sweat pierced pores to join the mist flying back at her off the rim. Her breathing and heartbeat drowned the sound of the Yampa and a spume of water loomed ahead.

There wasn't much room to maneuver between the approaching suck hole and the cliff face that formed the bank. They headed straight toward the cliff wall.

"Back off!" Glade yelled.

She fell into the boat to escape the scraping stone.

"You're strong enough when you're scared," Glade gasped.

The other boat approached the suck hole.

Both men paddled now, both wore life jackets. The one in front had more nose than the other and was more slender. His hair lifted as the boat scraped the mammoth boulder and swung around to enter the suck hole backward. Glade had been right. She knew them when she saw them. They were the men Leah had seen in the restaurant in Craig.

Chapter Thirty-five

GLADE raised his revolver and sighted along a tree limb. They had pulled over to shore and hidden the boat behind trees to watch for the goons.

"They couldn't have made it out of that suck hole." Leah licked the chalk of Maalox from her lips.

"Some types can get out of anything. What I saw of those two makes me scared as hell. When we're on the river they've got the advantage and the range. We'll wait."

They waited. No boat. No goons. Leah relaxed.

"I don't like it," he said. "I don't see any debris from their boat coming down river."

When they entered the river again, Glade was quiet. He kept glancing over his shoulder. It made her uncomfortable.

Surely the only danger lay ahead at Split Mountain Ramp now and on the river itself. Those men could not have survived that suck hole.

She'd forgotten their faces already. She could visualize

221

their boat and life jackets, their arms swinging paddles. . . .

"Glade, I feel a little sick."

"We forgot lunch. Have some granola. We'll stop at Jones Hole for tonight."

At dusk a sign announced Jones Hole. Leah had the odd thought that in no matter what outlandish place she found herself, there were always signs.

The Mormons' giant pontoons were pulled up on the beach and in the process of being unloaded. There was soon a crowd to welcome them in.

Dave helped Leah from the boat. "We didn't figure you'd make it out of Warm Springs in that little boat. We kept pulling over and waiting for you. Haven't been here long ourselves."

"We got a late start. Is the ranger here?" Glade pulled the boat out of the water and Goodyear took off through the trees.

"No. River's closed and he left. I just broke into his cabin and used his radio. The patrol's going to sweep the river for you two. Guess I panicked."

"Did all of your party get through?" Leah asked.

"Yes, but we've got several hysterical women. They're lined up at the outhouse."

Leah stumbled past the ranger's cabin and picnic tables to a clearing on the other side of a grove of trees. The women greeted her with relieved exclamations and she took her place at the end of the line.

Leah learned that she was now in Utah but that these Mormons came from Denver.

"You know," Rayleen said, "we were just taking a tally and realized that if we don't make it off this river, we will orphan a total of twenty-seven children."

They bowed their heads beside the foul-smelling building and Cindy, of the bedraggled pixy haircut, led a prayer of thanks that they had all survived their day on the river.

Leah prayed with them.

"You look positively green, Leah." Rayleen sat next to her at the picnic table. "You've sure got your work cut out for you. Any man who would bring a bride with an ulcer on a river-trip honeymoon . . . and then have nothing along to eat but granola. . . ."

Once again the Mormons shared their food with them. They'd boiled eggs for Leah. Everyone else had steak.

"How long have you had your ulcer?" someone asked from across the table.

"Since about fifth grade."

"How could you mistreat your body that much that early?" The entire table hushed to hear her answer.

"The doctor said it was because I was jealous of my younger sisters." Leah had the feeling no one believed her.

Dave changed the subject. "I called the patrol back to tell them you'd made it. But they'd sent a boat out already."

Leah wondered what the river patrol would think of the bodies scattered along the way. She took a tranquilizer, then found her sleeping bag and crawled off away from the Mormon tents while Glade helped them clean up.

The morning song of hundreds of robins awakened her, a warbling cacophony of bird song that filled the tall cottonwoods of Jones Hole. The natural symphony was ruined only by the itching of her sunburn and the giant Siamese sitting in the grass next to her head.

He was washing fresh blood and downy gray feathers from his face.

"How could you, cat? You bad, nasty. . . ."

Goodyear looked at her coldly. Not for the first time, he reminded her of Glade Wyndham. He crept forward to sniff her face.

Leah gathered him to her. "I know nature tells you to eat birds even if your stomach is full of Kal Kan, but I can't accept it somehow."

Glade walked toward her between two tents. He handed her a cup of milk and an egg. "I hard-boiled it for you last night."

He chewed Granola while she ate the egg. "We've got

223

to get out of here and to the Ramp before the Mormons do. It's only about four hours away. If there's any trouble we don't want to involve them." Tired worry lines creased the corners of his eyes and pulled down the edges of his lips. "But first there's one last thing I want to show you. It's early and I think we have time. How do you feel?"

"Pretty good, considering." She didn't like the sound of the one *last* thing.

He looked as if he'd slept little. This was the dawn of his big day. Today would prove if his "hapless little crusade" would bear fruit or end in disaster.

Because she had grown to care, Leah choked on the last of her egg. She didn't trust the people waiting at Split Mountain Ramp. She tied on river-stiffened tennis shoes and took his hand to follow him into the sweet, fresh morning. Goodyear stayed behind, curled up on the warm spot she'd left in the sleeping bag.

The smell of summer green, of cottonwood leaves, tall dewy grass, and earth came alive as sunlight lowered to the canyon floor. He led her across the clearing, away from the camp.

The richness of bird song followed them as they climbed a gentle trail to a rock-strewn canyon.

"If I don't die today, I must remember this," she thought and breathed in unsullied morning, felt through her jeans the cool wet of waist-high grass that overhung the path, saw the textured depth of sky, and tried to ignore the clouds gathering at its edges.

She tugged at Glade's hand to stop him, turned him around, and kissed him. "For this I could almost forgive you the Yampa River."

"But we're not there yet."

"What more could there be?"

"Indian pictographs."

Leah laughed. "We're not four hours from Split Mountain Ramp and you want to show me pictographs."

The sun warmed her shoulders, gentle sweetness enveloped them. The canyon walls took on a redder hue, adding to the rich colors of land and sky. Leah wished that they would never have to return to the river. She felt at peace with surrounding nature . . . a part of it rather than an alien.

"There." He stopped in the middle of the path and pointed.

She had to search the canyon wall opposite to find the dark scrawl on its face. Primitive figures of animals and people, one-dimensional and in fading black, defaced rocky grandeur. Undecipherable geometric patterns in peeling yellow orange . . . the mere scratchings of puny man.

"Probably four to six hundred years old," he said in wonder.

"Early American graffiti," Leah answered, unimpressed, and looked down the canyon that had outlived the Indians and would outlive her. Her own insignificance in the pattern of things was important only to her. For a moment Split Mountain Ramp seemed to matter less.

He turned to start back but she stopped him, wrapped her arms around him, and buried her face in his jacket. "Glade, I'm beginning to see why you're doing this thing . . . this mission you've chosen. But I still wish you didn't have to. I wish we could go off somewhere together, get to know each other without all the fear and danger."

"Hey, we will." He tipped her chin back so that she had to look up at his darkness against the blue brilliance of the sky. "As soon as this is over. Someplace nice and quiet. Who knows, I might even convince you to stop running away from things."

When "this" was over, Leah thought, they'd probably be under arrest at best and at worst. . . . But what if they did make it? What if the impossible happened?

"I came to Colorado to prove I could stand alone . . . and now. . . ."

"But you have proved it. Look at all you've survived. And you alone saved my life at Warm Springs. You've proved you're not helpless, Leah. I doubt you ever were." He pushed her away to look at her and tucked a strand of hair behind her ear. "You know, you're beautiful when you're a mess." And his voice was almost soft, almost dreamy as it had been once when they climbed toward the rim of the Flat Tops.

They dawdled on their way back, saying nothing, knowing that minutes counted yet unable to hurry.

The smell of burning bacon mingled with the first odors of the river and the outhouses as they approached. The Mormons were up.

They walked faster.

A woman screamed and a shot exploded ahead; the sky above the cottonwoods of Jones Hole filled with frantic robins.

Glade pushed Leah behind a thick tree trunk but not before she'd glimpsed the incredible scene near the picnic tables.

The Mormons stood in a long line facing two men who still wore their orange life jackets and had their backs to Leah.

Sunburned faces were shocked to ashen. Pairs of tennis shoes, streaked with dried river tan and their toes curling upward, still sat around a low concrete grill.

Breeze jerked at tent flaps, played with the paper wrappers of food on the tables, and hummed in whispers through cottonwood leaves.

"The next time will be for real," a rather undistinguished voice said clearly, "if you don't tell us where they are . . . and now."

"Stay here," Glade whispered against Leah's ear and moved with catlike stealth to the next tree and then to the next.

A coherent thought finally disengaged itself from the whirl in her head . . . had he remembered to oil the revolver in his hand since Warm Springs?

"They were here but they left before we got up," a sickened voice said.

"Their boat and their cat are still here. You're lying." His gun went off and again birds screamed overhead.

Leah peered around her tree in time to see Rayleen slump to the earth.

Leah tasted blood but she was past knowing if it was from her stomach or if she'd bitten her tongue. She stooped to dislodge the heavy rock at her feet from its dirty bed.

Partly in a dream stupor and partly in a rage, she stepped out of the shelter of the tree. Her feet seemed to float. Her skin tingled with the onset of shock. Her senses were stimulated beyond reason . . . sight, sound, color . . . even the feel of the cold rock in her hands seemed unbearably exaggerated.

Dave Randolf fell to his knees beside his wife, oblivious to the armed men.

Goodyear sat beneath a picnic table eating stolen bacon, unmoved by the horror around him.

Leah heard the faint click of Glade's revolver some distance to her left, saw one of the goons turn as if in slow motion . . . and fire.

Glade's gun went off at the same time and both men crumpled.

Glade Wyndham lay stretched out and still . . . with his face in the dirt of Jones Hole.

Leah registered loss and regret even as she raised the rock above her head. The man in front of her had turned slightly when Glade and the other goon fired, then snapped his head back to cover the Mormons, and as Leah jumped into the air, he began to turn again to check behind him.

Her full weight brought the weight of the rock down with a sickening crunch. The shock of rock hitting skull reverberated up her arms to her neck and shoulders. His gun fired as he fell and the sound jerked every muscle in her body.

The rock lifted of its own volition and came down again . . . up and then down yet again . . . and Leah's scream lifted to mingle with those of frightened birds.

She stepped back and watched the Mormons' eyes rise from the grisly mess at her feet to her face. Disgust and incredulity hardened to blankness as fourteen faces closed against her.

Chapter Thirty-six

FOR a moment, Leah Harper had stood alone. And there was blood on her hands.

She could smell it . . . it had spattered across her clothes. The man was truly faceless now.

"I wish . . . I wish we'd never met you," Dave choked. He stared at Leah and turned back to help Cindy tear away Rayleen's pants leg. "Her knee is shattered. She'll never walk on this leg again."

Rayleen lay unconscious as her friends stirred from their shock to help her.

Another man checked for a pulse on the man that Glade had shot. "Dead. I'll go use the ranger's radio."

Leah clasped bloody hands around the pain in her stomach and staggered to where Glade lay face down in the dirt. More blood, and she almost slipped in the dark pool by his shoulder as she turned him over.

There was a pulse in his neck.

She grabbed a dishtowel left to dry on a tree branch and stuck it under the hand pump on the concrete platform.

"Here, I'll pump. You hold it," Cindy said without expression.

They tore away Glade's shirt and washed the wound on his arm. Someone else wiped the dirt from his face.

Glade opened his eyes but he didn't seem able to focus.

"The bullet's gone through, I think," said a man she had met but didn't know. He made a tourniquet and twisted the knot with a kitchen knife, as he had done for Rayleen's leg.

People were cold but helpful. Glade was lifted from his

blood pool and transferred to his sleeping bag.

Leah crouched beside him, reeling through waves of nausea, her arms hugging her knees.

Cindy brought her a cup of milk. "If you hadn't . . . done what you did, they'd have killed some or all of us," she said in a daze. "It's just that . . . if we'd never met you we wouldn't have gotten involved in this . . . and . . . Rayleen has five kids and. . . ." She shrugged helplessly.

Someone brought a first-aid kit and worked on Glade's arm. He groaned.

Leah left to find her Maalox. When she returned, Glade was talking to the Mormons and Goodyear had stretched out beside him.

"I hear you killed someone," he said, when they were alone. His skin was deathly pale around the dark beard stubble.

The man and the cat stared at Leah with the same expression in different-colored eyes.

She rose to get him water without speaking.

"Don't," she said when he sat up to drink it.

But he took the cup, drained it, and lay back down. "We've got to get out of here."

"How? On angel wings? I'm sick and you're wounded."

"The river's not that bad from here to the ramp." Someone had taken the precaution to bandage him from the elbow to the tourniquet.

"You're delirious. There aren't just two dead men over there. There's a mother with a busted leg. If you think these people are going to let us leave, you're nuts. You should see how they've been looking at me. Besides, neither one of us is in any shape to face Split Mountain Ramp."

Glade sat up again and winced. "I told them that there was a possibility that more trouble was coming down the river, that they were better off without us."

Leah looked over her shoulder to find all the Mormons on the far side of the campground. "But they've radioed for help from the ranger's cabin."

"It'll be a while in coming and they know it." A corner

of black plastic showed where his shirt had been torn away. "Leah, please?"

"You don't know what the river is really like in flood. You've admitted that . . . I just want to live . . . in peace"—she thought of their brief morning idyl—"with you. And I promised to call my sister. . . ."

"Leah?"

"Oh, what the hell!"

Leah dunked herself in the dun-colored river to wash away the red of blood.

A strange boat had been pulled up on the beach. It was longer than the one Glade and Leah used and had two board seats with a large wooden box in between for supplies. Lettered in black across the top of the box were the words "River Patrol."

So the goons *had* lost their boats in the suck hole. But they'd lived to capture another boat when the patrol came down the river. And Leah was certain there were more bodies upstream where this boat had been taken.

The Mormons had helped to load the boat and Glade sat now in Leah's place at the front. He held a struggling Goodyear on his lap. Leah crawled into the back and felt strong arms push them off.

They left Jones Hole without good-byes.

The sweat of illness felt clammy on her skin, mixing with river grit and spray.

They entered a canyon where whirlpools played with the current, but troubled them little if Leah steered down the middle.

Goodyear sat on the duffels behind Glade, eyes squinted to slits against the glare of sun on water, tawny fur sparkling with mist beads.

She could see the end of the silly kitchen knife that still held a loosened tourniquet in place. The black head in front of her bobbed with the motion of the boat. "How are you feeling?"

"A little weak," he said thickly. "But the pain is strong enough."

"Well, don't climb the rim. I'll try to get us through.

230

You've lost a lot of blood and you'd probably get dizzy and fall off."

The whirlpool canyon ended and the river widened, sprawled, slowed. They had to pick their way around islands, some with bushes and a few live trees. A prehistoric setting. It seemed so remote from their planned destination that Leah relaxed and trailed her fingers over the side of the boat to wash away the vestiges of red that still clung to her cuticles.

Sun on pink-red buttes . . . an eagle floating in lazy circles, his shadow diving off sandstone and crossing the water.

She noticed the spreading stain on Glade's bandages and tightened the tourniquet. If only she hadn't had to kill. . . .

At least there shouldn't be any goons left and she felt more confident with the river. . . . "Glade, I've revived enough to want to start hoping again. Is there really a chance for us at this ramp place?"

"Well . . . the agency will be watching the bureau. And the bureau will be watching the agency. . . ."

"Who will be watching out for us?"

"Swords, I hope. Leah, we're not going to meet a firing squad at Split Mountain Ramp. I've said I'd hand over the papers to Welker if he could prove something would be done about them and they wouldn't get lost in the paper mill. What Bradshaw will do at the final moment, I don't know. He's got orders to get those papers, too."

"Why can't they investigate together? They work for the same government."

"They want to use them as leverage. In case there's a scandal, both agencies want to know what's going on and whom to threaten in case their organizations get pulled into it . . . it's called information gathering, CYA."

"And what can this Swords do?"

"He's the highest-ranking guy I know personally. He's also hard-core honest. Drives everybody nuts but he's powerful enough to get away with it. He can get us out of there at least. I'd rather be in his custody than theirs."

He lay back on the duffels. The dark brow had turned almost white.

"Which organization does he work for?" She reached around the Siamese to touch his cheek.

"Neither. He's part of a quasi-liaison group between the two, among other things. This group or committee was set up by presidential commission to coordinate the work of the two, but recently has been used to keep tabs on both the bureau and the agency." He drew her hand down to kiss her palm. "He's not a sure thing, Leah. But Swords is better than nothing."

"Does he really care about my elk and the places we've seen?"

"That I don't know." And Glade slept through the rest of the slow-moving island-filled park.

He awoke to help her through the rapids that followed, seated on the floor of the boat and resting during quiet stretches. The interminable morning wore on.

"Split Mountain Canyon," he said as towering walls moved in on them and he crawled onto the rim against her protests, almost toppling off more than once. A helicopter droned far above in a slit of sky.

Leah prayed to a faceless god called Swords. Cliff swallows flew about tiny holes far above. The red stain spread horribly across the bandages on Glade's arm.

"Split Mountain Ramp coming up," Glade yelled back at her and fell into the boat.

They shot out of the canyon.

Chapter Thirty-seven

HANDS pulled the boat ashore onto asphalt paving. Hands lifted Leah from it.

Hands helped Glade stumble up the asphalt rise.

Hands pulled duffels from the boat and searched them, pulled a sopping ball of fur from one and discarded it. Quite a crowd had gathered at Split Mountain Ramp to welcome them.

Leah faced Joseph Welker and Peter Bradshaw. She slipped a protective arm around the dripping, bleeding man next to her. "He must get to a hospital. The goons—"

"Where are the papers, Miss Harper?"

"Where's Swords?" Glade asked and then pitched forward, taking Leah with him.

More hands unscrambled their bodies and she was pulled to her feet. They rolled Glade over, tore open his shirt, and ripped the black plastic packet from his torso. Bradshaw removed the revolver from Glade's pocket.

Glade lay motionless on the asphalt, his eyes closed.

"Where *is* Swords, Mr. Welker?" Leah demanded.

"Apparently he's late." Welker took the letters from their waterproof packet and rifled through them, looking at the bottoms of the pages as if checking signatures. He winced more than once as he read.

"A deal's a deal, don't forget," Peter Bradshaw said and held out his hand. Welker divided the papers and handed over half of them. "You get copies of ours when I get copies of yours. And no substitutes, Joe."

"What about the deal you made with Glade?" Leah said it overloud, hoping that one particular man at the edge of the crowd could hear and that the man was Norton, the reporter. He was the only one who looked like a camper.

Bradshaw rolled his eyes in disgust.

But Welker said, "I'm afraid this is a little more involved than I thought, Miss Harper. These things take time. I'm afraid immediate disclosure would be unsuitable at present, but I assure you that matters will be investigated—"

"In other words, you're not going through with the deal as planned."

"There are extenuating circumstances here that. . . ." He continued with the meaningless jargon and wasn't even listening to himself as he glanced through the Enveco papers.

Leah caught a glimpse of the man in tennis shoes and rumpled sport clothes as he ambled off around the various cars at the top of the ramp and disappeared.

"Meanwhile, you're going to let this man lie here and bleed to death?"

"Of course not." Joseph Welker signaled absently to two of his men who carried Glade to the top of the ramp.

Leah started after them.

"Just a moment, Miss Harper. I want a full report of what happened to the others on the river with you. We found Brian." He didn't even look up from the papers in his hand.

"Warm Springs got Charlie, the goons got Brian, we got the goons, and there's a perfectly innocent woman with a badly wounded leg at Jones Hole, thanks to the goons. Put that in your damn file!" She turned away. "I hope those papers are worth the death count."

"Miss Harper, Leah . . ." Welker began patiently, but Leah didn't wait to hear him out.

She stopped only to pick up a drooping cat. Goodyear had lost weight on the river.

Cal Wyndham met her at the top of the ramp. "What's happened to my brother? He looks—"

"Somebody shot him this morning."

Glade lay on a picnic table. One of Welker's men cut

234

away soaked bandages. Another held a thermometer in his mouth.

"It's clean. He's lucky. But he's going to need blood."

Campsites, a few tents and campers. The outhouses here were fancier than those on the river and made of concrete blocks. Leah was beginning to dry, aware of the heat of the place.

"Who shot him? Why?" Cal hovered between Glade and Leah, his face red with heat and anger. "I wish I could understand some of this—"

"Cal, I don't think I could explain it right now."

"First they tell me he stole something and then. . . ." He shook his head helplessly and stomped back to watch Glade being rebandaged.

Leah sat on a bench and stared at the paved parking lot that seemed to undulate in the sun. In front of it was a phone booth of all things . . . or rather a phone on a metal pole with plastic shields enclosing the call box. The man in the tennis shoes hung up the receiver and stepped away.

"I must call Annette," she thought dumbly and started toward the parking lot. Dizziness overtook her and she leaned against a tree.

The tennis shoes blurred as they approached her. "Will Glade be all right?"

"I think so. Are you Norton?"

"Yes. Everything's taken care of. I figured he was unable to give any sign, but I heard your conversation. I put the call through just now. You've got three days. And"— he touched her arm—"thanks." The tennis shoes hurried away.

"Don't mention it." Leah slumped to the ground, her back against the tree trunk. Goodyear hunched next to her, eloquent bad humor on his chocolate face.

"Leah?" Glade called fuzzily from the picnic table.

But she couldn't get up to go to him.

Joseph Welker and Peter Bradshaw walked by, arguing in low voices, and stopped in front of her as a car drew into the parking lot. Two men stepped out.

"Mr. Swords . . ." Welker and Bradshaw said at once.

"Gentlemen. How are you?"

Leah stared at all the polished shoes milling around in front of her.

"I see you have everything under normally poor control," Mr. Swords said. "Will he live? Who's this?" Soft watery eyes stared down at Leah.

"His current. . . ."

"Do I take her, too?"

"And me!" Cal's anger had reached his voice.

"And who are you?"

"I'm mad. Damn bunch of John Waynes around here. Nobody's taking my brother without me."

"Hum, well it looks like we mustn't waste time." Swords turned to Bradshaw. "I assume you have what you want. Kindly help Frank here transfer Glade and . . . his assembly to my car."

"But—"

"Now!"

Arid, sun-bright scenery whizzed past car windows. Leah sprawled in a semisitting position next to Cal in the back seat, Glade's head heavy on her lap, his knees blocking the view on the other side.

She tried to focus on the face that turned to her from the front seat. The great god Swords was small, balding, and not particularly reassuring.

"Sorry I was detained," he apologized. "Tell me what has that . . . creature got to do with anything?" He pointed to the blimp sitting sphinxlike on Glade's chest.

"He's my . . . our cat. Mr. Swords, we have three days to disappear—"

"I have just the place in mind . . . nice and quiet and restful and. . . . Frank, phone ahead for medical help, will you? There's a plane waiting not terribly far from here. Three days? Why? Oh, I see. The proverbial feces will hit the proverbial fan . . . i.e., the press. I'm sorry to hear it's come to that. You're sure?"

"Yes, it's done. A deal is a deal and they reneged so—"

"Now, now . . . don't take it so hard. I'll arrange for an extended stay . . . in a most healthful clime."

"Leah?" Glade called again.

236

She bent over and kissed him and whispered. "We're with Swords now."

"Good." He relaxed and she combed dark curls with her fingers, but eyes filling with tears.

"You going to tell me what's happening?" Cal whispered, his hand balling into a massive fist where it lay over Glade's body. "I mean, is this guy all right? I didn't much like that last bunch."

"Glade seems to think we can trust him. I hope so. Neither of us is up to another fight." Leah hoped the whishing of the car's air conditioning covered the sound of her whisper as she tried to fill Cal Wyndham in on what had been happening. By the time she finished the car had pulled off onto a dusty track and stopped.

A wind sock flapped on a pole. A metal shed sat in a field where the sun had fried the tall grass to yellow. Two small planes sat in the middle of the field, one red and silver, the other larger and dazzling white.

On the fuselage of the white airplane in front of the wing a small painted gray heron stood serenely on one leg. . . .

Chapter Thirty-eight

LEAH wallowed in self-pity. Goodyear sagged heavily across her aching arms. He was all done, too.

Sun and nausea and an empty stomach and another final failure made her lean against the car. "But that's an Enveco plane. Glade said you were one of the good guys."

"Enveco? Oh, the heron. Don't worry now. They merely provided transport and a pilot in a difficult situation. There's nothing to worry about." Swords loosened his tie, wiped his forehead and pate with an immaculate handkerchief. "I've never known such unabated sunlight. . . ."

"Is something wrong again?" Cal had an arm around Glade, who was managing to stand, at least.

"Cal, that's the company that sent assassins to kill your brother. We can't get on that—"

"Enveco? That's ridiculous. It's an old established American company . . . merely offered help in my time of need. I needed a small plane fast. One that could use"— Swords waved an arm at sun-fried grass—"primitive facilities."

"What's the matter?" Glade raised a lolling head and finally took a fix on the white plane and the gray heron. "Oh, shit! Harry, I trusted you." His tongue stuck drunkenly on the "t's."

"Now, listen my friend, I'm a busy man. I agreed to get you out of this situation, throw my weight around . . . something I don't care to do often." Harry Swords removed his suit coat. His shirt was damp already but he wore no holster under his arm. "I think you need medical attention soon and I for one am getting on that plane. If you don't wish to come with me you needn't." And he walked off.

"Harry, Enveco was my cover company. . . ." Glade straightened, sweat dripping off the end of his nose.

Swords stopped, turned. "You didn't mention that. You merely said. . . ." He looked from Leah to Glade, his eyes widened. "So that's why they were so eager to lend me the plane . . . this is very hard to believe, you understand . . . even offered the pilot and Frank here . . . where's Frank?" He started back toward them and stopped. "Frank, put that away!"

"Everybody in that plane," Frank said behind Leah. "Or she gets it in the back and anybody else next."

Leah cried as she followed the others to the open door, where a face appeared briefly and then disappeared. The sound of the engine, the propeller beat dust clouds from the whipping grass, and Leah turned to see Frank's gun through tears.

She heaved Goodyear at his face and dropped to the ground in the same motion. She lay there waiting for the bullet.

But no shot was fired. Glade fell beside her and Cal's boots passed them both.

"What's happening?" Glade asked thickly.

"Your brother is swearing and jumping up and down on Frank."

Cal swooped back and scooped Glade off the ground. A moment later he came back for Leah and lifted her to the plane.

"Cal, no!"

Leah was inside and lying across Glade when Cal threw Goodyear and all his toenails onto her chest. "Cal, not you, too."

"Get them forward into the seats." A vaguely familiar voice from the front of the plane.

"Do we take Swords?" Cal asked.

"Yes," Glade answered and the plane moved under them.

"Glade, I can only say how sorry I am and admit that I was royally taken in," Swords said above the sound of the engine as they jolted over the rough field and the plane increased its speed.

Goodyear moaned terror and Leah clutched him tightly. Then they were airborne and it seemed quieter.

Cal sat in front with the pilot. "Ben, I'm glad to see you, but what the hell are you doing here?"

"Glade asked me to fly in here today and wait around to see if he needed any help. That's my plane we left down there. It wouldn't have handled this many," said the short stocky man Leah had met in the restaurant in Craig. He turned around briefly to grin at Glade, who slumped in the seat across the tiny aisle from Leah. "Listen, buddy, you told me to be ready for trouble, but Jesus. . . ."

"Where's the Enveco pilot?" Glade forced himself to sit up straight.

"He jumped me the minute I touched a foot to the field. I left him tied up in back of the hanger. Where do I fly this stolen baby?"

"I'm afraid the place I had in mind won't do now," Swords said from the seat in front of Leah. And he and Cal and Ben began discussing a fishing lodge in Canada that Ben knew of.

Leah turned to the man across the aisle. "Glade, why didn't you tell me you had another last card to play? I almost committed suicide by throwing the kitty at Frank back there."

"So much happened today, Leah, I forgot about Ben, too." He leaned closer to stare at her and the pallor of his skin made the dark eyes appear more shadowed than ever.

"What's the matter?"

"Poor Leah." His good arm reached across the aisle and she felt a stinging as he plucked a hair from her head. "Poor Leah. And barely ripe, too." He handed her the hair.

It was tough and wiry . . . and silver.

"What do you say, cat? Should we keep her anyway?" Glade reached toward Goodyear on Leah's lap.

And the fat Siamese spit and ran claws across the offered palm, leaving whitened streaks on the skin.

Glade Wyndham laughed. The man and the cat seemed always to understand each other.

Leah wondered if she'd ever understand either of them, but she knew she was committed to try.